GHOSTBUSTERS

GHOSTBUSTERS
GHOSTBUSTERS

NOVELIZATION BY NANCY HOLDER • BASED ON THE SCREENPLAY
BY PAUL FEIG AND KATIE DIPPOLD • BASED ON THE 1984 FILM
GHOSTBUSTERS • WRITTEN BY DAN AYKROYD AND HAROLD RAMIS
AND DIRECTED BY IVAN REITMAN

TOR A TOM DOHERTY ASSOCIATES BOOK | NEW YORK

GHOSTBUSTERS

Trademark and copyright © 2016 Columbia Pictures Industries, Inc.

A Tor Book
Published by Tom Doherty Associates, LLC
175 Fifth Avenue
New York, NY 10010

www.tor-forge.com

Tor® is a registered trademark of Tom Doherty Associates, LLC.

ISBN 978-0-7653-8843-8

Our books may be purchased in bulk for promotional, educational, or business use. Please contact your local bookseller or the Macmillan Corporate and Premium Sales Department at 1-800-221-7945, extension 5442, or by e-mail at MacmillanSpecialMarkets@macmillan.com.

First Edition: July 2016

Printed in the United States of America

0 9 8 7 6 5 4 3 2 1

In memory of Harold Ramis.

ACKNOWLEDGMENTS

Writing this book has been a terrific thrill, and I couldn't have done it without the help of a lot of people. My deepest gratitude to: my agent, Howard Morhaim, and his assistant, Kim-Mei Kirtland; my Tor team, including editors Christopher Morgan and Melissa Singer, art director Seth Lerner, cover designer Russell Trakhtenberg, managing editor Nathan Weaver, and copyeditor Faren Bachelis; publishing consultant Virginia King at Sony Pictures; and Eric Reich of GhostCorps/Montecito Picture Company. A huge thank-you to the *Ghostbusters* casts and crews past and present, and Ivan Reitman, Dan Aykroyd, Harold Ramis, Paul Feig, and Kate Dippold. Greg Cox, I definitely owe you one. *Grazie mille* to Mark Mandell, who answers every call, usually from the other room, and feeds me, loves me, and inspires me. You are my density.

GHOSTBUSTERS

It was a dark and stormy night. Perfect for a tour of one of the most haunted houses in America, the dread Aldridge Mansion, a Victorian brownstone steeped in shocking scandal and even better, bloody mass murder. A dark jewel of Manhattan's West Village, the historical estate loomed in deep shadows. Cue the lightning, the thunder, the terrifying howl of a wolf hunting down a hapless but leggy Gypsy maiden—

Okay . . . not so much.

Actually, it wasn't dark and stormy at all. A crisp autumn day blazed away in New York City, bursting with the blue skies and puffy white clouds that made the locals shrug and say, "Hey, it's really not so bad here, despite the overcrowding, high rents, and crooked politicians. It could be worse—we could be living in New Jersey."

On a glorious day like this, folks with a yen for the macabre could go out to the Edgar Allan Poe Cottage in a national park greenbelt in the Bronx and get a fright and a tan for what, five bucks? But luckily for Garrett and his impressive student loan debt, Aldridge Mansion's terrible reputation—and truly fine collection of period pieces—had drawn a sizable crowd for the last scheduled ghost tour of the afternoon. Garrett was their tour guide. They were grouped together in the elegant parlor, eyes wide, palms sweaty, hopeful and eager. Time to get to work.

Time to scare the pants off them.

Just like they wanted him to.

Tour Guide Garrett cleared his throat.

"The Aldridge Mansion is the only nineteenth-century home in New York City preserved both inside and out," he said in what he liked to think of as his *Sleepy Hollow* voice. He gestured to the original Aesthetic Movement settee and Clara Driscoll–designed Tiffany lamp, the neo-classical slate fireplace and the double-decker bookcases brimming with leather-bound volumes, including an original *On the Origin of Species* by Charles Darwin. When he wasn't brooding over his dismal rate of pay and the dead-end job's lack of health benefits, he had to admit that the mansion's sumptuous decor stirred him to his roots.

"This clock was on the *Titanic*. Sir Aldridge preserved it when he brought it with him into his lifeboat. That's his portrait." He pointed to the fine-looking fellow hanging above the fireplace mantelpiece.

"Over here you can imagine Sir Aldridge entertaining his wealthy guests."

One pretty twenty-something tourist glanced anxiously at the trio of headless mannequins in capes and a sailor's suit arranged beside a long table as he led them past. Her face noticeably paled and she looked seriously creeped out. Maybe she was a believer? Sometimes tourists showed him the photographs they'd taken during the tour that featured blips of light: "spirit orbs" or blurs, proof in their minds that the dead walked in Aldridge Mansion. He always acted surprised and intrigued, but seriously? The rooms were dimly illuminated night and day by period lamps and ornate wall sconces, and blurring in the snapshots was caused by using a flash too far from the subject. But of course he never told them any of that. Why ruin the fun?

Besides, gullible out-of-towners were generous tippers. And the tour guide biz was all about the gratuities.

Garrett led the throng down an extremely creaky hall at a merry clip. On every step, the ancient floorboards bowed ever so slightly underfoot, springing back sluggishly, bowing again. The overall effect hinted at imminent collapse. He smiled to himself as he heard a few gasps behind him.

"As you can see, even the wealthy get termites," he intoned over his shoulder with perfect delivery and timing. They chuckled. They always did. It was fun dissing the rich. But seriously, would the New York Department of Buildings allow anyone inside a structure that wasn't completely safe?

He paused in front of The Door. It was sectioned into elaborate panels and accessorized with an ornate brass knob, all original, and he thanked his lucky stars that it featured so prominently in the décor. It was one of two focal points of the entire tour.

He slowly turned to face his eager audience. Here was where he gathered in his cash money, tax free. It was decidedly not in the exquisite upstairs bedrooms, where he provided fascinating details on the lavish furnishings, the art, and the architecture. Thanks to an otherwise worthless four-year course of study at CCNY in art history, with a minor in drama, he could talk the talk and walk the walk. Nor was it in the cavernous grand ballroom with its intricate parquetry floor, or the period-accurate kitchen, or the rooftop solarium. Not even in the gilded, marbled, mirrored master bath suite. Those were just way-stops, diversions included on the tour to fill out the allotted time, to let anticipation build, and set the mood for the big finish.

The Door.

The imposing barrier encapsulated an unspeakable horror that passing decades could not erase, the same unspeakable horror that had lured this crowd of wide-eyed thrill seekers away from Manhattan's more savory sites. It was in fact Garrett's center stage, and in his fantasies perhaps a stepping-stone to something far more rewarding. Three weeks ago his cousin Lester had shot footage of him delivering a rousing rendition of his spiel in front of The Door. Lester's building super had mentioned he knew a casting agent who lived in a co-op down the street. Careers had been founded on less.

And for all he knew, someone in this afternoon's group would post the performance on YouTube, and it would go viral, and, and—

And action, Garrett told himself. Putting on his game face, he summoned up the necessary aura of the confidential and the mysterious.

"As you can see, this basement door is sealed shut." He made a show of trying to turn the brass floral-patterned doorknob, which had never so much as budged during his entire tenure as a tour guide. It was frozen in position, either welded or glued. The basement was strictly off-limits, even to the cleaning staff. Pausing a beat, he searched the goggle-eyed faces, forcefully selling the idea that what he was about to reveal was momentous. Then he spoke.

"One morning, Sir Aldridge awoke, furious when his breakfast wasn't waiting for him. He called to his servants but none of them responded. Why? Because during the night one by one they had each been stabbed to death in their sleep."

He let that sink in, right up to the hilt. As if drawn by an invisible magnet, the tourists leaned ever so slightly toward him. That's how hard they were hanging on to his words. Only one middle-aged man held back. Arms folded across his chest, he smirked as if to say: *I ain't afraid of no ghost.* Fine, be that way. The mass murder was a documented fact. Garrett had pored over the old sepia-tone photographs of the butchered cook and the eviscerated butler, the partially beheaded scullery maid and the shredded remains of the chauffeur—photos credited to Sir Aldridge himself. They were crimes of anger—no, of insane fury. Worse even than the photos he'd seen of Jack the Ripper's victims. As if the hand that had wielded the heavy blade wanted to erase the poor souls' very humanity.

The real details of the crimes were far too brutal for the

present crowd, of course. Grossing out the audience was a surefire tip killer. Instead of hanging around after the tour for a nice chat with the friendly guide and the transfer of commensurate compensation, they stampeded for the front doors as if school had just let out.

"It was later discovered they were murdered by his eldest daughter, Gertrude Aldridge." He pointed to her large oil portrait on the wall. Her dark hair was upswept and she was dressed in an elegant ball gown decorated with rosettes and ribbons on the puffy sleeves and the corsetlike bodice. She wore long white gloves. It had been painted several years before she went lunatic with the knife, and even then she had an expression that could curdle milk.

He often wondered if the artist had asked Gertrude to smile and that bone-chilling grimace was the result. And those eyes! How could a painter stare into those bottomless pits day after day without going mad himself? They blazed with a mixture of fury, hate, and contempt that made tourists avert their gaze. It was like facing down a tigress. Had Gertrude fancied the likeness? Had she directed the pose herself? Why else had the painting been kept and not destroyed? Garrett had walked past the thing five days a week for four years; to him it was just a late-nineteenth-century portrait by a pupil of Thomas Eakins of a dead crazy woman.

The atmosphere in the room grew close. He had their full attention.

"According to the old man's diary, by the time Gertrude had finished her mission her nightgown was so saturated with blood that it had left a two-foot-wide trail up the stairs to her bedroom. To spare the family public humiliation, instead of turning her in to the police, they locked her in the basement and fed her through this slot." With a flourish he indicated a metal rectangle that had been inset in the thick wood. His intent listeners had questions, of course. He was leaving great gaping holes in the story. What did Sir Aldridge do with all the bodies? How did he conceal the crimes from the victims' families and friends? Who cleaned up the incredible mess? How long did Gertrude live in the basement dungeon? Did she wail and scream night and day? Did she die there of natural causes or did she take her own life?

Excellent questions all. The answers to which Garrett withheld until after the official tour ended, when the guests who wanted to know more would be obliged to dip into their billfolds. "Years later," he said with barely a pause, "when a new owner moved in, they dug out her remains. But after repeatedly hearing strange sounds emanating from the basement, he sealed it shut. That's right. No one has opened this door since." While he doubted that was the whole truth of the matter, he'd never been in the basement to test it. "And thank god," he went on, "because I can't imagine what she would look like after all these years. She wasn't looking too good before."

He nodded at her looming portrait. The group laughed, but a bit nervously this time. None of them could hold Gertrude's maniacal gaze.

As if on cue, a silver-plated candlestick—a Paul Revere reproduction—fell off a bookshelf and hit the floor with a clang. The tourists jumped at the sound and let out a unison yelp.

As if on cue.

The last tour guest lingered. She was the twenty-something believer blonde. She had shown no inclination to tip him, hadn't even touched the clasp of her ridiculously tiny purse, but Garrett didn't mind in the least. A hottie, she had a head shaped like a lightbulb, which as Garrett had read in *Success Secrets of Hollywood,* was a big plus on TV. People with lightbulb heads looked way better on the little screen. His own head was relatively normal sized and shaped. On TV it would look like a bowling pin. Head expansion surgery was elective and costly, health insurance wouldn't cover it, and he had no health insurance anyway. It was a catch-22 or something and his cross to bear.

"That was amazing," she said in a breathy voice with a deep southern twang as sweet as pecan pie. "You should be on TV."

"Well, thanks. That's the dream, anyway."

She blinked at him, then nodded rapidly. "Oh yes. You should totally go for it. The tour was great. So scary."

"Thanks. Do you like to be scared?" he asked, letting an arch tone creep into his voice. The only thing about Aldridge Mansion that scared him was the thought of working there for the rest of his life.

Her big blue eyes glittered. "Oh yes."

"Why?" he said, moving close enough to get a whiff of the Juicy Fruit she was chewing.

"Because it's *fun*."

"Well, I know a lot of even scarier stories. Some of them have happened to *me,* right here in this mansion. If you're not busy maybe you and I—"

"Samantha June, let's *go*." It was the rude dude who had smirked at him during the tour.

The girl—Samantha June—pulled a moue of distaste and gave her hair a toss. "That's my daddy. We're going to Central Park."

"There's a couple of ghosts in the park by the boathouse," he said in his *Sleepy Hollow* voice. "If you go there at night, sometimes they manifest."

"That would be so cool," she said eagerly.

"Yeah. Really cool."

She cast a glance up at the portrait and shivered a little. "Unless they look like her."

"Back in her day they couldn't fix what she's got."

"What she's got?"

"Can't you see it? Those big bags under her eyes and the saggy chin?"

"Uhh, no . . ."

"It's butt face!"

Samantha June choked hard on her Juicy Fruit.

Garrett tried to pat her on the back, but she moved out of reach. "Are you okay?"

She nodded and gave him a forced little laugh before she resumed chewing. "Maybe you should be more careful," she said earnestly. "I mean, I know this is all probably just pretend, but it's not nice to speak ill of the dead . . ."

"In case they're listening, you mean?"

"Uh-huh."

"I guess you're right. There's no way of telling what they can hear." He fought the urge to grin like an idiot. Gullible chicks were so totally hot.

Samantha June glanced down at the candlestick, which was still lying on its side on the floor, then at him as if trying to decide if he had made it fall over, or if it had happened spontaneously. The strain of the problem made her frown a little and chew faster.

He would never tell. Those things had a way of winding up on Yelp.

"Was that a true story?" she asked out of the blue. "About the murders?"

"Yes, for sure. In fact, we have to kind of clean it up for the tours. The truth is much more extreme. It didn't come out until the 1940s, when Sir Aldridge's personal effects were made public."

"Like what?" She took a step toward him. From the huskiness in her voice, he knew that delicious little tingly tangly chills were working their way up her prim little backbone. Some people really did love to be scared.

"Well, she took a knife from a drawer in her father's gun case. It was a Paget hunting knife, actually very rare, and—"

"Samantha June!" her father bellowed. "The tour bus is going to leave!"

"Rats," she said.

And the spell was broken.

"Coming!" She beamed at Garrett and said, "Well, bye. See you on TV sometime."

"Maybe so." He flashed his most winning smile at her, but she missed it, having already turned away. She didn't even look back as she hurried out the front doors. He was disappointed, but only mildly so. There would be more cute tourists tomorrow, and besides, he had to rush to his second job.

Ol' Gertie Pants glared down at him. Her expression hadn't changed of course, but the context had. To Garrett she now looked insanely triumphant, pleased that his flirtation had come to nothing, and she had him all to herself again. As he often did, he wondered what could have happened to Gertrude Aldridge to make her so crazy. So *wicked and violent*. He wasn't sure he believed that people were born bad. To flesh out his repertoire as tour guide, he'd learned a lot of legends about evil spirits, curses, hauntings, and they rarely occurred because someone simply had been misunderstood or something trivial like that.

"So what was it, Lady G?" he asked the glowering portrait. "Did someone steal your fave tiara? Or was it your way of getting out of an arranged marriage to some fat, rich old bastard? Were you really in love with the gardener, whose face you turned into mulch?"

Ed Mulgrave, his boss, had already left for the day and he was alone in the cavernous mansion. How many times had Gertrude Aldridge "watched" him shut down for the night? He had lost count.

He picked up the candlestick, made sure the spring mechanism was loaded for next time, and set it back on the mantel. There were four scheduled tours tomorrow. At the same precipitous moment in his spiels the rigged candlestick would "suddenly and inexplicably" fall over— triggered by a concealed bit of spinning wire. Sometimes the cheapest tricks were the most effective.

He checked that the lights upstairs were off and windows locked, alarms set. He did the same for the ground floor. All was secure. He wondered if he should text Lester tonight, see if his super had made contact with that casting agent and given him the video. Or maybe it was it too soon to press the issue? There was a fine line between eager and stalker. No doubt about it, Samantha June's compliments had warmed his ambitious soul.

He grabbed his backpack and was about to head for the front door when something rattled behind him. The mansion was settling. It happened all the time. One of the reasons people thought old buildings were haunted was because of all the noise they made just succumbing to the force of gravity. He turned to look, saw nothing, and started walking.

Another rattle.

He paused. He hoped it wasn't rats again. They could make a terrible mess that he'd have to clean up in the morning before the first tour. They chewed up anything and everything, and they weren't housebroken. He decided that he really should check. He'd have to let Ed know as soon as possible, maybe text him tonight—

He turned around.

Rattling again.

The sound appeared to be coming from the locked basement door. Rats on the other side of it? His breath caught as he drew closer. The knob was *turning*. The knob frozen since forever! A chill shot up his spine. *Someone on the other side is trying to turn it.*

How had someone gotten into the basement? Was it one of the tourists? All the entrances and exits leading down there were sealed tight.

The knob stopped moving.

"What the . . . ?"

Then, without warning, *bam*!

The Door jolted from a powerful impact on the far side, as if someone large and powerful had crashed a shoulder against it. The suddenness and the violence rocked Garrett back on his heels. Sawdust and plaster rained down from the top of the doorjamb. The wooden center panels of The Door bowed outward. No human being could do that unless they had a battering ram.

Bam, bam, bam!

And between the jarring crashes, something was thrashing and scraping on the other side as if desperate, furious—

The pack slipped from his hand to the floor. As he turned and ran across the room, the rhythmic bashing continued behind him, echoing through the empty house. The thing wanted out.

Wild to get away, he grabbed the knob of the entrance door. It didn't move—it was frozen solid like the knob to the basement had been. He tried again, throwing his full weight against it, and the knob suddenly glowed red hot in his grip. Searing pain ripped through his fingers and raced up his arm. With a howl he jerked his hand away.

The frantic noises behind him immediately ceased.

In the smothering quiet all he could hear was his own panting. When he glanced back at the basement door, the blood drained from his face and a moan of disbelief escaped his throat.

The Door, sealed shut not a minute ago, hung open.

Wide open.

An icy breeze rushed through it. He could smell the dank, chilly air rising from the basement. Someone had opened The Door that couldn't be opened.

From the inside . . .

What was racing through his mind was not possible. There had to be another explanation. It had to be a trick, some kind of elaborate practical joke. He looked down at his hand. The palm and underside of his fingers were bright red and they throbbed painfully. No way was he going to try the superheated doorknob a second time. As he hurried back to the living room the rigged candlestick levitated from the floor, hovered for an instant, then flew straight at him, barely missing his head.

The whoosh of air as it hurtled past turned a skeptic into a horrified believer. As unlikely as it seemed, there was no denying the evidence of his five senses. The madwoman's portrait loomed over him. *Don't look up. Don't look up. Whatever you do, don't look up.*

Grabbing a heavy chair by the arms, he hammer-tossed it with all his might at the leaded bay window. The chair stopped in midair just short of its target, and instead of shattering the glass so he could crawl out, like a demented boomerang it reversed course and slammed into him squarely, knocking him onto his back.

He rolled onto his hands and knees and scrambled under the only protection in sight: a circular dining table. The table legs screeched on the floor as the heavy piece of furniture slid away from his cowering form, scraping across the room and leaving him completely exposed. A glowing green substance oozed from the walls. It was thick and gooey, and it moved counter to the laws of gravity, spreading up and sideways as well as down the historic and irreplaceable butterfly chintz wallpaper. A wave of dizziness swept over him and he thought he was going to faint.

He pushed to his feet and ran in a blind panic, crying, "I have a family!" He whirled left and right.

And then there she was, gliding through The Door. Gertrude Aldridge, mass murderess, hauntress of the dark. Madness blazed in her eyes, evil in her predatory advance. She was floating, gliding toward him, shimmering, transparent . . . and wacko. "Okay, I don't have a family, but I have roommates!"

He was so frightened he had no idea where he was heading—until he found himself on a narrow wooden staircase. He had never seen the stairs before, and under the mansion's ground floor there was only one destination. It was the last place he wanted to be.

"Oh no!"

He was in the basement. The floor was cracking; an unnatural green light pulsed and shot upward through the fissures. A lavalike substance burbled. The staircase was coated with it and the ooze dripped, sticking to him. As Garrett spun on his heel to run back upstairs, his foot slipped on the stuff and he started to fall facedown. He caught himself on a tread above with his hands, which plunged them in goo. It was cold and pulpy. Pulling himself free, fingers trailing bubbling strands, he willed his legs into motion. His shoe made a sucking sound as it popped from the slime. He lurched upward, one step, then two.

His foot broke through a termite-weakened tread. As his ankle, then shin, slipped into the void, the rickety staircase trembled and fell to pieces under him. He held on, staring up at the top of the stairs where The Door, once a symbol of the dread unknown, was now his means of survival and escape.

Something was moving in the darkness toward him.

Adrenaline shot through his veins and he shouted in fear, legs windmilling as he fought to pull himself up.

That gum-chewing girl, she was wrong, he thought. *Being scared isn't fun at all.*

Shivering violently, but unable to stop himself, he looked over his shoulder.

Glowing. Brilliantly. Hideously. She was reaching for him, reaching—

Garrett screamed and screamed.

2

"**D**a da DA da, dadada DA da . . ."

Erin Gilbert smiled over at the TV as she finished spraying the clothes in her closet with freshener. On the screen was the cute cartoon ghost show she used to watch when she was little—back before a ghost had ruined her life.

No time to dwell on that now. I have a lecture to give. And it might be the most important presentation she ever delivered. The fate of her wonderful, reinvented life depended on it. She adjusted her plain skirt and blouse before checking herself top to bottom one last time. The überconservative style choice projected an image of a serious scientist committed to teaching and research, and on a fast track to tenure at a major university.

Tenure! Go, Erin!

She grabbed her messenger bag and hurried off to her first lecture of the morning. As she left her apartment, she cast her mind back to The Incident, the catalyst that had ultimately led her into a life—and a brilliant career—in the world of hard science. She had been eight. So young to go through so much . . .

Second-grader Erin Gilbert was in love with life. She and her mom and dad lived in a picturesque little town in southern Michigan, a suburb of Battle Creek. She enjoyed being in the second grade and riding her bike back and forth under the canopy of tall trees on her street. Most of all she loved her little black dog, Corky. Her father said he was "part Spaniel, part who knows." Her father worked as an executive in a big cereal company. Her mom stayed at home and volunteered with the Soroptimist club. Their house was built of white wood and brick, two stories with a wide, wraparound front porch and a two-person swing, tall, narrow windows, and it looked brand new, inside and out.

The house next door was also two stories, but with a very plain front like a box, and a few little bitty windows. It was painted a yucky yellow with ugly dark brown trim, and there was always smoke and a bad smell coming from the backyard because the old lady who lived there burned all her trash. Mrs. Barnard was short and round, with sunken eyes and wrinkles in her pale cheeks. When she wasn't dressed up for Sunday church, she wore an apron over her housedress and stomped around in big clunky shoes.

Mrs. Barnard kept chickens in her backyard on the far side of her burn barrel. She fussed over all her poultry, but most of all over her beautiful rooster named Ernesto. He had shiny black feathers on his back and wings and a copper-colored chest. She carried him around the yard cradled in the crook of her arm like a big cat, stroking his head and back, and talking to him. He cackled and clucked back at her.

Mrs. Barnard had no close family who visited her, but Sundays she drove to church in the '52 Plymouth sedan she kept in her sagging garage. Church and chickens and lots of smoke. That summed up Mrs. Barnard.

Plus *grumpy*.

Every morning at sunrise, Ernesto woke up the Gilberts with his crowing. And when he started to crow, Corky started to bark. It made her parents angry (and sleepy), but there was nothing they could do about it, really. At least, that was what they used to say.

Corky was very interested in Mrs. Barnard's chickens, which were kept safe in a sturdy wire mesh coop, and there was a four-foot-high wooden fence separating the sides of the two yards. He'd tried to dig under the fence any number of times, but Erin lined the fence with stones to keep him on the Gilberts' side of the fence.

One day after school, Erin was playing with Corky in her yard, throwing an old tennis ball for him to fetch. He was a very energetic who-knows Spaniel and it took a lot of fetch to tire him out. She had just extricated the soggy ball from his mouth when a loud commotion at the fence made her and the dog look up. Waving his black wings to keep his balance, Ernesto perched on top of the fence, pretending to be an eagle.

Mrs. Barnard rushed up to the rickety wooden slats and tried to catch him, but she was too slow. The bird let out a squawk and flapped clumsily down into Erin's yard. Realizing the danger, she made a grab for Corky's collar. Her fingers couldn't get a firm grip and he shot away. In a blink, the dog jumped on the chicken. Over the terrible squawking and growling as the two fought, Erin could hear Mrs. Barnard screaming at her, and she saw the old woman trying desperately to climb over the chest-high barrier.

Then Corky got hold of Ernesto by the back of the neck and bit down. Bright blood started squirting in all directions as the two of them rolled on the grass. Ernesto stopped squawking and flapping. When he went limp, Corky ran off to his doghouse with the rooster in his mouth, dragging it inside with him. He was madly wagging his stub of a tail.

On the other side of the fence, Mrs. Barnard shrieked and screamed for the longest time. "You!" she shouted at Erin, over and over again. "You better watch out!" Her face throbbed bright red and her nose ran and she sobbed and wailed. She kept stopping in the middle of crying to put the ball of her fist against the middle of her chest and she closed her eyes like something in there hurt.

Then Mrs. Barnard disappeared into the house. A little while later, Animal Control came out and she ordered them to take Corky away and put him to sleep. But the lady told Mrs. Barnard that Ernesto had flown onto private property so it was trespassing and fair game. And Corky was licensed with all his shots, so there was nothing to be done.

After that, every time Mrs. Barnard saw Erin and her dog she yelled threats at them: "You better watch out!" And she took to burning her trash at all hours, so the nasty smoke would blow into their house. She seemed to get angrier and angrier by the day. Erin asked her father if she should apologize or send her a card, or maybe they could get her another baby rooster, but he said that would only stir her up more.

The Incident created a very tense atmosphere on the quiet, tree-lined street. At her parents' request Erin stopped playing in the backyard with her pup. Poor Corky got very restless and barky, which made her parents cranky. They said they didn't blame him, but Erin was worried. What if *they* called Animal Control and ordered them to put Corky to sleep?

Then Mrs. Barnard started parking her junky car in front of their driveway, blocking it, and instead of just burning her trash she took to throwing it over the fence.

Erin's father had to call the police. The officer took notes and then went over to talk to Mrs. Barnard. It was very exciting and at the same time scary.

The day after the policeman came, when Erin walked home from school she saw an ambulance parked in Mrs. Barnard's front yard. She got a glimpse of the old woman laid out on a gurney as people wheeled it out of the front door. She was covered up to her chin with a warm, soft blanket and an oxygen mask covered the bottom half of her face.

Erin's mother hurried out and pulled her inside their house, so she didn't see what happened next, but later she overheard her parents talking about how Mrs. Barnard had died in her front yard with the paramedics trying to save her. They took her dead body away in the ambulance very quietly, without running their siren or lights.

"That old lunatic won't ever bother us again," her father said.

But that night, Erin was awakened in the middle of the night by the sound of a cock crowing. She recognized the rooster's voice at once—it was Ernesto. She listened with her covers pulled up to just below her eyes, but the noise didn't repeat. And Corky hadn't heard it or he would've started barking downstairs. It couldn't have been Ernesto, she assured herself. She had watched her father pull his mangled body out of the doghouse—a rooster that would never wake up anybody ever again.

After a minute or two, she decided she must've dreamed it. She slipped further down in the warm bed and closed her eyes. She was just drifting off again when she smelled something icky and familiar—burning trash. Her heart started to pound. With eyes tightly closed she was suddenly wide awake.

Then something touched her on the nose. Cold like an ice cube or a snowball.

"You!"

She jerked and her eyes flew open. She would have screamed, but her throat closed up.

Death had changed Mrs. Barnard, and not in a good way. Her skin was gray and her eyeballs were white. Her compact, grandmotherly body was stretched like a funhouse mirror; she was sticklike and tall, legs and arms so long that she could stand flat on the floor at the foot of the bed and reach over it to grab both sides of the headboard. Her fingernails scratched into the wood as she shook the bed. Erin flopped left and right, struggling not to fall off.

"You better watch out!" the apparition shrieked down at her.

The burning trash smell blasted from Mrs. Barnard's

gaping mouth and as it washed over Erin, she held her breath to keep from inhaling it. She was terrified and at the same time fascinated by the strange turn of events. If Mrs. Barnard was dead, was this really her ghost? The old woman's face seemed to pull this way and that, milky eyes by turns bulging then sunken, and Erin could see through the shifting form to the curtained bedroom window behind it.

"You better—uh, uh . . ."

The ghost convulsed above her, as if choking on something deep in its guts, eyes squeezed shut, mouth gaping, strange narrow tongue extended onto its chin.

"Uh, uh . . ."

Then the dam broke. With a mighty lurch that quaked the bedframe, Mrs. Barnard threw up.

A torrent of what looked like blood gushed from her mouth and poured onto Erin's face and chest. It was red like blood but it wasn't warm, and it was so gooey and sticky it was barely liquid. Mrs. Barnard kept retching and the stuff kept splattering down. Erin struggled for air, thinking for sure she would drown in it.

Somehow she twisted away and slipped out the side of the covers. She ran out of her room, barefoot and screaming down the hall to her parents' bedroom. They were already awakened and sitting up in bed when she burst into the room. She burrowed into the covers between them, burying her head and pleading, "Don't let Mrs. Barnard get me! Her blood is all over my bed!"

Her father jumped out of bed while her mother held her and tried to comfort her. When he came back he said, "There's nothing there."

"You just had a nightmare, Erin," her mother said. "No more ice cream for you after 7 P.M."

"Nightmares just happen sometimes, honey," her father said, trying to assure her. "They're nothing to worry about. They're perfectly natural."

After the perfectly natural nightmares—the cock's

crow, the smell of burning trash, the angry spirit barfing buckets of red goo on her face — repeated night after night for the next month, her parents told her they were going to get her some help. She assumed they meant that they would help her get rid of Mrs. Barnard. But she was wrong.

Erin sat alone in the backseat of their car as her father and mother drove her to see a new doctor. She was scared when they first told her, but her parents promised she wouldn't be getting any shots because this wasn't a "shot doctor." They pulled up in front of a one-story house in a different suburb of Battle Creek. It didn't look like a doctor's office. They went up the walk to the front door and her father rang the bell. When the door opened, it smelled like someone was baking cookies inside.

Erin thought Dr. Marsha Malone was pretty. She had beautiful chocolate skin and gold jewelry. And she was fun to talk to. She made jokes while just the two of them played board games, asked a lot of questions, and unlike her parents, never seemed upset by the answers Erin gave her. Her office was like a living room, only in a separate part of the house off the driveway, and it always smelled like ginger cookies.

"Why do you think you're having the nightmares, Erin?" Dr. Malone asked one day.

"I don't know."

"Your family had some problems with Mrs. Barnard before she died, didn't they?"

"She wasn't a very nice neighbor," Erin said softly, staring down at the game board. "After Corky ate Ernesto she got even meaner. I was afraid of her. So was Corky."

"Do you feel guilty about Ernesto?"

"If I had kept Corky in the house it wouldn't have happened. Ernesto wouldn't have gotten killed."

"But you didn't know Ernesto was going to get free and hop into your yard," Dr. Malone said. "You had no way of knowing that. And you couldn't have stopped him from flying over the fence. So that isn't your fault. What about Mrs. Barnard? Do you feel guilty because she died?"

Erin fidgeted in her chair, squeezing a game piece. "Kinda."

"She was an old lady, and she had a bad heart," Dr. Malone said. "She wasn't taking her medicine. You had no control over what happened to her, either."

Erin looked up at her. "Then why doesn't Mrs. Barnard know that? Why is she after me?"

"Erin, do you believe ghosts are real?"

She met the doctor's gaze and nodded emphatically. "Will she get me? What will she do to me? Can you make her stop?"

Dr. Malone sat quietly for a moment. Then she inclined her head as if she had decided something.

"Erin, could you please wait here for a moment while I speak with your parents? I'll be right back."

After she left the room, Erin started to feel weird being alone. She got up and went down the hall after Dr. Malone, hoping to find the source of the cookie smell. On the right was another room with the door slightly open. She could hear the doctor talking. She stopped outside and listened.

"Honestly, Mr. Gilbert, there seems to be no family history of mental illness on either side of the family. I don't think this is something you and your wife need to worry too much about. I think this is a passing phase. It could be an attempt to remain a helpless child and draw your attention. A final burst of infantilism is not uncommon at her age. I think the dreams will stop when she realizes she's not going to lose your love if she grows up."

"So she's lying about the ghost in order to manipulate us?" her mother said.

"This goes much deeper than that, below the conscious level. I don't think Erin is at all aware of the need she's actually expressing. She sincerely believes what she has seen is real."

"We're not getting any sleep," her father complained. "It's worse than that damned rooster. Can you give her something to calm her down?"

"I'm sorry, I don't prescribe sedatives for children her age. Perhaps some warm milk and a bedtime story might do the trick. That would make her feel more comfortable and loved, and make her drowsy as well."

"Is that *all*?" Her father sounded mad.

"I would like to keep seeing Erin on a weekly basis, monitor her progress in the short term to make sure nothing else is going on with her. There could still be an underlying organic cause for her hallucinations."

Erin tiptoed back to the doctor's office, crying softly. She didn't understand half of what she had heard, but she was wounded to learn her mother thought she was a liar and scared there was something wrong inside her. It was all Mrs. Barnard's fault. Everything. She wiped back her tears and steeled herself, determined to ask Dr. Malone for the shot, no matter how big, that would just make it go away.

nough thinking about that, Erin told herself. But the memories always stayed with her at a slightly-less-than-conscious level. Like a rash, but from the inside. There were things you could buy at the grocery store for *that,* but not for what ailed Erin.

It was deep autumn, and she was happy to see the biochemistry of the season in full swing—the chlorophyll in the leaves breaking down while at the same time, the development of red anthocyanin and other pigments went full throttle, thereby producing the traditional colorful fall foliage. In her sensible plaid skirt and jacket, she strode at a spritely pace across the venerable campus of Columbia University, her place of employment, her place to shine. Students in sweaters sat in group discussions on the rolling lawn, watched over by bronze sentinels of knowledge such as the enthroned *Alma Mater* and *The Thinker,* lost in deep thought. Columbia was one of the most prestigious schools in the country—6.9 percent undergrad acceptance rate—and she was a professor there. And soon, if all went well, Christmas would come early this year: she would be a professor there *forever.*

Today was a stepping-stone toward that goal. Make that a milestone. A day she had marked on her calendar. V-Day. For validation. All the years she had suffered as "Ghost Girl" were far behind her. Here she was respected for her fine mind, her research skills, and her dedication to the scientific method. For being a scientist.

She nodded pleasantly at a few colleagues as they passed her. Did they know what was happening today? She was going to speak in the department auditorium—"the big hall." It was such an honor. Only the best professors delivered their lectures there. But she was up for the challenge. Oh *yes*.

Poised and confident, she sauntered into the clubby alumni hall that led to the faculty lounge, with its gleaming dark wood paneling, oil paintings, and statuary. Perks for the possessors of high IQs. She beamed as she watched the academic elite milling about in weighty conversation en route to the big lecture hall. They were her colleagues. She was their peer.

She got down to the pit—the front of the room—and wrote the equations she planned to discuss on the whiteboards. As the number strings stretched across the shiny surfaces, she couldn't stem the pleasurable thrum that came from knowing that she knew what she was doing. Yes. She launched. Full speed ahead. She put down the marker.

"As my calculations show, we will soon be able to combine general relativity and quantum theory into a—" Hmm, her voice was a little squeaky there. "Muwaaaaaaa. Muwaaaaa." Time to stretch the vocal cords. And do some lunges. Yes, some lunges so that everything *flowed*.

The room was empty, but it wouldn't be for long. She put the turbo on her exercises—*muwaaa, lunge*—sharpening both body and mind. Like a fencer: parry, lunge, riposte, yodel—

"*Muwaaaaaaaa—*" she sang out. "*Muwaaaaa—*"

She turned on her heel and let out a shriek. There was a man standing behind her. Sixty-something, quite attentive.

"Yes?" she said, grabbing a folder and perusing it in an attempt to recapture her dignity.

"I'm sorry for interrupting you," he said. "But I need to speak with you. About something you wrote."

To conceal the fact that he had scared the living daylights out her, she began to pack up her things, belatedly realizing they were unpacked because she had yet to deliver her lecture. But she would look foolish if she un-unpacked them in front of him.

"All right. Which publication?" He couldn't mean her article in *Nature*. It wasn't out yet.

"I'm talking about your book."

Erin froze. Surely she had misheard him. *No one* knew about the book. It didn't even exist in this space/time. She began to get dizzy again.

"I'm not sure what you mean," she said as neutrally as she could.

"You're Erin Gilbert?" he asked.

She waited. Her heart had ceased beating. Or was beating too fast. Or something. She couldn't even remember what state she was in. New York. A state of high anxiety. And anger, yes.

"Coauthor of—"

He must not speak the title. The title is poison. Listeria for tenure.

But he had a copy! In his hand! Huge, hardbound, real! He squinted and began to read:

" '*Ghosts from Our Past: Both Literally and Figuratively: The Study of the Paranormal.*' "

Each syllable was like a knife through her heart. *Oh god, god, my tenure review is next Thursday,* she thought wildly. *I buried that book years ago. This can't be happening.*

"I'm sorry," she said stiffly. "That must be a different Erin Gilbert."

The man cocked his head as he compared her face to the photograph on the dust jacket. She looked a lot younger. And stupider, even though she was trying to look smarter.

"This really does look like you," he observed.

I have to make this go away right now or I am dead.
Had she actually just been warming up? Her entire professional life was now passing before her eyes in a freezing cold sweat.

"Okay, listen, Mr. . . ." *Ghost of Christmas Past . . .*

"Ed Mulgrave."

"Listen, Mr. Mulgrave." She strained to be pleasant. "That book was just sort of a joke. No self-respecting scientist really believes in the paranormal. That was a long time ago, just a gag between two friends." She almost choked on the last word. That friendship was also a thing of the past. She ignored the pang of guilt centered in a vortex of building apprehension.

He frowned dubiously. "A four-hundred-and-sixty-page gag?"

It was clear that he was not going to go away without a fight. Or a discussion.

She surrendered. "What do you want?"

He claimed his victory as he lowered the book. "Well, I'm the historian at the Aldridge Museum and I believe it's haunted," he announced, with no small modicum of drama.

"Don't you give ghost tours? Isn't that the whole point?" She tried not to sound snappish. But why not? She could sound snappish if she wanted to.

"Yes," he conceded, "but that's just for fun. And ticket sales. But this has never happened before. It scared my tour guide nearly to death. If you could just take a look." He shrugged helplessly. "I tried the police, but I just sound crazy."

And I won't? Days away from my tenure review?

"I'm sorry, but that book you're holding is nonsense." She gave her head a quick shake. "I don't know how you found it anyway. I thought I burned both copies." Then threw the ashes into the Hudson River in a weighted garbage bag.

He blinked in surprise. "Oh, I bought it online. It's on Amazon. Both hard copy and e-book."

What?

WHAT?

Shock smacked her like a slap; then rage ignited like a Roman candle. *No way no way no way. I will murder her. Maim her and—*

She remained poised.

"Is it now," she said calmly.

Then the students began to file in.

Ninety-seven minutes later, her lecture was finally over. Erin had killed it, but she didn't know if she had done it in a good way or a bad way. She couldn't remember a word she'd said. The students hadn't asked any questions and had filed out silently. That had given her a chance to race back to her office and go online. One, two, three, and she was on Amazon and—

She gasped. "No."

It was there, just as Ed Mulgrave had said, on its own Web page. There was no mistaking the cover. Or her name as coauthor. And the other author? Who else: *Abigail L. Yates.*

The final blow was the three words in huge letters above a photograph of Erin that dominated the screen:

GHOSTS ARE REAL!

Her fury doubled. Tripled. There weren't enough exponents to adequately quantify it. She was *pissed.*

"Son of a—"

There was a knock on her door. It opened, and Harold Filmore, her department chair, stood on the threshold. In the pantheon of the Mount Olympus that was the Physics Department, Dr. Filmore was all the gods. He held her fate in his hands. His was the sword that could cut the string— or sever the neck—of her career. *He cannot ever, ever see that book.*

"Erin," he began, and she quickly turned the monitor, angling it away from his line of sight.

"What? Yes," she blurted. Then took a breath to calm herself. "How is your day faring?"

His brow furrowed and at first she thought he was angry, but then she realized he was confused. Trying to parse what she had just said. She had to get ahold of herself.

He took a step in and she pretended to stretch her wrist, bumping it into the monitor to angle it farther away. She thought about knocking the monitor onto the floor, but what if it didn't break? Then if he tried to help her retrieve it, and saw the screen and *oh my god, oh my GOD*—

She ordered herself to stay calm. Or at least to appear calm.

"We're set for the final review of your tenure case next Thursday," he said, as if this was good news. Two hours ago, it had been. "But I saw that you had a referral from Dr. Brennen at Princeton. Their science department just isn't what it used to be. I'd consider getting a referral from a more prestigious school."

She was baffled. "More prestigious than Prince—" And then she caught herself. This was not something she should argue about. "Yes, of course." She faked a little laugh. "I can't believe I almost did that."

He appeared to relax, satisfied that she could sail over this speed bump. Behind her, the monitor glowed like a piece of plutonium. She body-blocked it and maintained her focus on his face.

"I think you're an asset to modern physics and I'd hate to see you throw it down the drain," he told her.

I've heard that before. She kept her focus without blinking, smiling tightly. He turned to leave and she almost let go, collapsing into a puddle, when he spun back around. She stood at attention. He looked her up and down.

"Oh, and about your clothes," he said.

She was unnerved. "Um, what about them?"

He stared at her. Just stared. She stared back. It was a staring thing. Her heart was pounding. The monitor was glowing. The book was on Amazon. Her clothes . . . what, what was wrong with her clothes?

"Never mind," he said.

She looked down at her outfit. That was not the priority here. The book of doom was the priority.

She whirled around and clicked on "Abigail L. Yates." Then she leaned forward, and began to read the horrible revelations that spewed forth:

"Abigail continues her passion for the study of the paranormal at the Kenneth T. Higgins Institute of Science . . . "

Ooof! The eigenvalue of her outrage was unquantifiable.

She sailed out the door. Abby. Abby Yates. What would her life be like if she had never met Abby?

4

A long time ago in a high school far away . . .

Erin Gilbert, her well-worn briefcase clutched to her chest, serpentined between the long lab tables, and took a seat on a stool near the windows at the back of the classroom. On the stool beside her sat a girl she'd never seen before—eager, alert, but also a little shy. The class was Honors Physics, but for lack of available space at C. W. Post High, it was being held in the chemistry lab. The other students were excitedly chatting and joking, with the occasional piercing shriek; the noise was quite loud. She set her briefcase on the counter beside the stainless steel sink and Bunsen burner, and took out her notebook and pen, trying her best to be invisible.

That rarely ever worked for her, but she had no other option except to stay home from school—and she had pretty much played out that hand with her parents by third grade.

The boy sitting at the lab table in front of hers slowly turned on his stool. He smiled wickedly at her, revealing his braces. Pudgy, blemished, pasty-faced Carl Lund was her science and math class nemesis. Because they were both college fast-tracked, he was in every period of hers except PE.

"I'm going to kick your butt in this class, Gilbert, you giant loser," he sneered.

Erin wanted to say, "Good luck with that," but she knew better than to provoke him.

Not that it ended up mattering anyway.

Carl straightened his signature slouch, and loud enough for someone in the hall outside to hear, bellowed, "Hey, Gilbert, see any ghosts over the weekend?"

She could feel the new girl staring at her in astonishment. Erin's cheeks burned.

"Look out, Ghost Girl!" Carl said. "Here it comes . . ." He opened his yap, stuck out his tongue, and made gross barfing noises.

The whole class cracked up. Some of the kids caught the fever and mimicked Carl, pretending to vomit. Which made everyone laugh even louder.

The joke apparently never got old.

Way back in second grade, Erin had made the mistake of confiding her experience with the spirit of Mrs. Barnard to Darla Murray, a girl she had desperately wanted to be her friend. Darla had promptly told the other popular girls in the class, to secure her place as their reigning queen. The story spread around the playground like chicken pox. No one believed Erin. They all thought she just wanted to sound important and special when she wasn't. So not only was she geeky and friendless, she was a mental case to boot. They started calling her "Ghost Girl," behind her back at first, then to her face, and the name had unfortunately stuck.

As the class bell rang, the physics teacher hurried into the room with an armload of notebooks. He was a big man with a tight crew cut. He wore a short-sleeved dress shirt and a bow tie that clashed with his slacks.

"Welcome to Honors Physics," he said. "I'm Mr. Puccini." His baritone, no-nonsense voice silenced the laughter and talking. He glanced down at a three-by-five card in his hand. "We have a new student with us today. From Indiana, isn't it, Abby?"

"Yes, Mr. Puccini."

Erin looked at the smiling girl one stool over.

"Let's give her a special welcome to our school," the teacher said.

"Ahh, ahh, ahh . . ." Carl pretended to sneeze as he shouted, "*Fat-butt!*"

Everyone laughed; everyone but Erin and Abby.

Although Erin felt really bad for the new girl, part of her was relieved the focus of derision had momentarily shifted.

"Enough of that, Mr. Lund," the teacher said, staring him down. "On your feet. Get up here. Let's see if you can solve the problem I've written on the board. If you can't, maybe you don't belong in an honors class . . ."

The students made appreciative "ooooooh" sounds.

His freckled face red, Carl slipped from his stool and stepped up to the blackboard. He looked at the equation and snorted.

To Erin's chagrin, he had no trouble solving the problem, which she had solved in her head, too. The jerk gave the class a show-offy deep bow before retaking his stool.

Mr. Puccini ran the remainder of the hour like a well-oiled machine—no interruptions, just physics, and plenty of it, keeping everyone on their toes with pointed questions and corrections of the answers given. After the bell rang, Erin let most of the others file out for next period before she picked up her briefcase.

The new girl hung back, too. "Why do they call you Ghost Girl?" she asked softly. "I'm Abby Yates, by the way." Which of course, Erin already knew.

The eagerness in her eyes to learn Erin's most embarrassing not-so-secret secret made Erin groan inwardly. *Another torturer joins the inquisition.* Abby Yates was short; her nerdy, shapeless attire accentuated the roundness of an already somewhat too-round body. Her striped wool socks flopped loosely around her ankles, but perfectly matched her purple Birkenstocks.

"I've been interested in the paranormal like for-ever," Abby confessed breathily. "That and conventional physical sciences fascinate me. Are you into the paranormal, too?"

"I've got Honors Calculus next period," Erin said, biting off her words. "Gotta go."

As she breezed around the end of the lab table, Abby called to her back, "Calc with Mr. Bennett? That's me, too. Can I walk with you?"

It was lunchtime after math class and Abby followed Erin to her locker, then outside. To be honest, she hadn't tried all that hard to ditch her—assuming she actually could have; Abby clung to her like a life preserver. Having sat through a second class together, Erin was less certain of her kneejerk analysis, that the new girl just wanted to be in on the in-joke that had everyone else in school in stitches. Abby seemed as lost as she was, and maybe more than a little scared, too, what with it being her first day at C. W. Post and coming from out of state. Erin got the feeling that Abby just wanted someone to hang with. They had a lot in common, at least superficially. They shared the same fashion sense. The same disdain for boys, because boys weren't interested in them. And the same level of smarts, or they wouldn't both have been in the honors science program. It was great to be needed, but Erin refused to get her hopes too high—she had been burned too many times in the past.

"So, come on and tell me," Abby said as they sat down on a bench in the quad to eat their sack lunches. "How did you get that 'Ghost Girl' nickname?"

Erin lowered her peanut butter and jelly sandwich. "Everybody else in school knows, so you're going to find out sooner or later," she said dismally. "Might as well get it over with."

Then in a low tone of voice and highly compressed

fashion, she told Abby the story: Corky, the dead rooster, the dead neighbor, and the haunting.

"You had actual *visitations*?"

Erin nodded glumly, returning to her sandwich, which had turned completely tasteless. She chewed the mouthful to paste, waiting for the other shoe to fall, for her new friend to make fun of her like everyone else.

"That is so amazing!" Abby said, beaming at up her. "Do you still see Mrs. Barnard's ghost?" She sounded almost . . . hopeful.

"I saw her every night for a year when I was little," Erin said. "Then her empty house burned down and I never saw her again."

"Damn!" Abby said, slapping herself on the thigh.

Erin flinched at the smack. *Here it comes*, she thought. *I knew it. She's a crazy person.* She had to be.

"Think what we could have done if we'd had the right equipment on-site."

"What?"

"The questions we could have investigated," Abby said. "I mean, come on! What kind of radiation was it giving off? Infrared? EM? Ionizing? Was the energy constant or fluctuating? Did it reflect or refract light? Or did it project its own light? Was there chemical trace left behind at the scene? Perhaps phosphorescence? Maybe radioactivity? Even if all we accomplished was to eliminate the obvious possibilities, it would have been a major breakthrough in the understanding of spectral phenomena."

Erin was dumbstruck. "Do you believe me?"

Abby looked her in the eye. "I saw how you handled yourself in Advanced Physics and Calculus. You're not some whacked out, woo-woo doofus. You got game. So if you aren't a dimwit, and you don't think I'm a dimwit, why would you repeat something to me everybody else thinks is total BS? There's nothing to be gained from a lie like that at this point, is there?"

Erin just stared at her, unable to speak.

"Okay," Abby went on, "there is no physical evidence to examine, no way to confirm that you saw what you saw, but I'm willing to suspend disbelief in the absence of falsifying proof."

Popper, Erin thought, with a catch in her throat. *She's quoting* Karl Popper, *one of the greatest scientific philosophers of the twentieth century.* And a personal hero of Erin's!

Abby leaned closer, her face suddenly flushed with excitement. "Please tell me what you saw and heard and felt during the experience. Everything you can remember. Was there a rush of cold or slamming doors or lights flickering on and off before the spirit materialized? What was the ectoplasmic deluge like? Was it actually wet—were your clothes soaked by it? What was its consistency? Did it have an odor or taste? Did the ectoplasm completely disappear when the presence vanished? Did the vomiting happen every night? Was the specter's appearance, performance, and exit the same every night? Did your interaction with it change anything it did in the present moment or the next time it appeared?"

Erin did her best to explain what happened and how it happened—like a holographic tape loop every night for a year.

"Good grief!" Abby exclaimed when she was finished. "That's a humanoid Class Four!"

"A class what?"

"It's an application of Linnaean taxonomy," Abby explained. "An interest of mine since middle school. One way to make sense of the disparate spectral phenomena is to note all associated facts surrounding their individual appearances and classify each into main and subcategories. I've started the process but only really scratched the surface."

"Science is all about clear, precise definitions," Erin

said. "That is so totally Baconian! Oh my god, I don't believe it—you're really into this! I never though I'd meet
any—"

"Ahh, ahh, ahh, fat-butt!" The fake sneeze came from
behind them on the senior lawn.

They turned to see Carl Lund grinning fiendishly. He
was backed by a coterie of nerdish hangers-on.

"Ahh, uhh-ahh, uhh-ahh . . ." He pretended trying to
hold back a second sneeze, waving his hands like flippers,
closing his eyes, and wrinkling his nose. When he let it
burst forth, it echoed around the quad: "Fat-butt! Fat-butt!
Fat-fat-butt-butt! Fat-fat-butt-butt!"

Abby jumped to her feet and rounded the bench with a
ferocious growl, swinging her heavy backpack overhead
like a mace. There was no doubt she meant business. Carl
and friends turned and fled, laughing.

Erin applauded her as she returned and dropped into her
seat.

"Do I have a nickname now, too?" Abby said, slightly
out of breath.

"I'm so sorry . . ."

"Don't be," Abby said. "Ghost Girl and Fat Butt. We
sound like comic book superheroes."

It was the start of a beautiful friendship.

And collaboration.

Oblivious to everyone else, and mostly in secret, they
set about making the first truly scientific study of the
paranormal. Like Erin, Abby was very organized, self-
motivated, and disciplined. First they read the standard
"ghost hunter" works: *Spates Catalog, Tobin's Spirit
Guide,* and *The Roylance Guide.* Then they began cata-
loging everything they could find on the Internet, including the confirmed fraudulent incidents, so they could more
easily and quickly identify and discard them. The sheer
volume of information was daunting—ninety-six million
search results on the word "ghost" alone. Clearly, they
needed some help. But whom could they ask? And how?

They couldn't pay someone else to do the work, they didn't have that kind of allowance money, and they were just kids, what adult would work for them?

Abby finally came up with a novel solution. They both belonged to the Physics Club at Post High, so why not start a Metaphysics Club, too, and have members help with the research? They wouldn't even have to pay them. Mr. Puccini provisionally allowed them the use of school property because he thought the idea was funny and that it was all about debunking the spiritual and unscientific. But that was only part of it—the public part.

They held three club meetings after school in the chem lab and no one showed up except the janitor, and all he wanted was to wipe down the lab tables and stack the stools. Of course word got around school about the club and the empty lab, and the yahoos like Carl made the most of it. Strangely enough, nasty remarks didn't seem to bother Erin as much anymore, not with Abby to turn them into their own private jokes.

Erin never told her therapist about the interest in the spirit world she shared with Abby—she had fibbed when the question had come up and said physics and higher math were the hobbies they had in common. She didn't want her parents to find out about the scientific ghost hunt she had embarked on. They had been so relieved that she had finally found a friend and that she seemed happier about high school in general.

It was weird; she had been thankful when Mrs. Barnard had stopped haunting her, but sometimes wished she had her back, bloody barf and all, to confirm that the experience was real—and that she wasn't crazy. She knew searching for ghosts in order to prove she wasn't crazy would make her look deranged in the eyes of her parents and her therapist, as if the years of analysis had all been for nothing. It would crush them to discover what was really going on, but she couldn't help herself. She wanted an explanation for what had happened to her, even though she was afraid of what she might learn about herself in the process.

Even though they used special algorithmic tools they had designed to refine the searches, the task was just too much for two people. Plus they had schoolwork to complete. After a couple of months, they gathered a lot of useful information to make some generalizations about forms of spectral anomalies. But clearly the Baconian approach would take the rest of their lives simply to compile the data, let alone analyze it.

"We've got to try a different method," Erin said. They sat on her bed amid heaps of printouts and charts and empty candy wrappers. The debris flow spilled onto the rug on either side of the bed frame.

"Okay," Abby said, "I'm listening. What have you got?"

"Screw empiricism. Let's try rationalism."

"Descartes, Descartes, Descartes . . ." Abby chanted, pumping her fist in the air.

"In the absence of evidence to the contrary," Erin continued, "we assume that ghosts are real and proceed from that as a general rule to test what makes them appear the way they do to us. Bigger-picture stuff. What could they consist of, where do they go when they aren't here, what keeps them from commuting back and forth when they want?"

"Those hypotheses could all be tested with limited experimental variables, if we had the right gear," Abby said. "I'm loving this—real science applied to the paranormal. Gilbert, you're a frickin' genius!"

Instead of merely collecting data for later analysis, Erin and Abby began extrapolating and synthesizing from the paradigms of conventional science in an attempt to explain the observed phenomena. Those theories included quantum and nonquantum physics, Lagrangian mechanics, string theory, parallel universes, interdimensional membranes, and ionization caused by the friction of cross-dimensional transfer—like a thermonuclear static charge.

Night after night, seven days a week, they stayed up late on the phone giggling and laughing and evaluating their progress.

Erin's parents thought they were talking about boys.

As the memory burned a hole in her stomach lining, Erin scowled through the window of her taxi. Apparently that wasn't the only time Abby let people think she was doing one thing when she was actually doing another. No one was supposed to know about the book.

And now everyone did.

5

E rin got out of the cab. She was in the Bronx, standing before the Kenneth T. Higgins Institute of Science, an academy of higher learning that she had never heard of before. It was housed in a large, run-down building fronted by three arches; pennants above them read Imagine. Invent. Inspire. As she walked past the threadbare patch of front lawn, a lively student discussion deteriorated into a multicombatant brawl.

Indignation over Abbey's treachery was the fuel that propelled her into the dismal structure, down a narrow flight of stairs, and along a dim, dank basement hallway until she reached the door she sought: number 25. There she halted, suddenly out of steam.

The door was marked PARANORMAL STUDIES LABORA-TORY—DR. ABIGAIL L. YATES AND DR. JILLIAN HOLTZMANN. A piece of paper was taped to the door. On it, in thick capital letters, were the words DO NOT WRITE STUPID THINGS ON THIS DOOR. The word "stupid" had been added in red marker.

I have to do this, Erin thought. But she didn't want to. She really, really didn't want to. Taking a deep, dread-filled breath, she knocked.

"Enter!" a voice called. It shocked her that she knew that voice almost as well as her own. Actually, better, since sound was a wave and the vibrations of one's own voice were created inside the cranium in the ear canal, then sent to the auditory nerve for interpretation by the brain.

Don't stall.

She went inside. Blinked. If this was a lab, then the lunatics really had taken over the asylum. She was staring at a huge junkyard for geeks piled with all manner of machines, motors, monitors, ducts and duct tape, speakers, copper wire and steel housings, wires of every color and thickness, rivets, tablets, tools, blue component shelves, yellow component shelves, and scratched-up tables loaded with computers, computer chips and potato chips and chocolate chips, and was that a jet pack?

And there was the damned book itself, proudly on display for all to see. She gulped down a bitter pill of guilt and shame.

"I've been waiting a long time," the voice she remembered said sternly.

"Oh, Abby," she said. "That's exactly what I was afraid of—"

"I hope I got more than one wonton out of you."

She tried to parse that. "Excuse me?"

A deliveryman had come into the room behind her. He was carrying a plastic bag and inside, a soup container. She got it: wontons.

"Oh," she said.

Then Abby walked into the room from between yellow plastic curtains. She was still the same old Abby: green eyes, little turned-up nose, and a complicated, antenna-like helmet on her head that resembled an old-fashioned hair dryer belonging to a fifties housewife from the planet Xenon. It was covered with toroid magnets, circuits, bristling filaments, coils of wire, and possibly a Ginzu knife or two. Those days, those old days of scientific questing—

Abby spotted Erin and instantly slowed, a fire smoldering in her eyes. Erin had had dreams and nightmares both about this moment of confrontation and retribution. She held her breath.

"Well. My old friend, Erin Gilbert."

Erin couldn't look Abby in the eyes. She lowered her gaze to the floor—was that a fishing rod? Why would they have a fishing rod?—and soaked in the tension.

"What's on your head?" the deliveryman asked her.

"An advancement in science," Abby replied. She handed him some bills and took his delivery order. "That'll be all. And please show *her* the exit. I'm sure she was already looking for it."

Abby turned away as the confused man took Erin by the elbow and began to lean her to the door. "It's the same door we came in," he explained. "It's very simple, really." Erin brushed him off and walked after Abby's back.

"Abby," she began, "we need to have a conversation."

Abby pointed to the thing on her head. "Well, I'm trying to have a conversation with the constant frequency signal I'm relaying through spectral foam. If you can be more interesting than that, be my guest."

Erin's attention was diverted. According to their hypothesis, localized ether excitation, known as "spectral foam," could result in regions of seemingly unphysical occurrences and the appearance of "specters." Ghosts. Abby had access to spectral foam? How in the world had she managed *that*?

Erin, refocus, she ordered herself.

"You put the book online without my permission." There. Plainspoken and to the point.

Abby raised a brow. "I wasn't aware I needed your permission."

She was going to make this difficult. Erin was going to have to play through. Just like in miniature golf.

"Yes, you do, Abby. I really need you to take it down."

Abby defiantly pulled herself to her full height, which wasn't much. The fire in her eyes reignited. "Absolutely not. It's a great book. Or have you forgotten?"

Abby sat down and pulled her Chinese food out of the delivery sack. She wasn't going to make this easy.

"Look, I'm up for tenure right now," Erin said. "This is the first thing that comes up if you Google my name." She showed her the book. "If my colleagues see this, I will be the laughingstock of Columbia University."

Abby was about to pry the lid off her Chinese food. She shrugged. "So?"

"*So,*" Erin pressed, "there is no experimental backing for anything in that book. No one has ever been able to prove the existence of the paranormal! That book just makes us look crazy."

Abby lifted her chin. "Guess what? If all theories had experimental backing, we wouldn't be anywhere! You tell Columbia University that! You give them that from me!"

She looked down at her soup. A scowl shadowed her face. "There is only *one* wonton! Unbelievable!"

Erin remembered the many all-nighters they had pulled, subsisting on wonton soup and meat-lovers' pizza. And the time they had gone shopping for the black turtleneck sweaters they were wearing in their author photo . . .

She sat and sighed. That embarrassing photo. She was standing behind Abby with her elbow on her shoulder. *Behold. We are brainy.* They looked like teenage-girl versions of one of their heroes, the late, great astronomer Carl Sagan, who had sent a golden record on one of the *Voyager* spacecraft for the aliens to listen to. They also looked like beat poets. And Simon and Garfunkel.

They did not look like serious scientific investigators.

"You carry a lot of tension in your shoulders," a woman's voice said, startling her. Erin turned.

The speaker was sitting at a worktable with her boots up. She was blond, her curly hair billowing upward, and she was wearing glasses that looked like an oversized pair of safety goggles. She was playing with a small blowtorch. Over a stretchy olive crop top she wore a pair of gray overalls splattered with paint; over that, an army jacket. She had on a pendant that was a big screw angled through the letter U. Screw you. Har-har. The woman was surrounded by piles of miscellaneous metal parts, what appeared to be scavenged electronics components, and conglomerations of the two that looked like weapons. Behind her, a pegboard was overloaded with more junk on hooks.

Already on the defensive, Erin felt her dander rise. She said, "Okay who are you?"

Abby acknowledged the woman, saying, "Holtzmann works with me in the lab. She's a brilliant engineer. And *loyal*." She emphasized the last word. "Would never abandon you. Unlike some people I know—"

"Yes, I *get* it," Erin snapped. Even a guilty party could only take so much, well, guilt.

"She specializes in experimental particle physics. She almost got into CERN."

That was the European Organization for Nuclear Research, and infinitely harder to become a part of than Columbia University. Erin said, "Almost?"

Holtzmann was still playing with the blowtorch. *Pffft, pffft,* on and off. "There was a lab incident." She grimaced slightly, but her eyes twinkled. She seemed a bit like one of those feral children you saw in documentaries from France.

Abby glanced over at her. "He'll wake up."

"They said he moved a finger yesterday," Holtzmann said, brightening a bit.

"Oh, good."

Erin couldn't figure them out—if they were toying with her or all this was true. Abby seemed genuinely pleased at the news. She returned her attention to Erin. "She and I are bringing the ideas in our book to life. We're close on a hollow laser for the reverse tractor beam."

Oh my god, she's serious. That's what's on the table. And the walls. And the floor. I'm surrounded by bits and pieces of our shared delusions.

"Terrific," she bit off.

"It is terrific," Abby said coldly.

Holtzmann cocked her head. "Abby, why don't you just let her listen to the EVP?"

Abby shook her head. "Absolutely not."

EVP stood for electronic voice phenomenon. As in recordings of ghostly voices. Despite herself, Erin said, "What EVP?"

Holtzmann flashed a cajoling smile at her colleague. "Let her listen. It's the only way she'll know."

Know? Know what? That they're both insane?

"Fine," Abby said. "But she doesn't deserve it."

Holtzmann and Abby walked over to a tape recorder on one of their crowded worktables. Holtzmann gestured to it. "A few months ago, we spent eight days at the Chelsea Hotel."

A registered national historic landmark, Erin filled in. Home to musicians and avant-garde celebrities for decades. Of course, such a place was said to have its share of ghosts. Sid Vicious's girlfriend, Nancy, had been stabbed to death there.

Holtzmann continued. "We didn't get anything—"

Of course not, Erin thought, but she was beginning to get uncomfortable.

"—or so we thought," Abby cut in. "We found this later, going through the tapes." She was looking at the device.

Without thinking, Erin said, "Did you use only one recording device? If you had multiple ones you could've located the source—"

Abby snorted. "Did we only use *one* recording device? I'm not a moron, Erin."

"I should warn you . . ." Holtzmann leaned forward and hit play. "This . . . it's upsetting. What you're about to hear . . . it's just not from this world."

Erin leaned in. White noise, static, jittered from the speaker. Holtzmann turned up the volume. The static grew louder, but it seemed to be more organized, containing a rhythm, perhaps even a pattern. The skin on Erin's face prickled. Her chest tightened as she caught her breath, alert, listening as hard as she could. Had Abby really done it? Finally made contact?

And then . . . the unmistakable *blat* of a fart punctuated the ambient vibrations. Holtzmann and Abby cracked up, and Erin's cheeks flared with heat.

"Wow," she said, not wanting for anything in this world for Abby to know how disappointed she was. Because she *was* disappointed. "Really? That's disgusting."

Holtzmann's eyes glittered with mischievous humor. "Is it more or less disgusting if I tell you it came from the front?"

"Cool joke," she snapped back. "You guys are just killing it in here."

"Oh, we have fun," Holtzmann said.

"I'm so glad we could have an adult conversation about this," Erin said irritably. She was outfunned and outgunned.

Abby regarded her, hostility resurfacing in those familiar eyes. "If you really don't believe in this stuff anymore, why were you looking for the book? Huh?"

"I wasn't," Erin said. "Some man came to see me because he thinks his building is haunted."

Abby and Holtzmann traded looks.

"What building?" Abby asked.

"Aldridge Mansion," Erin replied.

Abby and Holtzmann burst into action, zooming over to a computer and beginning to type. Batman and Robin. Frankenstein and Igor.

"See, that's the problem, Abby," Erin said. "This book . . . this science . . . it encourages troubled people to indulge their delusions. People who need real help, not stupid theories . . . Okay, you're not listening."

Abby wasn't listening. Neither was Holtzmann. They were quietly murmuring to each other as they hovered over the computer. Finally, Abby stood and said, "Let's go see some ghosts."

As if they had completely forgotten that she was there, they started packing a plethora of strange-looking equipment into a large duffel bag. Erin fought to remain a detached observer, but she couldn't help checking out everything, trying to remember the various diagrams and sketches they had put in their book. Crazy ghost-hunting equipment. Useless and preposterous. But was that an enhanced MEL meter? And what about—

Abby zipped the bag shut. Thusly prepared, she and Holtzmann made a beeline for the door. Then Abby looked over her shoulder at Erin.

"All right, let's move."

Erin gave her head a shake. "I'm not going on your mission." Although for a second there, she had really wanted to . . .

Abby looked at her sourly. "Well, thank you for sending your regrets, but I didn't invite you. I just can't lock this door until you're out of the room. Move it. Or you can just lock it and shut it on your way out."

Erin was stung. "Oh. It was an understandable mistake." She was fully aware that the reason for her visit was getting buried in this so-called "mission." *Why* had she provided such a detailed explanation? All she'd needed to say was that someone had seen it on Amazon. That was it. It was the scientist in her, the *good* scientist, dealing in facts. Ed Mulgrave was a fact. But ghost hunting?

Fiction.

Dangerous fiction.

Trying to maintain her dignity, she walked past Abby toward the hallway.

"That's a beautiful suit, by the way," Abby said.

"Oh. Thank you." Erin was pleased. Inordinately so. Still, it was the first kind thing Abby had said to her after all these years apart.

My doing, she thought. *My fault.*

She trailed after Abby and Holtzmann as they staggered down the street with their stuff. They giggled and chattered. They were having fun.

If you want tenure at Columbia, she reminded herself, *you cannot have fun.*

Abby hailed a cab and looked back at Erin. With mock obsequiousness she said, "Oh, I'm sorry. Did you want to take this cab and leave us behind? You've always been so good at that."

Erin rolled her eyes, but inside, her feelings were hurt. She'd thought the compliment on her suit had been an olive branch, not a wooden stake.

"That was very pointed," Holtzmann declared, and Abby inclined her head.

"Thank you."

Erin called after her, "Abby, please take down the book." *Please, please, please don't ruin my career.*

Abby looked at her and seemed to see her for the first time. Erin began to seriously lose it. Yes, what she had done to warrant Abby's present behavior—and she did warrant it—had been churlish, backstabbing, thoughtless. But she had been very young then. And maybe she had gotten some bad advice. She wasn't sure. After all, she was up for tenure at Columbia. And Abby was mired in the boondocks of weirdness at the Kenneth T. Higgins Institute.

My career is my life. The esteem of my colleagues is crucial to my future. Please, please, please, Abby, this punishment does not fit my crime.

Something in Erin's chest wrenched, and wrenched hard. And Abby's face softened, as if somehow through the white noise of bad history she could hear Erin's distress call.

"All right," Abby said. "Introduce us to this guy at Aldridge Mansion, and if we don't pick up anything there, I'll consider taking the book down just until you get your tenure to Bullshit University."

"Thank you," Erin breathed, deflating like a popped

balloon. She was saved. And maybe, just a little bit curious about Aldridge Mansion . . .

No. No, no, no, I. Am. Not.

But it did look like fun. Back in the day, it had been a lot of big, scary fun.

Erin got into the cab. Next stop, Aldridge Mansion—with a side trip down Memory Lane.

6

This is going to be fun. In an it-might-kill-us way.

Bundled up for the cold, college freshman Erin sat side by side with Abby on the bus from the University of Michigan at Ann Arbor to the town of Ypsilanti. The side windows were fogged with condensation, but against the darkness on the street she could see dim white mounds of snow banked up in the gutters. There was hardly anyone on the bus so late on Thanksgiving Day. A drunken man was talking to himself in the backseat, but she couldn't make out what he was saying because the engine noise was so loud. There were a couple of teenage boys in hoodies jacked in with earbuds and a thin middle-aged woman in a knit beret with overstuffed shopping bags who was trying to read a yellowed paperback book while the bus lurched and swayed sickeningly.

The ride between campus and Ypsilanti took about fifty minutes, and though Erin wouldn't admit it to Abby, she was terrified out of her mind the whole way. Their ultimate destination was Depot Town, which lay north of the gentrified section of Ypsilanti, a place where two freshmen girls had no business after dark. Instead of being home for Thanksgiving dinner surrounded by family and love, they were risking robbery, rape, and worse.

On top of that, they both had lied to their parents about the reason for not coming home for the holidays: they said they had to hunker down and study—a lie of omission. What they were studying was not the science or math their parents would naturally assume, but the paranormal.

"This is it," Abby said, pulling the stop cord for Depot Town.

They trundled off the bus, backpacks loaded with scientific equipment and recording gear. Abby took the lead, turning north on the empty sidewalk, leading them away from the lights and life of the restaurants in Depot Town's historical buildings, and toward the address on Norris Street.

They speed-walked through a mixed neighborhood of stark Victorians, bungalows from the 1930s, and small, bunkerlike brick homes from the 1950s. The lots were big, full of bare mature trees and drifts of snow that almost completely buried the underbrush. The sidewalk was cleared and salted, but icy in the shadiest spots. They both had their flashlights out because the streetlights were sparse. Erin could see into some of the houses that were close to the sidewalk. Some looked warm and comfy. Others were dark, dead, and forbidding.

Every time a car's headlights flared behind them, Erin cringed, waiting to hear the screech of brakes and the sound of car doors banging open. The route was dotted with empty lots and abandoned houses: convenient places to commit murders and hide bodies. How had she ended up here? The answer was simple: Abby had talked her into it. With the sheer force of her personality, her friend had convinced her they had no choice but to come here Thanksgiving night, which meant blowing off going home for the holiday and risking their own safety. Abby had the ability to pull Erin past the edge of what was comfortable and into the realm of what was decidedly not. Abby wasn't fearless or stupid; she was just willing to take a calculated risk.

"This could be the big time," she said. "We've got to go for it."

And so they had.

Cold seeped into Erin's feet and hands and her eyes watered. The lower part of her face was wrapped in a muffler. After walking for what seemed like miles, they finally saw the street number they were looking for. It belonged to a 1950s ranch house with narrow, high-set horizontal windows. Gang tags covered the redbrick veneer. The entrance was on the side, up the driveway, the entire property enclosed in a rusting, six-foot-tall hurricane fence decorated with No Trespassing signs. The snow-mounded yard was studded with unidentifiable junk that had been either dragged out of the house or thrown over the fence.

"With all that tagging, there's got to be a way in," Abby said. "Maybe it's around the side." She shined her light on the ground and it cast a bright ring in the snow. She set off across the empty space between the fence and the side of the darkened Victorian next door.

Erin followed her through the snow, turning her own light through the fence, onto the plywood nailed over the house's front door and picture window. KEEP OUT had been spray-painted on the plywood, but was barely visible beneath the graffiti.

They had embarked on the field trip because something horrible had happened at the Norris Street address on Thanksgiving Day 1966. According to news accounts, the man of the house went berserk after the Detroit Lions lost to the San Francisco 49ers, fourteen to forty-one, and chased his family out into the icy street with a baseball bat. After locking the door, he threw the cooked turkey out of the oven, blew out the pilot light, stuck his head in, and gassed himself. Ever since, and particularly on Thanksgiving, supernatural events had been reported at the house: an eerie green glow from inside, crashing noises, moans, curses, shrieks, and most disturbing of all, the unmistakable smell of roasted turkey. That's why the place stood abandoned—people were afraid to live in it.

"Over here," Abby said. "I knew it. There's a break in the fence."

They had to take off their backpacks to squeeze through the slit in the wire, then reach back to retrieve them.

Abby reshouldered her pack and hurried for the boarded-up back door. "It's loose," she said as she pulled the edge of the plywood aside and reached into the gap. "The door isn't locked. Let's go in."

Erin followed her through and into a little mudroom with a curling linoleum floor. Beyond it, their flashlights lit up the spot where the washer and dryer had been.

"Kitchen must be just ahead," Abby said.

Their breath steamed in the light of the flashes.

"Stove is gone," Erin said, noting the gap in the counter under the range hood and the capped-off gas pipe sticking out of the foot of the wall. "But that's where he died. Those Formica countertops are original."

"Nice cigarette burns," Abby said.

Erin swept her flashlight around the room. Some of the acoustic tile ceiling had fallen out and pink fiberglass insulation was strewn all over the floor. "Rats have been in here. Ugh."

"Let's check out the rest of the place," Abby said.

They moved through the dining room and into the living room. The walls had big holes kicked in them and they, too, were tagged. Glass from broken windows glittered on the floor. Plumbing fixtures had been ripped out of the bathroom, the mirror shattered into confetti, and all the bedroom doors were gone. Someone had dragged an old, stained twin mattress into one of the rooms. Their flashes lit up empty whiskey bottles and fast-food trash. Someone had been camping there. Not recently, though—the dates on the moldy newspapers on the floor were a year old.

"This is so cool," Abby said, taking it all in. "Do you feel the vibe? Spooo-ky! We're going to catch us a ghost; I know it. We've got to spend the night!"

"It's freezing in here and the floor is disgusting," Erin protested. "We didn't bring sleeping bags, or even blankets."

"We can take turns on the mattress."

"You've got to be—"

"Wait," Abby said in a hushed voice. "Did you hear that?"

A faint creaking sound came from the other side of the house.

Erin's heart began to pound.

"Hurry, get out the gear," Abby whispered.

Erin dug the video recorder out of her pack. Abby unwrapped the unwieldy, portable photoelectron spectrometer they had cobbled together from parts filched from U of M physics and chem labs.

When they tiptoed back to the living room, a greenish glow was moving around in the kitchen, very erratically. From the doorless doorway came a sharp clatter and disembodied curse.

Erin breathed in the aroma of roast turkey and a wave of dizziness swept over her. This was it. This was really it. She was about to see her second ghost, only this time with a witness. Her legs went weak. She suddenly realized she wasn't ready for prime time. She was all talk and none of the walk.

Abby grabbed her shoulder and shoved her forward. Erin instinctively aimed the video camera at the dancing light on the other side of the doorway as she was pushed bodily through it.

Intense light blasted into their faces as they burst into the ruined kitchen, and Erin was momentarily blinded.

"Who the heck are you?" said a shrill voice. "I'm armed!"

Erin's eyes quickly recovered and she saw a diminutive woman in an olive-brown down hat and matching parka holding a portable lantern in one hand and a dinner fork in the other.

"We're scientists from U of M," Abby said, stretching the truth with what sounded like absolute conviction. "Who are you?"

"Martha Kinsler. I'm a writer, doing research for a book."

"A book about ghosts?" Erin said.

"Well, it's sure as hell not interior decorating," Kinsler retorted. "Why are you here?"

"Ghosts, same as you," Abby answered. "Only we're using applied science to uncover the mechanisms of the spectral plane. We have some theories . . ."

"What's that smell?" Erin gasped. "Is that *him*?"

Kinsler showed them her open Tupperware container and the still-steaming turkey, gravy, stuffing, and mashed potatoes. An insulated bag sat on the floor. "My Thanksgiving dinner. Sorry, there's not enough to go around."

"No problem." Abby lowered the PKE spectrometer's nozzle. She carried the makeshift analyzer on a webbed strap over her shoulder.

"That thing's kind of intimidating." Kinsler nodded at the ten-inch black probe. "What does it do?"

"Samples the air, and what's in this box measures the ionization energy," Abby said. "We believe that could be a component or maybe the chemical signature of spectral appearances."

Kinsler raised her brows. "Wow, you weren't kidding about being scientists. Have you taken any readings yet?"

"We just got here," Abby said.

"What do you know about Charles Lemayne?"

"Got mad after the Lions lost and killed himself right there," Abby said.

"There's a bit more to it than that," Kinsler said. "I interviewed his widow a few years ago. He was about to lose this house to the bank—because of a serious gambling problem—when he had a vision about the outcome of the Thanksgiving Day game. Not a hunch, but a real vision, according to the widow. Came to him while he was brushing his teeth two days earlier. He saw something in the bathroom mirror—she wasn't clear about what it was— but it told him to bet his last nickel on the Lions. He was so scared by the experience and so financially desperate that he did what he was told."

"His widow was convinced this was the truth?" Erin asked.

"I am certain she believed it," Kinsler said. "Even talking about it forty years later shook her up so badly she could hardly speak."

"Do you think he had been contacted by something from the other side, something malignant?" Abby said.

"That's for you to find out," the little woman said. "And when you do, you'll want to write a book about it; everyone does, and sensational paranormal is hot with publishers right now. If you ever decide you need a ghost writer— ha-ha—to help you, here's my card."

As she passed it to Abby, blue and red lights flashed through the narrow windows at the far end of the living room, spinning over the ceiling and walls.

"Crap!" Kinsler cried. "It's the Ypsi cops. We've got to get out of here fast or we're going to get busted. I can't do more jail time."

"We are so in for it if we get caught," Erin told Abby. "We could even lose our scholarships."

The three of them barreled out the back door, squeezed through the gap in the fence, and didn't look back as they ran across the snowfield behind the house. They got about a hundred feet across the field when a dog started barking; it was running close behind them.

"Police dog!" Erin cried. "Oh my god, the cops sicced their dog on us!"

Abby broke out in laughter. Erin turned and saw a poodle fighting hard to keep up through the deep snow— it was apricot colored and about knee high. When they reached the street on the far side of the field Abby was still giggling.

Erin didn't think it was funny at all.

In the years that had passed since that crazy night a lot had changed.

Erin and Abby had both graduated from U of M and Erin had entered graduate school at Princeton. Abby decided to find someplace in New York to further her research on the paranormal, and Princeton wasn't it. While other undergrads had been partying at the frats and sororities or tailgating at football games, the two of them were sneaking into supposedly haunted houses looking for ghosts, conducting experiments, and theorizing how quantum and nonquantum mechanics might define what was on "the other side." Based on those original concepts, they had developed a brand-new technology for ghost hunting and capture, albeit mostly hypothetical. And spurred by Martha Kinsler's comment on that cold Thanksgiving evening, they had compiled a massive book on their scientific investigations of the paranormal.

The book had seemed like such a good idea at first. It came together in a string of no-sleep, overcaffeinated weekends, a compendium of their field notes, hypotheses, and foundational equations. Erin and Abby had a unique synergy—each one's excitement and inspirations fueled the other. The arcane science and math challenged and stimulated them both. It was thrilling to feel they were on the cusp of doing something truly novel: taking the paranormal out of the Dark Ages.

At first.

Now, not so much.

As Erin hurried across the Princeton campus to a crisis meeting with her physics department graduate advisor, her heart was filled with dread. What she was considering

doing was not just cruel, it was unforgivable, and she hoped
the advisor could provide her with alternatives that had
eluded her.

Initially she and Abby had tried to get some interest in
the book project from university and mainstream science
publishers, but no one wanted to touch it. The academic
reviewers' comments they got back on the partial manuscript were painful and eye opening:

"Made me a believer. After reading this manuscript I
know what being dead feels like."

"Science, this is not; incomprehensible rubbish, this is."

"A hodgepodge of science and science fiction. This
effort proves the old saw: a little education can be a dangerous thing."

"How old are these authors? Twelve?"

Abby wasn't put off by the possibility—or the fact—of
rejection and ridicule. Keeping the anticipated goal in sight,
she simply ignored it. If she had self-doubts, they took a
backseat to what she saw on the horizon. So they had agreed
to publish it themselves. But with the ghastly academic reviews, Erin felt herself withdrawing intellectually and
emotionally from the enterprise. She hadn't told Abby or
her parents, but she'd gone back to therapy, which was offered through the Princeton student health program. The
therapist had helped her reassess what had been going on,
her own motivation and mechanisms since childhood.

In fact, after six years of diligent searching, Erin and
Abby had not found a single ghost. With no car at their
disposal, as undergrads they had traveled all over southern
Michigan on foot, bike, bus, and train, and still could not
confirm that the spectral plane they were researching
even existed. Part of her was relieved, because her memories of Mrs. Barnard were so deeply disturbing she didn't
want to see another ghost. Part of her was terrified, because
not finding any ghosts meant she had probably been crazy
as a child, that what she'd experienced had been a recurring, violent hallucination. If she gave up the search, she'd

never know the truth about herself, whether she was a nut job or not, but to the rest of the world, including her parents and her academic peers, the searching for ghosts in itself was the act of an irrational person.

Her therapist asked her to consider the possibility that she was caught in a repeating, self-generated, irrational loop fueled by fear and guilt. She was afraid of finding out the truth, and guilty about pursuing it. It made perfect sense to her.

Writing the book had been great fun, and so far at least, hardly anyone knew about their private research, their secret adventures. Publication and its implications were bringing the underlying issues to a head. The book's impending release threatened Erin with exposure and made her vulnerable. Deep down she knew she had come to a fork in the road, that she couldn't combine a career in conventional science and the science of the paranormal without paying a dear price.

Putting it all out there was exactly what she'd done with Darla Murray back in elementary school, and look how that had turned out—she had become Ghost Girl, a perpetual joke. Her therapist helped her to see that beyond the very real concerns about her future professional life, she was afraid of history repeating itself. The early ghost experience had left Erin wounded. The fact that her parents hadn't believed her and thought she might be mentally disturbed had undercut her self-confidence and shamed her. What happened in grade school and after had only made it worse. Whom could she trust to protect her? The lesson she had learned was: no one.

Despite the ghastly reviews, they persisted with the book, primarily because Abby wouldn't let it drop. Unlike Erin, she didn't give a damn what people thought of her. Unlike Erin, she wasn't in graduate school at a prestigious university. The harder Abby got pushed, the harder she pushed back. Erin still felt there was solid science behind their work, but the prejudice against the subject matter was too deeply ingrained for it ever to be taken seriously. She began to have doubts about the wisdom of publishing it at all, and tried to get Abby to delay. But she wouldn't hear of it.

"Someone will find it and take notice if we just put it out there," Abby said. "Stuff like that happens all the time. If we get some interest, we can get funding and push forward faster."

In the end they agreed to self-publish the manuscript using a print-on-demand site. After the costs of editing, layout, and promotional package, they each had enough money left over to buy two bound copies. And they were on their way.

Without telling Abby, Erin had given the manuscript to her graduate advisor for a quick, confidential read. Professor Emil Hazan's office was on fifth floor of the sprawling—and intimidating—redbrick and concrete Jadwin Hall complex. The office itself was much less impressive, a windowless cubbyhole so tiny and narrow that Erin wondered how he got the desk in—by disassembling it in the hall first? She also wondered whether he had to climb over it to reach his office chair on the other side.

Hazan was fiftyish with gray in his close-cropped beard and hair, and definitely not a neat freak. The floor-to-ceiling bookshelves were crammed with books, folders, and physics journals turned every which way, and the carpet was covered with heaps of printouts, books, and folders that wouldn't fit in the overstuffed bookshelves.

There was no chair for her to sit on—no room for a chair, either—so she stood in a small clear space on the floor, which the inward swing of the door made necessary.

Her advisor clapped a hand down on top of the massive manuscript perched on the edge of his desk, the cover page of which had somehow become badly coffee stained. "You can't let this get out," he said emphatically. "If you do, you'll never land a position in a reputable institution; it could make you unemployable except in a city college somewhere unpleasant. What on earth were you thinking?"

There was anger and negative judgment in his small, dark eyes. She felt she had to put up a defense and answer his question. "It's been an interest of mine since I was little, so I've pursued it."

"Some interests should be kept private," Hazan said. "The preposterous subject matter aside, your main conclusions are shaky at best. Using particle beams of an as yet indeterminate type to repel or hold hypothetical spectral forms 'because they are polarized'? Really? You present no evidence that ghosts exist, let alone have polarities. The proton packs and wands you describe are bad pulp science fiction. Assuming you could actually 'trap a ghost,' what would you do with it? Keep it confined forever in a polarized field? Try to return it to its own natural environment? Based on the logic of the math you've used throughout, that kind of, for the lack of a less dramatic term, *membrane breach* could create an instantaneous black hole. What you're suggesting here cannot even be safely tested without risking the end of the world!"

At least it seemed Professor Hazan could follow the math.

There was a related issue, something that had to be dealt with immediately, so she gamely pressed on. "I'm supposed to do an interview on TV later today, part of the promotion—"

Hazan slapped the stack of pages, creating an avalanche of piled folders and magazines off the side of his desk. "There's a lid on this now," he said. "You told me there are only two extant printed copies, plus the raw manuscript. You can just take the book down off the Web site. No one will know it ever existed." He paused and gave her a deep, soul-searching look. "Erin, you've worked too hard and you're far too talented to throw your career away with this nonsense. As you know, we physicists live in a fishbowl. Word will spread beyond Princeton, that is guaranteed. If that happens, you might as well drop out of grad school and put your application in at Walmart."

That was the last thing Erin wanted. She loved science too much.

"Everyone in the graduate department here will think you're crazy," he went on, "and treat you accordingly. You will become a pariah. There's no way you could stay and succeed."

She flashed back on her childhood shame and her fear of being delusional. And in that instant saw the only feasible route out of the situation was the one she herself had already come to.

Denial.

There was no ghost of Mrs. Barnard. There were no ghosts, period.

There was no book about hunting ghosts, either.

She was normal if she acted normal. And if she acted normal, the world would embrace her, not reject her. *If I don't let this go any further,* she told herself, *I have a shot at a dream life. A life without fear of what I might discover, or that I will be discovered. No one will think I'm crazy, so I won't be crazy.* She was intelligent and talented, and she could find a way to fit in. *It's not faking if you pull it off.*

"This is a big turning point for you," Hazan said. "You have to decide what you really want. I can't do it for you."

But he already had. If she had come here looking for permission from the Princeton Physics Department to dump on her best friend, she had received it. A wave of complicated relief washed over her.

She thanked Professor Hazan and walked out of his office. Before she reached the elevators, the relief was gone and anxiety kicked in. How was she going to tell Abby? She knew she couldn't say the words to her face. Not just because it would break her best friend's heart. Abby was too strong, too committed. She had no doubts they were on the right track. As had happened so many times before, she would simply bowl Erin over, the book would come out as scheduled, and her professional career would be irretrievably ruined.

The answer was cowardly, but necessary under the circumstances: she stayed home the rest of the day, did not go to the TV studio, and shut off her phone to avoid reading Abby's frantic texts in the final moments before airtime.

Back at her studio apartment, she watched a few minutes of the show and was proud of the way Abby presented herself and their ideas. When the interviewer got mean, she had to shut it off; she couldn't bear to watch. She knew she should have been there; if she had any guts at all, she would have stood by her friend.

Erin ran into the bathroom with tears streaming down her face and barfed into the sink.

7

That was then, this was now.

Abby and Erin, ghost hunting again. And Dr. Hazan's prophetic words had been made manifest: their fascination with the paranormal had ruined Erin's career.

As the trio reached the gates of the illustrious Manhattan brownstone, a young man crossed the street and nervously approached them. He looked like he wanted to be anywhere but there, moving his gaze from the building beyond them to their faces and back again. As if he were watching Aldridge Mansion's every move.

"Can I help you?" he asked querulously.

"We're here to see Ed Mulgrave," Erin told him. "He visited me earlier today."

His face went white. "Ed Mulgrave? But Ed died fifteen years ago."

Holtzmann cried, "Whaaaaaaaat?" at the same time that Abby exulted, "Yes. This is it."

Erin huffed. "That's ridiculous. I just saw him."

Then the sixty-something man who had approached her in the auditorium walked up. He acknowledged Erin with a bob of his head.

"Okay," she snapped. "Who's that, then?"

The younger man collected himself. "Oh, that's Ed's son, Ed Junior."

Was this some kind of setup? She was abashed that she'd

allowed herself to experience the tiniest twinge of anticipation. "All right, that's obviously who I meant."

Mr. Mulgrave approached the three of them and
said, "Thank you so much for coming. We've been so
frightened."

Abby took a step forward, establishing primacy. "When
is the last time the paranormal entity was sighted and what
on a scale of T-One to T-Five was the level of physical in-
teractivity?"

Mr. Mulgrave gestured to the younger man. "Garrett
here saw it Tuesday and I believe it made him soil himself."

"Jesus, Ed, really?" The guy—Garrett—flushed to his
roots.

"That's a T-Three." Abby was jubilant. "Awesome. Let's
set up inside." She turned to the young man. "You can give
us a tour."

Garrett shook his head. "I'm not going back in there.
Here." He reached into his pocket and hurled a set of keys
on the ground in front of the mansion so hard they bounced.
With that he turned for the sidewalk. Though he quickly
stuffed his hands into his pockets, Erin saw how badly they
were shaking. His walk was shaky, too, as if his knees
were about to buckle under him.

Wow, he really is frightened. Erin looked up and studied
the windows. *What is in there?*

After unlocking the front door, they entered the parlor.
Erin knew it was the parlor because like every other item
in sight it was clearly labeled. It was spookily dark inside,
and she guessed that the drapes were always kept shut to
prevent sun damage, and very little sunlight ever penetrated the gloom. Holtzmann had already started filming
with a camera. Abby pulled out something that looked like
a cross between a tuning fork and a whirligig.

"What is that?" Erin asked.

"PKE meter," Abby replied, holding it aloft. "If there's
a ghost around, this baby'll let us know."

Erin scrutinized the apparatus closely. PKE stood for Psychokinetic Energy Meter, which they had theorized would detect the presence of paranormal entities. "Does it work?"

"Umm, yeah, it works," Abby insisted, a little affronted. Then under her breath she added, "We just haven't seen it work because we haven't had direct contact with the paranormal. *Yet.*"

Same old, same old, Erin thought.

Holtzmann's camera panned toward her. The book was dangerous enough to her career; Erin sure as hell wasn't going to be caught dead—so to speak—on camera. She nudged the lens in the other direction, making sure she was well out of frame. Abby held out the PKE meter like a dowsing rod and followed its readings through the parlor. Erin watched as she reached a door on the other side of the parlor. Abby tried the knob. It was locked. She cocked her head at her meter.

"Sealed shut," she announced. "We'll come back to this. Erin, be useful and find a sledgehammer or something."

Erin threw up her hands, unsure how to deal with her ex-bestie at the moment. Was that a joke, or did Abby seriously intend to destroy a national historic landmark door? They should have gotten more information from Ed Mulgrave before they'd entered the house. Abby had insisted that they had to go in blind, or their expectations might affect their results. That was a sound scientific approach, given the unknown range of variables they faced. Why did it rankle her so much to admit it?

She decided to give herself some space to think things through. But just as she drifted out of Abby's orbit, she happened to glance up at a portrait on the wall. *Yikes.* Chills washed down her spine. A truly horrifying face with a rictus smile like The Joker's glared down at her. She had never seen insanity rendered so perfectly in two dimensions. It had to be none other than Gertrude Aldridge, the family psycho who had murdered all the servants.

Holtzmann and Abby had pulled up the museum's Web site back at the lab before they'd left to come here. Gertrude was apparently the resident ghost and main tourist draw to the museum.

Freaked by the sourpuss glaring down at her, she walked back over toward Holtzmann and Abby. Holtzmann, standing nearer, said quietly to her, "It's a fantastic book, you know. Nothing to be ashamed of."

No doubt, if you're teaching someplace like Kenneth T. Higgins Institute of Science, Erin thought. *Shame is relative.*

They followed Abby as she slowly scanned everything in the room with the PKE meter. Eyes on her readout, she said, "We got asked to be interviewed on University of Michigan's local news show, you know."

Holtzmann perked up. "Oh, really?"

That's just wonderful, she's not done with me, Erin thought dispiritedly. *She's going to tell Holtzmann the whole miserable thing.*

Abby nodded. "That's right. Erin had started grad school, but she was gonna come back for it. Man, it was exciting. I was so proud of that book."

She is never going to let this go.

"Well, I'm nervous this is headed somewhere bad." Holtzmann didn't sound nervous at all; in fact she sounded like she was having a blast.

"No, it was fine," Abby assured her. "I saw some people snickering—it turned out they didn't really take it seriously. But it was all right because Erin showed up and we showed them."

Erin sighed.

"Except that she *didn't* show up!" Abby announced, setting her jaw. "And I was made fun of all by myself and I never even heard from her again!"

"I left you a message that I couldn't make it," Erin blurted. "It's not my fault that your machine didn't record it!" Oh god, what a stupid thing to say. It was also a lie.

But how could she go into the full story here? There was a valid reason she hadn't shown up. A very *personal* and *private* reason. And as it turned out, her decision to boycott the show had proven a good call. Abby still wouldn't be able to see that, to understand why she should have allowed the ashes of the only two physical copies in existence to rot at the bottom of the Hudson River. The career-destroying albatross was her pride and joy. Had Erin tried to explain it on that fateful evening, they wouldn't have remained friends anyway. Abby would have been just as hurt and angry, would have talked Erin into participating, and her career would have been demolished before it had even started.

Abby shook her head sadly at Holtzmann and said, "Let's go check out the parlor. Too much negative energy in here."

Erin watched in dismay as Abby and Holtzmann swept through a large archway into the parlor. No, she couldn't just leave it like that; it made her seem so pathetic. She had to try to explain; she owed Abby the truth. When she started to go after them, her shoe slipped on something. She stopped and examined the sole. It was coated with something green and slimy.

"What is this . . . ?" she murmured to herself.

She looked up at the ceiling for the source of a drip, and then shifted her gaze forward. What she saw made her whole body jerk.

The basement door stood wide open.

She started to lose it, big time. Then she caught herself. It was another prank, of course.

"Wow. Really. Again?" she said, rolling her eyes.

Erin walked into the parlor. Abby was hard at work with her PKE meter. Holtzmann was filming and munching on Pringles potato chips. Exasperated, Erin said, "Is there anything that *isn't* a joke to you guys?"

Abby and Holtzmann looked at each other as if confused. Erin wasn't buying it for a second.

"Well, that's rude," Abby said.

She sounded genuinely affronted. Now it was Erin's turn to be confused. "You didn't open the basement door?"

Abby's eyes widened with excitement. "The basement door is open?"

There was a noise, muffled and distant. Maybe a creak. Or a footfall. Or a foot creak. Or all three. Whatever it was, it made them all jump in unison. When they slowly turned and looked through the archway into the foyer, it was just as Erin had said: the basement door stood wide open.

The absolute surprise on their faces told her it hadn't been any of their doing. Erin provided the only other obvious explanation: "Well, if it wasn't you it's probably just Ed or the—"

Then Abby's PKE meter lit up and the antenna started to spin. It looked like a fuchsia and teal Venus's-flytrap. Abby flinched at the sudden movement and stared down at the machine in amazement.

"I didn't even know it did that," she confessed.

Creeeakkk. Erin caught her breath at the screechy sound. Abby's and Holtzmann's eyes opened comically wide. Someone was coming up the rickety remains of the staircase, from the basement where the tour guide had sworn he'd seen a ghost.

Creeeakkk.

When Abby and Holtzmann cautiously moved forward, Erin followed.

"Oh my god," Abby said. "My ears just popped. Definite AP-xH shift. I don't think we're alone. Holy crap, holy crap. Give me the camera."

She grabbed the video recorder from Holtzmann and advanced, with Erin close on her heels. As Erin continued to move forward there was a loud *crunch* right behind her. She jolted, then half turned, every fiber of her being dreading what she was about to see. But it was just Holtzmann, munching another chip.

Erin said beneath her breath, "How are you still eating?"

Holtzmann mumbled back through a full mouth, " 'Once you pop' . . ."

You can't stop. Erin knew the Pringles slogan.

She was about to admonish Holtzmann when a dim greenish light began to glow and pulse from down the stairwell. Erin's mouth fell open. So did Abby's and Holtzmann's—with an uneaten Pringle stuck to her lips. Abby's face turned red with excitement.

A spectral form began to float upward in the stairwell. A vague, filmy presence at first, it rapidly thickened and took a human shape: the figure was a young woman's, and though her facial features were strikingly beautiful, there was a definite hint of a resemblance to the monstrous portrait on the wall. She was wearing the same fancy gown.

"Please tell me you're seeing that," Abby said.

Erin was. *Oh. God.* She was.

"Good god," Abby wheezed. "It's a Class Four, distinct human form apparition."

In other words, the Holy Grail they had been seeking for so long.

Erin's heart hammered. She couldn't move. She could only stare at the shifting form, overwhelmed, struggling to summon a defense. Her highly trained rational mind tried to squirm out of the logic trap it found itself in. Mass hysteria, she reasoned, that had to be it. They were seeing what they expected to see, based on past experience and the situation they found themselves in. Or maybe their very presence was altering the normal course of events— Heisenberg's uncertainty principle to the max.

"This isn't happening," she murmured.

"Oh, it's happening all right," Holtzmann said.

"And it's the most beautiful thing I've ever seen." Abby's tone was awed, reverent.

Erin had to know, one way or another. Her life, her sanity

depended on it. She somehow found the courage to take a step forward. "It can't be real," she said, as if denying it could make it vanish. It didn't vanish. She reached out her hand.

"Careful! It could be malevolent," Abby said. "We've never made contact before."

Apparently caught up in the thrill of the moment, Abby had forgotten all about Mrs. Barnard. Erin had survived her previous spectral experience, despite being scarred for life by it. As scary as this situation was, she saw it as a chance to take control in the moment, to cease being a victim for once.

"No," Erin said. "She looks peaceful somehow." She took another step forward, approaching the floating form with respect and all the humility she could muster. "Hello, ma'am. My name is Erin Gil—"

The ghost tipped her head, seeming to notice Erin for the first time. Erin stopped dead in her tracks.

As she watched, spellbound, the phantom's sweet, tranquil face blasted into a skull adorned with two bulging gleaming eyeballs. It shrieked. Terrified, Erin tried to take a step back, but her feet were rooted to the floor. As the specter raged and reached for her with stretchy arms and claw fingers, it opened its mouth wide and a torrent of glowing green goo sprayed Erin with the force of a fire hose, knocking her back on her heels.

"Get down!" Abby cried, way too late.

Erin stood dripping in slime. She could feel it sliding from her matted hair down her face and neck; it squished between her fingers. At least she'd had the foresight to close her mouth. It was a familiar sensation, like Mrs. Barnard all over again, except the goo wasn't red this time. *What the hell,* she thought, *how did I become the designated slime target?*

Then without warning the ghost flew straight at Erin, arms outstretched. To avoid further contact, she dropped to the floor with a thud. So did Holtzmann and Abby. The ghost sailed over their heads, flew straight at the opposite wall, and seemingly disappeared right into it.

In unison, Erin and the others leaped to their feet and dashed out the front door. She was stunned to see the ghost flying down the street away from them. No way could it be a prank or a trick. It was visible in broad daylight. A Class 4 distinct human form apparition.

"Dear lord!" Abby cried as it vanished around a corner. She snatched the camera from Holtzmann and frantically hit the rewind button.

"Did we get it?" Holtzmann cried. "Lemme see." She leaned close to Abby and together they peered into the tiny view screen.

"Yeah, but it only appears as a color form," Abby said, somewhat deflated. Erin could barely process what they were saying. Her brain was so overrevved it felt like it was vibrating, a tingling that matched what was going on in her fingertips and toes. Almost to herself, she said, "What just happened?"

Abby looked up from the camera. " 'What just happened'?" She grabbed Erin and shook her. "We saw a ghost!"

That rattled her right out of her stupor. "We did!" Erin cried, goo sluicing off her in swaying strands. Not just goo, she realized. Ectoplasm! "We saw a ghost!"

They jumped up and down, shrieking with joy. "Ghosts are real! Ghosts are real!" Their chant echoed down the street; pedestrians turned their heads, passing drivers looked puzzled.

For Erin it was more than the most astounding discovery in the history of humankind, it was redemption, absolute redemption. *I'm not crazy! I was never crazy! I didn't make it up!*

Ghosts are real!

8

The Mercado, one of Manhattan's iconic Art Deco structures, loomed over Forty-ninth Street like a falcon on a cliff. Commuters rushed through its wide shadow, absorbed in the mundane and the trivial, unaware that deep in the bowels of the building, doomsday had already dawned.

He could see them in his mind's eye—the staggering drunks, the bullying teenagers, the women decked out like fashion models, the Wall Street wolves—sheep, all of them, lambs to his slaughter. He fervently hoped in their death throes they suffered the torments of hell, but he knew advancing The Plan was far more important than the extremis of individual agony. To everything there was a season—and an expiration date. The time was nigh to open the mythic gates, and he could not miss his window of opportunity.

Soon, he thought, the word both a promise to those insectoid humans scurrying inanely several stories above him, and the mantra that animated his every waking moment. But it was not a prayer. Prayers were never answered; he had firsthand knowledge of that. All through middle school, he had prayed for an end to the bullying, the beatings, and the shame of his public torture. Although the little Ohio town of Middlebury had been started by Quakers, there was no brotherly love anywhere in sight. Night after night he had fervently prayed for a towering volcano to emerge like a monstrous pimple from the flat ground of the town square and spew white-hot lava all over every inch of it, paying special attention to the football stadium. No volcano had appeared.

Nor had the zombie apocalypse.

And Julia Roberts had ignored his selfie video inviting her to prom.

But down through history many of his fellow Illuminati had been similarly abused, scorned, and reviled. He saw now that his trials and tribulations had been tests, and that he had proven himself worthy by reaching deep down to find the means to survive. And to prepare his unthinkable revenge.

The headquarters of this impossibly great but nearly invisible man was located in the apartment building's cluttered basement maintenance room. The humble cot and rust-stained sink told one story about his life, but the framed diplomas from Stanford and MIT on the cracked and peeling wall told another: here dwelled authentic genius. Unappreciated, overlooked, hounded, ridiculed. They would pay for dismissing him so easily. Those who had directly done him harm and all their kin—down to the last monkey standing, they would pay. If only Dr. McNulty, his old physics professor at MIT, could see him now, on the verge of rewriting the very nature of existence, he would have been so proud.

Donning his official jacket, he meticulously fastened the row of brass buttons. Chin lifted, he gazed at his reflection in the mirror and recited his morning affirmation:

"You will do a great job today."

Though he wore the uniform of a high-end maintenance man, to him it was a kingly robe, the mantle of his station. Though his face was a little on the round side, his bearing and the unholy light in his eyes was that of an emperor. His name was Rowan North, and no power on earth could stop The Plan. As had become his habit, he continued programming his brain:

"Your potential is matched only by your ambition. Trust in your abilities and the universe shall bend before your will."

A voice blared from the tiny speaker hanging from a nail on the wall.

"Rowan, we've got a clogged toilet in eighteen forty-three. It's bad. Like, biblically bad. Get on it ASAP."

"Absolutely," Rowan said. "Nothing would make me happier."

With a flourish he picked up his tool kit. Couldn't forget the rubber gloves and plunger, though; he'd definitely need them. Soon he would use a far more powerful plunger and send this planetary cesspool swirling and sluicing down the drains of hell. The very same hell that was constantly moving and shifting behind the many mirrors in his room—agonized shapes, melting faces, claws, immense scales, yellow fangs, leaping flames. As he smiled into it, his own reflection was superimposed upon the shadowy creatures of the abyss. Oh, how he would rejoice when the world burned.

"And the universe shall bend before your will," he finished in a voice gravelly with emotion.

As he turned for the door, ready to go to work, the things in the mirror slithered, rustled, and pulsated, pushing against each other impatiently.

Erin Gilbert's fingers dug into the arms of Dr. Filmore's office chair as she stared in horror at the video playback the dean of her department was showing her. Never had one woman soared to such dizzying heights of discovery only to plummet to the depths of abject horror. There she was, jumping up and down with Abby and Holtzmann, shrieking, "Ghosts are real! Ghosts are real!" at the top of her lungs, like she'd just won the Powerball.

Dr. Filmore put the video on pause. Her face was in

close-up, smeared across the entire screen. To quote some of her students, she looked "way dorky."

"Dr. Bronstein saw this on Reddit." The dean's expression was stern. "It was reblogged from a Dr. Abigail Yates's Web site—Ghost News. I hadn't heard of that publication."

Think fast, Erin told herself. She forced what she hoped was a look of sheer, flabbergasted astonishment onto her face. "Wait. You don't think that's *me* in the video, do you?"

The dean turned to look again, and after satisfying himself, he stared at her without blinking.

Denial was second nature to her. She had learned that survival meant denial. It meant that therapists eventually stopped asking questions and left you alone, and that the kids at school finally got bored and found someone more interesting to bully. And with that in mind she said:

"But this isn't something I'm really involved with. Truly." She added a couple of head bobs to hard sell it. But it didn't appear that Dr. Filmore was in the market for prevarication. His blank expression did not change.

"I hope you understand that when we give someone tenure, they represent this institution," he said. "They affect such things as grants and our standing in the collegiate rankings."

Oh no, not my tenure. But this should not affect my tenure. It's not like the book. It was a spontaneous moment. He doesn't know the context. We could be practicing for a play, or playing a joke on someone, or—or—

Her only option was to try to shift the context, put a different spin on the video. She forced a wide smile, leaned back, and made her hands into a pair of finger guns.

"Gotcha! Ha!" she said. "You should've seen your—"

"Please, don't pretend this is a prank," he said.

"—face," Erin finished weakly. "Okay." Deflated, she lowered her hands to her lap.

"I'm sorry," the dean said. "This just isn't what this institution is about."

"It's not what I'm about, either!" she pleaded. "I'm about real, serious science. And I want to work at a university that takes that as seriously as I do." She swallowed down her fear and cranked up the wattage on her fake smile even higher. "That's why I conducted this test, so congratulations, Dr. Filmore."

She extended her arm to shake his hand.

"This is just uncomfortable now."

Deny that this is happening. And it won't be.

"Well, my class starts in an hour, so I'd better get back to it."

Dean Filmore said nothing as she jumped up from the chair. The way he looked at her she could have been a bug on the wall or a bit of loose fluff on the carpet.

The box containing the gathered contents of Erin's office was very heavy. She shifted it in her arms and trudged through the hallway of the physics building. Students and faculty milling in the corridor watched her, and she could hear them whispering. Her cheeks blazed.

The whispering and snickering behind her grew even louder. At least this was her last trip through the gauntlet.

It was a true walk of shame.

She turned and looked down the hall a final time, a game smile plastered on her face—and once again let fly with a denial:

"Just taking my plant for a walk," she proclaimed to all the people staring at her. She raised and lowered the heavy box. "Getting a little exercise. Woo-hoo!"

I have lost it all. This is the dark night of my soul. At three forty-seven in the afternoon.

The corridor was as endless as her despair.

And her anger.

It did not abate as she caught yet another cab, briefly panicked at the thought that she no longer had an income, and clenched her hands tightly in her lap. The contents of her office, of her entire academic life, sat beside her. So few objects when you considered how long she had worked at Columbia. It was all so wrong, so unjust.

"I have an article coming out in *Nature*," she growled through clenched teeth.

"Hey, that's swell," the grizzled cabbie said. "Is that like *Playboy*? Because you know, they're going to stop having nudies."

"No." Tears welled. She was so frustrated, and that was such a stupid question. "But that's very forward thinking of them," she managed to say. "Women should not be objecti—"

"Can't compete with the free porn on the Internet," the cabbie elaborated.

"Oh." She chewed the inside of her cheek and stared out the window. The world was no longer her oyster. It wasn't any kind of shellfish. It was a gasping, dying striped bass yanked from the Hudson River.

"Throw it back, throw it back," she whispered. If only she could start this day over. This day should have been illegal from the get-go.

"My brother-in-law told me once him and my little sister thought about making a sex tape," the cabbie informed her. "To make some dough, you know? Like them Kardashians. I liked to deck him."

Erin balled her fists and dug her nails into her palms. Abby had promised to take down the book. How had she not realized that posting that idiotic video would be just as problematic for her, if not more?

Because she is obsessed and self-centered, and always has been. As Erin answered her own question her simmering fury spiked and hit boiling point.

"You'd do okay in the free stuff," the man said, still prattling on about pornography. "Well, here we are."

Erin handed him some money, grabbed her carton, and slid out of the rear of the car. The cabbie frowned at her. "Hey, there's no tip."

"Here's your tip," Erin said. "Don't be a pig anymore."

"Hey, what's your problem?" the man shouted through his open window as she walked away. She wobbled under the weight of the carton, ignoring the cabbie's long, colorful string of X-rated words.

Perfect, just perfect, Erin thought. She staggered into the hallway and headed toward the stairway to the basement. Her back muscles were screaming. When she reached the door to the Paranormal Studies Laboratory, she set down her box, straightened, and kicked open the door.

Hell hath no fury like a college professor fired.

Abby and Holtzmann were bent over a piece of equipment. They looked up in surprise as Erin stormed in. The sight of them sent her even further around the bend. She was so angry she was frothing at the mouth, as if she had rabies.

"Well, I hope you're happy," she snarled. They were puttering away, their TV on, not a care in the world. Oblivious to what they had done to her with their stupid Reddit. She needed to smash something, anything, but preferably something expensive and irreplaceable. Snatching up a likely contraption from a worktable, she raised it in blind fury.

"Noooo! We'll all die!" Abby and Holtzmann shouted together.

Erin froze. Very carefully she set down the device, then grabbed an ammeter to throw.

"Noooo! We only have one of those!" the two yelled.

She put that down, and feeling suddenly desperate, snagged an empty soda can.

"Okay," Holtzmann said. "But can you throw it at the recycling can?"

"Rinse it first, please," Abby added.

Erin stomped over to the sink and turned on the water, began to rinse the sticky can.

"How could you *do* that?" she ranted into the sink, but

loud enough for the people on the floor above to hear. "How could you put that online? I was *fired!* Everyone was watching. I was completely humiliated!"

She heaved the can into the recycling bin and slumped onto the couch.

"Maybe all this is a bad dream," she said hopefully. Then she started lightly slapping herself on the face. "Wake up, Erin."

Holtzmann hurried over, and pretending she just wanted to help, started slapping her, too. Erin shoved her away.

"All right, knock it off," Abby said in a tone that said she meant it. "Now, I'm sorry, but we saw a *real ghost.* How long have we been looking for that? And she was beautiful, Erin." She nodded at her friend. "Well, until she dislocated her jaw and ectoprojected all over you. But even that was beautiful."

Erin opened her mouth to protest. A real ghost, all well and good, yes, but in the *real* world—

She caught herself.

Except that this was the real world. And in the real world, she had seen a real ghost before and no one had believed her. She had stopped believing it, too. But this time, two other people had seen it. And they knew that she was not delusional.

In her mind's eye, she saw Gertrude Aldridge floating up eerily from the basement. She was indeed very beautiful and very strange. She changed right before their eyes, shifting form as if made of green smoke. Followed by the all-too-familiar barfing and then fluttering away down the street, as real as a runaway kite.

I was never crazy.

The anger and the urge to do battle left her. For better or worse, she had to play the hand she was dealt. Without being asked, she started to debrief.

"There was a heavy ionization discharge," she said. "I could smell it. Somehow it got energized."

Abby enthusiastically picked up the olive branch. "Full-torso transmogrification with corporeal aggression. Right before our eyes." Her expression hardened as she added, "And we're supposed to be quiet about it? We've been working our whole lives for this. And we got almost a hundred comments. And not just crazies." She led Erin over to the desktop. "Read this one."

Erin squinted to read the small type. " 'I wanna slap them wit dis dick.' "

Abby stabbed her finger at the monitor screen. "Below that. This lady describes a Class Three haunting in her home. She's scared, she lives alone, and she can't afford to move. We can provide a real service here. She can't call the police. She can't call a friend. Who is she going to call? We're on the cusp of discovery here." She zeroed in on Erin. "And I know you love the cusp."

Erin nodded. That was why she had gravitated to quantum physics. "I do. I love the cusp."

"Now, I know this isn't Columbia," Abby said. "But the Kenneth T. Higgins Institute—"

"Uuuuugh," Erin said. The you're-making-me-puke sound kind of popped out of its own accord. This place was no more an "Institute" than the Large Hadron Collider had debunked string theory.

"That is *insanely* rude, but I'll ignore it," Abby said. "The Higgins Institute grants us money and they let us study whatever we want. They don't even ask what we're doing. We have been left alone for almost a year." She grinned confidently. "Watch. I'll go ask them for more funding right now."

Abby's dean's office was shabby but not un-dean-like. Erin watched his puzzled face as Abby petitioned him for more money. About halfway through her pitch, it seemed to slowly dawn on him exactly who she was. When the lightbulb went on, he grimaced.

"I honestly just didn't know that your department still

existed," he confessed. "I can't believe this has gone on this long."

Abby appeared stupefied. "What?"

He shrugged his shoulders and then shook his head. "I'm sorry, but ghosts? No, no, no. We simply cannot let the twelve-year history of this institution be smeared by this."

"Oh, come *on*." Abby huffed. "Suddenly this school has a classy reputation to uphold? You're wearing shorts."

"You teach a whole class on Rihanna," Holtzmann added.

As the dean's face reddened, he half rose from behind his desk. "Well, then how 'bout you get your candy asses out of my office?"

"My god," Erin blurted.

As they made a beeline back to the lab, loaded up their equipment, and made an undignified exit pushing a very short parade of wheeled carts, a kind of euphoria swept over Erin. They truly had nothing left to lose. How did the song go? "Freedom nothin' left to lose?"

"You know what?" she said, suddenly energized. "We're going to show everyone we're not crazy. We just have to capture an entity and bring it into a controlled environment." She turned to Abby. "When you said the equipment was close, how close did you mean?"

"Well, that's a great question," she replied, panting as she labored to keep her cart moving. "See, we have no lab. But the good news is we also have no money."

Total freedom!

"I have some savings," Erin told her. "Do either of you have any savings?"

"I was planning on asking if I could borrow some," Holtzmann ventured.

"We can do this," Erin said. "We're gonna be the first scientists to ever prove the paranormal exists." *And we will have the last laugh. Those stupid deans will* beg *us to take our jobs back!*

A huge smile lit up Abby's face. "That's the Erin I used to know. Welcome back. Now let's get out of here with this stuff before they make us give it back."

With impeccable timing, the front doors to the college flung open and slammed back. The dean ran out of the building wielding a baseball bat. "Hey!" he shouted. "Bring that shit back here!"

Abby threw her weight against the cart's handle, driving with her legs.

As Erin put on a burst of speed, she saw the man step on and trip over his flip-flops. He went down hard on the pavement and lost his grip on the bat, which rolled away.

Whoa, some serious scuffed knees there, Erin thought. *That'll teach him to wear shorts to work.*

Pursuit was not forthcoming. Gleefully the trio zoomed out of sight around the corner.

This time next year, everything will be different, Erin told herself as she pushed her portion of the liberated gear down the middle of the sidewalk. *We will be famous and respected. Every talk show in the world will ask us for interviews—and I will always show up.*

9

Time flies when you're having fun.

But when you're bored? Not so much.

The Seward Street subway station seemed especially quiet today. It wasn't a weekend or a holiday, so Patty Tolan didn't know what to make of it. She did know how to take advantage of the occasional slow times, though. She loved to read and had turned the ticket booth into her own private library. Her favorite topic was New York. So much had been written about the city and its history, it was hard to know where to start or when to stop, so she had decided to specialize. As usual she was halfway through one book—*The Gangs of New York*—and she had three more in progress stacked on her desk. There was a fifth book in her lunch bag, and she'd lost count of how many at home. Working for the MTA was a great job for someone who liked to read, but it sure did get lonely sometimes.

She perked up at the rumbling approach of a subway train and the rush of gritty air it pushed ahead of it into the station. A few seconds later, the debarking passengers began to pass in front of her window. She leaned into her microphone and hit the speak button, hungry for some human conversation.

"How you guys doing?" she began. No answer.

A woman in a blue shirt passed close by, moving to the right. "I have that same shirt," Patty told her with a big grin. "Except mine is purple and long sleeved." The woman didn't break her stride. "You know what? It's just a different shirt."

The woman was gone.

Patty deflated.

"Get home safe," she said wistfully.

Something moved in the corner of her eye. When she looked to her left, she jumped in her seat. A man in his thirties with an ample face was right up against the glass, staring in at her. His superintense gaze and pinpoint pupils rang all her alarm bells and she carefully rolled her chair back from the window. She was a New Yorker born and bred, and while she sought out conversation, she never looked for trouble. And this dude was on drugs or a day pass or *something.*

"You scared me," Patty told him, which was a nice way of telling him not to scare her anymore.

"They will always ignore you," the man said. "Because they are walking sewage focused only on their own trivial matters."

Wow, you must be New York born and bred, too, she thought. *You've got the whole attitude down.*

"Uh-huh. Everything good?" she asked pleasantly.

"You take pride in your work." His inflection was flat, like he was trying out for a part in a horror movie as the hypnotized minion or something. And his expression, which mixed distaste, anger, and obsessive focus, was off-putting in the extreme. No way around it, this one was just plain weird.

"Well, I don't know about that," she said. She sold subway rides in a ticket booth. Occasionally answered a question or gave directions. There wasn't much there to be proud of, except being friendly and courteous.

Still he stared in at her. And did not move. He was so close to the window that his exhaled breaths slightly fogged the armored glass.

"When the Fourth Cataclysm begins," he continued,

"the laborers will be among the last to the butchery. So make the most of your time."

Who are you, my union rep? Nope, that dude's got a tic in his right eye and a crooked little mustache; you're just another nutcase on the loose.

"Oh, okay, my man," she cajoled him. "Thanks so much. You have a great day."

Pleased with himself, he nodded like a robot as if to say "You're welcome." That was some serious medication. She went back to reading *The Gangs of New York*. It was well researched. She enjoyed a well-researched book. . . .

There was blurring in the security monitor beside her, indicating movement. She glanced over at the screen. It was Mr. Crazy Man, of course. He walked along the platform, then climbed down and walked straight into the subway tunnel.

Patty exhaled. "Oh, come on . . ."

Concerned despite her irritation, she put down her book, picked up her flashlight, and left her booth. She could have alerted the transit police, but she needed to stretch her legs anyway. She had her portable radio clipped to her uniform belt; if anything looked dicey, she could give them a holler. The loony tune had only seen her sitting down; on her feet she was much more impressive, intimidating even. She had backed down more than a few would-be subway villains just by standing up straight and giving them the stink eye. When she entered the platform, she spotted her favorite pest, a young graffiti artist she had nicknamed "Tubesy" after "Banksy" in London. He was busily spray painting the platform wall.

"Hey!" she yelled at him. "No graffiti! I already told you!"

He looked at her and shrugged. "I'm just trying to help out." He pointed to his latest masterpiece, the words No Graffiti. Spelled correctly this time.

Extra credit for that.

"Oh, I get it. You're just being a nice guy, huh?" The

tone of her voice said, "You are not fooling me one bit." She craned her neck, checking out the otherwise deserted platform, and then stared into the inky darkness at the far end of it. No sign of Mr. Crazy Man.

"Just get out of here before I call this in," she told Tubesy, and patted her radio like a sidearm for emphasis.

He sauntered off toward the stairs, aerosol can in hand, spray painting the floor as he went.

"Oh, come on, man!" Patty groused, exasperated by the younger generation. Shaking her head and blowing out a puff of air between her lips, she started walking toward the end of the platform.

As she approached it, an odd flash of light pulsed from down the tunnel, and then was gone. Patty shined her flashlight in that direction and called out a hopeful, "Hello?"

Was the blast of light from a shower of sparks? A frightening vision of Mr. Crazy Man accidentally touching the third rail blazed through her mind. Although she had never seen a crispy critter in person, there were pictures in the history books she'd read. There was no more arcing, if that's what the flash was from. Either it was nothing or it was something, and if it was something it wasn't moving. She walked down the steps at the end of the platform and entered the tunnel. She played the light beam over the track a few feet ahead and on the walls, which were decorated with pipes and conduit—everything was grimy black. She wasn't too concerned about the rats—they were afraid of light and people—but she didn't want to go in so far that she couldn't get back out when the next train slid around the distant corner. There were emergency niches spaced along the walls a person could duck into to avoid being hit, but they were filthy with grease and soot, and she wasn't sure they were of sufficient size to keep a large woman such as herself from getting clipped. She wasn't about to back into one to test the fit, either.

Patty played the beam deeper in the tunnel. Mr. Crazy

Man was nowhere to be seen, not standing, not curled up on the death rail in a fetal position. But something else caught her eye, something strange and definitely out of place. Attached to a pipe on the wall, it was round like a pie pan and thick like a Bundt pan, and it looked to be made of brass. There were things attached that looked like gauges and canisters. Oh, and cylinders and coiled wires. The top was domed, and it was pulsating.

Her blood ran cold. First thing she thought was: bomb. But looking closer, she realized it was some kind of electronic device, decidedly homemade and evidently not all that well put together. Sparks were shooting out of it like it had a short. She decided to take a closer look before calling it in as a suspicious package. When she pointed her light at the ground so she could see where she was stepping, she noticed something even weirder—a glowing wave of energy flowed from the device. She'd never seen anything like it.

"What the . . . ?"

Suddenly she had serious second thoughts about it not being a bomb. If it was, she realized she was already so close she couldn't get away if it went off. Or maybe it was intended to disrupt the electronic signals in the trains? Feeling like she had nothing to lose at this point, she moved even closer, and as she did she became aware of another glowing object, this one much bigger, not attached to anything, and moving on its own.

Squinting hard, she saw it was a man—a glowing man, walking away from her down the tunnel. He was freakishly tall and thin, and he was wearing a black-and-white-striped prison uniform. From her copious reading, Patty knew that New York State had abolished that style in 1904. He had a sparking metal object on top of his head. It looked like the skullcap placed on a condemned prisoner's head during an old-time electrocution.

From what she'd gleaned, they hadn't worked very well.

Was the guy an escapee from some off-Broadway show? What the heck was going on?

It worked!

As Rowan watched from the deep shadows of the subway tunnel, he could barely contain his elation. *The prototype worked!* He had succeeded in drawing forth and freeing one of the long imprisoned—and so became his master in the present malaise and the eternal kingdom to come.

Rowan wanted to rush out and claim his first prize, but had to hang back because the happy laborer from the ticket booth would see him. Thus far, he had not taken the opportunity to send a living soul across the vast barrier to the land of the dead. No, his armies would do that for him, come the dawn of resurrection day—

He couldn't figure out why the laborer was spending so much time snooping in the tunnel. Didn't she have more important duties to attend to? Filing her nails? Talking on her cell phone? The device had withstood its first field test, but he didn't want to overtax it. He was very concerned about the sparks. Perhaps a contact had been jarred loose when it flared and came online? The harmonic vibration of the waveform could be causing an intermittent short circuit. He needed to examine it and make the necessary repairs before further damage was done, but he couldn't move from hiding until she was gone. He shifted his weight impatiently.

The device began to hum, and the hum grew louder and louder; he could hear it clearly from down the tunnel. Then without warning, it exploded in a shower of sparks. Pieces of his work of genius flew in all directions. Rowan watched in horror as they ricocheted off the walls and spanged against the metal rails. It couldn't have been just a short. The power conversion must have been off; or the charger had been too powerful, or too weak, which allowed back-wash from the other side to enter the system. He had to collect the pieces to learn what had gone awry. But how could he manage it with that stupid cow nosing around? Why hadn't the shrapnel cut her down?

Must I kill her? If so, she brings it on herself.

The explosion caught Patty by surprise. In the millisecond between the bang and the stinging spray of fragments, she was sure she was dead. She jumped, but after the fact, and to no effect. There was some smoke and it made the tunnel smell even worse, though she would never have thought that possible. She shined her flashlight at the tall man in the costume who was still calmly walking away as if nothing had happened. Had he set off the explosion with some kind of remote detonator? Had he planted more of those things? Should she call the cops and get the heck out of there? She knew if she turned her back on him, they might never find him again in the labyrinth of tunnels.

It was all down to her. It didn't matter that she was an unarmed ticket seller with a fantastic vocabulary. Hers were the only eyes and ears on the glow-in-the-dark weirdo.

"Hey! You can't go down there," she shouted at him.

He stopped. She knew that was the point, but now she wasn't sure what to do with—

She gaped as she looked down at his feet. They were not touching the ground. *He is hanging in the air like a . . . no, he can't be . . .* She couldn't think straight. *A ghost. A mother-flippin' ghost.*

In no apparent hurry, the floating man turned and seemed to study her intently. She stood her ground and studied him right back. His prominent teeth were clenched tight, mouth and cheeks frozen as if the electricity was still flowing through the cap on his head, and his eyes burned with malevolence; everything about him screamed *evildoer, evil-*

doer. What he'd done to rate a seat on Old Sparky was a mystery, but she was certain he'd earned every single volt. If he drifted toward her, oh god, if he got anywhere near her, she was going to have a heart attack. She had never seen anything so horrible.

Then he locked on to her gaze and smiled like a hungry wolf.

Which set a new benchmark in horrible.

She gasped a quick breath and shouted at him: "Go wherever you want. They don't pay me enough for this."

Dropping her flashlight on the track, Patty ran for her life.

10

A couple of days had passed. Erin squinted up at the bright sunshine, feeling the warmth on her face. It was another glorious autumn day, and the leaves were even more splendid. The world was filled with hope.

And so was their rental agent. "I found a fantastic spot for your business," she gushed.

Erin had to agree. Most definitely. She, Abby, and Holtzmann stood on the sidewalk in front of a gorgeous firehouse conversion. Erin hadn't realized there was even such a thing, but at first glance she knew it was perfect for them, with its large double doors and towering cathedral ceilings. They could double, triple, maybe quintuple the volume of random parts, groundbreaking inventions, and ghost-catching paraphernalia they kept on the premises. There would be room for the isolation chambers vital for equipment testing and refinements. From the outside, the building actually sparkled, wood gleamed, brass fittings shone.

"This firehouse was converted to a loft in 2010," the rental agent told them. The merry glint in her eyes made Erin think she was already planning how to spend her commission on the deal.

Abby and Holtzmann craned their necks to take in the sizable structure.

"Wow," Holtzmann breathed, and Abby cried, "Yes!"

When the agent opened the front doors, the two of them

ran inside together like excited little girls. Erin watched as Abby bounced around the cavernous room like a super-charged particle. Because she held the purse strings by default, she felt she had to maintain a façade of reserve. Sheesh, someone did.

"Look at that floor-to-ceiling height for equipment!" Abby crowed. "Okay, we'll put the accelerator over there . . ."

I feel so empowered by my savings, Erin thought with no small bit of pride. She'd socked away as much of her Columbia salary as she could—but living in Manhattan as a single person was ridiculously expensive. And she made about half what a tenured professor did—she felt a sudden twinge recalling that fact. Without hesitation, Erin turned to the agent and said, "We'll take it."

"Great," the woman said, giving her a big smile. "The rent is twenty-one thousand dollars a month."

"Fuck you," Erin blurted. Her sense of empowerment vanished as she realized her life savings translated into a mere sixty-four days of sumptuous firehouse living.

The agent blinked at her in astonishment. "Excuse me?"

Erin regrouped. "I'm sorry. That just came out." Then she winced. "That's the monthly rent? No one could afford that. Why are you even showing us this?" *To make us suffer?*

The agent shrugged. "You gave me no parameters. All your friend said was you needed a place to 'explore the unknown.'"

Erin did not miss the sarcasm in the woman's delivery. She said, "Well, help us explore frugally, okay?"

And you tell them we can't stay here, she thought, looking on as Holtzmann and Abby gleefully danced and cavorted.

The real estate agent's Operation HQ reboot was nothing like the firehouse loft. It wasn't converted. In fact, it was condemned—a run-down, two-story, stand-alone Chinese restaurant in a part of Chinatown that made Erin clutch her purse in a death grip and mutter, "Are you sure you got the address right? Maybe we should rethink this."

But street numbers did not lie.

Gone was the firehouse exuberance. Grim faced and silent, they filed into the dim stairway and climbed to the second floor. *This* was all they could afford: a wretchedly dilapidated restaurant dining room, mess and disrepair rampant. The Chinese fittings on the doors, lamps, and skylight were dusty and shopworn. The green tiled order window was cobwebbed. The red-and-white floor was sticky. That combined with Abby's and Holtzmann's over-flowing boxes of assorted junk made Erin feel like she was breaking out in hives. She was allergic to *chaos*—at least, that was *the theory*.

A little physics humor there, to attempt to lighten the revulsion.

It failed miserably. Her allergic reaction just as easily could have been from glue residue on the peeling wall-paper or the ghosts of smoked tea ducks. The place was really gross. She was afraid to sit down or stand, for that matter.

When she looked over at the doorway, she was slammed by a wave of déjà vu. Abby was getting into it with the same Chinese deliveryman Erin had encountered on her first visit to the Kenneth T. Higgins Institute. His name was Benny, and apparently he had been delivering Abby's Chinese food for years, and pissing her off for just as long. Why she hadn't just picked another restaurant from the hundreds available was a puzzle too complex for Erin to unravel. As she listened in on the conversation she re-alized that by a strange twist of fate, they had Benny and his extended family to thank for the state of their new headquarters—having abandoned the restaurant's up-stairs dining room as a lost cause, the family had kept open the ground floor, take-out kitchen. Abby appeared as frustrated and confrontational as ever with the delivery guy.

"How does it take you an hour to walk up a flight of stairs?" Abby flung at him. "I move above you and you still can't help me out?"

Benny didn't answer, only watched as she pulled her carton of soup out of the bag and opened the lid. She looked first at it, and then at him. His face was a mask of disinterest.

"This is just broth and one shrimp," she complained. "That's not soup. That's a pet."

Behind her, Holtzmann plugged in her boom box and quickly got to work. She had donned a hazmat suit and her blond hair was piled atop her head. The equipment she was in such a hurry to test was sensitive and expensive, and Holtzmann was taking all reasonable precautions— by dancing to "Rhythm of the Night" by DeBarge with a small blowtorch in each hand, firing them toward the ceiling like six-shooters. As she twisted and dipped to the driving beat, one of the torches accidently swept over a paper towel dispenser and it immediately burst into flames.

Erin wildly jabbed her fingers at the fire that threatened to crawl up the flocked red wallpaper. What with the layers of ancient grease that had been allowed to congeal on every surface, the room was a fireball awaiting ignition. Unruffled, Holtzmann winked at her and danced over to the extinguisher. Busting what was by far her best move, she reverse-grooved back to the flaming dispenser, took a moment for one last spin, and with a whoosh of retardant put an end to the danger.

Jeez, Erin thought. Everything was a joke to Holtzmann—she was like a continuously charged positive ion. Erin had occasionally wondered about the "lab experiment" that had blocked her acceptance at CERN and the man whose finger had miraculously moved. That morning Holtzmann had bought him a get-well-soon card and scrawled "Happy Anniversary!" above her signature. What was *that* all about?

After the unrepentant Benny left, Abby's ire evaporated. She put down her soup and carried a sheaf of brightly colored paper over to Erin.

"Okay," Abby said, "I've got a Web site up. And I've been passing out these flyers all over town. Draw in some business."

Business. The private sector. Money exchanged for goods or services provided, not cajoled out of foundations with grant proposals. It was a brave new world.

Erin took the flyer Abby shoved at her. Their phone number and address was printed on it under a banner headline: "IF YOU SEE SOMETHING, SAY SOMETHING!"

Erin hesitated. Then she said, " 'If you see something, say something'?" That's the antiterrorism logline."

Abby sighed. "I thought that sounded familiar. At least we now know why people keep calling to report suspicious bags. Dang it!"

She snatched back the flyer and marched away, shaking her head.

Maybe she was hungry? Erin thought. She might think more clearly with some shrimp—correction, a shrimp—in her stomach.

Erin looked around the room, unsure what to do with herself. Abby and Holtzmann were simply continuing with what they'd been previously funded to do. They were still being funded to do the same thing. The only thing different was that Erin was now the funder. She didn't really have a place in the new order of things. She supposed it was up to her to make one. Taking in the debris and disarray and general filth that surrounded her, she knew she could always start tidying it up, but, blech . . . a PhD in physics from MIT (she had transferred from Princeton) reduced to cleaning lady? Besides, from the look of it the job could take months. The sterilization alone . . .

A knock on the door broke her train of thought. As Erin turned, an insanely buff and handsome man opened it and walked across the threshold. He was tall, with exquisitely styled blond hair, and blue eyes framed with lashes. His face was a study in angles—high cheekbones, square jaw, hollows in his cheeks—and he had that sought-after man-triangle physique: broad shoulders, narrow waist, non-existent hips. He was so impossibly stunning that for a few microseconds Erin was actually afraid that he might be another day-walking ghost, about to turn into a demon and barf ectoplasm all over her. Then as her pleasure centers became drenched with the sheer delight of his presence, her mind emptied of thought as if it had been flushed.

"Excuse me," he said. "I'm here about the receptionist job?"

What Erin heard was this:

Nothing.

His amazing lips moved, but no sound registered in her brain. All she could do was stare at him.

He bent down and gently said, "Hello?"

His voice broke through her endorphin haze. She realized he had an accent, Australian, she guessed. And suddenly of all the accents in the world, hands down that was the one she loved most. If he asked her to do anything in that soft voice, she would have done it without a moment's hesitation. What she said in response to his one-word question was again: nothing.

And then *he* repeated himself a bit more forcefully. "Hello?"

His gaze was hypnotic, but the shift in tone penetrated her consciousness and broke the spell. She said, "Of course. Let's go to the conference room."

Just then, Abby popped her head in.

"Are you Kevin?" she asked the man. "Fantastic. We spoke on the phone. Follow me."

He did. Erin gaped at his lovely butt, unable to move her feet.

Abby said, "Erin!"

The Mercado.

It was his world headquarters, in the short term.

What far grander establishment would he commandeer once the barrier had been completely torn asunder? The White House? The Kremlin? Tokyo Disneyland?

They all had their merits.

He didn't yet know why the device in the tunnel had exploded. It was difficult to determine without recovering most of the pieces, and when he went back for them a good deal were mysteriously missing, perhaps gathered up by rats—who knew. But he did know the device was working perfectly before it blew up. Ask him how he knew.

He smiled to himself. It was good to have secrets. Powerful secrets. It made him feel he had absolute control, delighted to go about his day among the mindless rabble knowing they had no idea that he alone held their fate in his hands. He could barely contain his glee while unblocking toilets and clearing kitchen sink P-traps. His day job consisted primarily of getting rid of waste created by wastrels too lazy or stupid to deal with it on their own. The simplest way to stop the endless flow of crap, cutting to the chase per Occam's Razor, was to lay waste to the wastrels.

He stepped out of the elevator, toolbox in hand, with his favorite song earworming. *You should be dancin', yeah . . .* He cut a nifty 360 pirouette, paused on the upbeat, and then continued on.

Love among the crab Rangoons . . . Erin was so smitten.

She, Abby, and Holtzmann sat on one side of the rectangular table in the center of the restaurant with Abby. Kevin, who was there to be interviewed for their receptionist position, had the other side of the booth all to himself. Abby had a notebook open in front of her. Even in the restaurant's dim "mood" lighting, which was in part due to burned-out bulbs, Erin could see the vast numbers of question marks written on the page. The earth was still moving under her feet, but Abby seemed all business, oblivious to Kevin's charms.

But there was one question Erin wanted to ask first. She smiled into those dreamy eyes and said, "So, Kevin, are you seeing anyone?"

He smiled. "Yeah. I'm seeing all of you sitting right there." Oh *god,* that Australian accent. It was so sexy.

"No, um, anyone . . . *special*," Holtzmann said in her occasionally madly dangerous-sounding drawl.

"You're all special." He smiled. He was so not getting this.

"Like . . . are you in a thing? A relationship?"

"Erin?" Abby queried, looking bewildered.

"Okay, sorry." Erin flashed Holtzmann a look. They were on the same wavelength. This hunky man would be incredibly distracting and they had serious work to do.

"First off, congratulations." Abby said, beaming at their prospective employee. "Your walking through this door already tells me that you have a daring and curious mind."

Kevin's brow furrowed; he looked momentarily bewildered by both the compliment and the conclusion. Recovering, he smiled and said pleasantly, "Sure."

"Everyone has an unyielding passion to answer the unanswered questions. A lifelong dedication. Well, most of us." She nodded at Erin. "She's in and out. But for the most part, everyone here is fiercely dedicated—"

"Okay, he doesn't need our history," Erin said, not loving the fact that Abby was dissing her in front of *him*.

"Well," Abby said, affronted.

"So you must be curious about what we do," Erin said, abruptly changing the subject.

"Definitely." He gave her an earnest look. "Do you work Wednesdays?"

That took Erin by surprise, but she managed a reply. "Uh, yes. Yes, we work Wednesdays."

The frown that passed over his face wrinkled the bridge of his very handsome nose. "Shoot. That's tough for me."

Holtzmann chimed in. "What's your background, Kevin? What were you doing before this?"

That seemed to stump him, like she had asked for the solution to a complex problem in calculus. As if doing the math in his head, he was quiet for a long moment and then he said, "This and that."

Abby nodded and wrote that down. As she did so she murmured, "'This *and* that'? Great. Multitasker."

Ooh, she likes him, too, Erin thought. *How will we get any work done if we're all swooning over Heavenly Kevin? Maybe we won't care.*

"This comes with room and board, right?" Kevin asked, his Australian accent so sexy in the lilt given to the last word. "I need a place to crash. With my hat."

What? No, Erin thought. *We're not paying for that.*

"Yes it does," Abby assured him. She paused. "Your hat?"

"Mike Cat," he corrected.

"Oh, you have a cat named Mike."

"Actually, it's a dog named Michael Cat."

Abby wrinkled her nose. "I'm sorry, but you can't bring a dog in here."

"Hmm, okay. I can't get here before ten," Kevin informed them in a matter-of-fact tone. "And I'll need some flexibility. I'll have auditions here and there. Improv rehearsal. And saxophone lessons."

"Oh, you play?" Erin asked. Saxophone meant great breath control, which translated into stamina. And of course, strong lips.

"My uncle does. I just watch."

But he must do other stuff, Erin thought. It looked like his six-pack had a six-pack. And his arms, they looked like—

Abby tapped her finger on her notebook to reclaim control of the interview. "Well, let's get to it. Big question. Do you believe in ghosts?"

Erin laughed, Holtzmann laughed, and Abby laughed, too: of course he must.

Kevin gave his head a shake. "Um, not really," he admitted.

Abby's eyes widened. "Oh? Oh." She quickly flipped through the rest of the pages of her notebook; when she got to the last one she slowly closed it. "All these follow-up questions were based on a yes . . ."

The implication was clear: the interview was over. Kevin would have to crash elsewhere.

But he was bright enough to realize how badly he'd blown it. Clearing his throat, he said, "Well . . . you mean like Casper?"

Abby leapt on his feeble attempt to salvage the interview. "Yes! Like Casper." She beamed triumphantly. "Okay, he gets it."

Erin remained skeptical. "Does he, though?"

Abby ignored her. "Kevin also dabbles in Web design, so I asked him to try a couple of logos out for us. Show us what you've got, Kevin."

Erin's heart fluttered a little. Not only gorgeous, but he was an artist, too. That explained so much—his apparent distraction, his discomfort with a conventional interview process, his odd responses to Abby's questions. They were lucky that he had applied. Why someone like him would even consider such a lowly job raised a flock of other questions . . . But back to the logo. Of course they would need one for their company. Something professional would help them advertise their business online. And that way they could show up at their clients' locations instead of having them enter this den of crawling bacteria.

Kevin eagerly opened his laptop. The three leaned in. The image was of a ridiculous cartoon ghostette with enormous boobs. Erin wasn't the only one whose smile drooped.

But Abby was not going down without a fight. "Well, look at all that effort," she said. Her cheeks were flaming red. "Sometimes it's not about the end product but the journey."

Erin was not about to sugarcoat something so important to their company's public image. "Kevin, you do see how that makes us look bad, right?"

When he cocked his head and appeared to consider that question, Erin dared to hope. Then he said, "If your problem is with the boobs, I can totally make them bigger. Here's another option."

The next sketch was of a man staring down at a gravestone, his upwelling of grief at that instant evident in both facial expression and body language. It was actually pretty good.

"You know, that's not half bad," Holtzmann said. "It does make me real sad, though."

"Yeah, that's a bummer," Abby concurred.

"Don't be sad," Kevin countered. "The grave belongs to a murderer."

Yikes. So not where I was going in my head, Erin thought. *Or where we should be going.*

They all looked at him. Kevin shrugged, and with a tap on his keyboard opened door number 3: a picture of a bunless hot dog floating over a house.

Now Erin was massively confused. "Is that supposed to be for us?" she asked.

Kevin gestured to Abby. "She said on the phone 'a ghost or miscellaneous.'"

Abby was quick to cover for him. "Oh no, actually I said 'a ghost but nothing *extraneous*.' Okay, so just a misunderstanding."

Abby, you can't be serious. Erin felt sorry for her. The

desperation behind her maneuvering was painful to witness.

Holtzmann looked bemused. "I still have so many questions about this choice." She pointed at the hot dog.

Enough, Erin decided. She smiled sweetly at the job candidate. "Um, Kevin, could you excuse us for a moment?"

He nodded, slid out of the booth, and walked a short distance away. He seemed fascinated by a large brownish stain on the wall, something that was revealed by the peeling wallpaper. Holtzmann thought it looked like Switzerland, but she kind of had CERN on the brain.

Erin murmured to the others, "As much as I like to look at him—"

"*What?*" Abby said, aghast.

"You don't find him attractive?" Erin asked.

Abby gave her "the look," which brought back a flood of memories. "Kevin?" she said. "Ugh."

Erin tried another tack. "We can't do this. We are scientists. We are trying to do something real."

"He's the only applicant," Abby declared.

Erin's brows shot up. "Really?"

Abby became deadly serious. "Erin, he chose us. That means something. And we of all people should know better than to judge others. We don't know what's in there. I see a natural curiosity in him."

I'm surprised you can see anything, Erin thought. *My best guess is there's a perfect vacuum in there.*

They turned to look at him. "He's trying to get through the glass," Erin said.

Indeed, his focus had shifted from the wall stain. Now he was bumping his head against the aquarium, a place where doomed crustaceans had twitched antennae and scuttled to and fro. There were still some fish. Kevin was trying to get at the broken phone that had been dropped inside. Perplexed, he said, "How am I supposed to answer the phone in there?"

Case made, Erin thought triumphantly.

"Look, Erin, everyone has something to offer," Abby re-iterated. "This is not a place of judgment. You walk into this laboratory/Chinese restaurant and you will be welcome. I'm telling you, there's something in there."

Kevin hit the dust-coated Chinese gong.

Abby's cheeks colored again but she kept going. "I am never wrong about a person."

Holtzmann half raised her hand. "What about the Nigerian prince—"

"We might still hear from him!" Abby insisted. She looked over at the applicant. "Kevin? You got the job!"

Erin gave him a thumbs-up instead and forced a smile.

"Welcome aboard!" she said cheerily.

"Cool." He seemed far less excited at the prospect than she was upset. "Can I bring my suitcases up?"

"Yes, you may," Abby declared grandly.

Kevin headed out the door. As Abby watched him go, she did a double-take. Erin stepped forward to see what had startled her. A very tall dark-skinned woman in a uniform was sitting on a chair outside the door at the top of the stairwell. She was calmly reading a magazine.

"Ma'am," Abby said, "if you're picking up takeout, wait downstairs."

The woman looked surprised. "Oh, I saw this magazine and thought this was your waiting room."

She put the magazine back on the floor and walked through the doorway. After giving the room a cursory once-over, she said, "You know this building is built in the same spot as the first Chinese gambling den in New York?"

Erin and the others stared at her as if to say, "The point being?"

"Also," she went on, "I was just chased by a ghost."

The tall woman's name was Patty Tolan, and she worked in an MTA ticket booth. In an even voice Patty told them about the weird guy who had stopped by her window to tell her that the Fourth Cataclysm was coming, and then about the graffiti artist she chased off, the sparks in the tunnel, the device that exploded, and then she finally got around to the ghost. The latter sent Abby and Holtzmann into a frenzy of activity. While Erin and Patty stood idly by, they ran around the dining room gathering equipment and other gear seemingly at random, and squabbling over which piece of junk was most appropriate under the circumstances.

When they had what they needed they all hurried out of their "office"—Erin had to use that term lightly or lose heart; it was just temporary, she told herself. They had pluck on their side, and "pluck" was "luck" that had peed on itself, or so her uncle used to say. Which, now that she thought about it, made absolutely no sense. Anyway, as they went down the stairs out of the Chinese restaurant onto the street, she realized what a pleasure it had been to listen to Patty talk; she was a voracious reader, thoughtful and well spoken, and that made Erin think fondly on the good old days at Columbia where she was surrounded by articulate, bright, nonchaotic people.

Not that Holtzmann and Abby weren't intellectually curious. It was the expression of that curiosity and their lack of traditional boundaries that left something to be desired. As they accompanied Patty to the scene of the incident, Erin found herself walking beside a collection of gear that looked like it had been ripped straight out of a low-budget science-fiction movie. Holtzmann was wheeling a large metal cart piled with equipment as well as their silver duffel bag with its HIGH VOLTAGE shoulder strap, modded with an array of decals patches: a cute skull and crossbones; a biohazard warning; an embroidered toxic waste circle. There were various probes and remote sensors that looked like electronic harpoons and prods meant to herd Paul Bunyan's ox.

As they clattered along, New Yorkers, being New Yorkers, pretty much ignored them, but a couple of young women in ripped jeans and stylish padded jackets—one black, one charcoal gray—trailed right on their heels, murmuring to each other and giggling.

Erin hung back a little, allowing the girls to catch up to her. Ahead, Holtzmann and Abby were peppering Patty with questions, and although Erin knew she probably should be listening, she recognized what could be a teachable moment for her and a learning moment for the two young women. They were smacking gum and wore tons of heavy sparkly eye makeup and enormous matching earrings that spelled out Fuck You in rhinestones, but still . . .

"That is extremely precise, very cutting-edge scientific equipment," Erin informed them, gesturing at Holtzmann's cart. "We are all high-level researchers. Breaking new ground. Big ideas."

The girls pulled in their chins and raised their brows. The shorter one's mouth twitched. Erin could read their expressions: they were skeptics. Doubting that a team of women scientists could be so empowered.

"Girls can be scientists, too, you know," she insisted. "Do you know what STEM is? Science, technology, engineering, and mathematics. Women are underrepresented in these fields in part because they lack sufficient numbers of role models. I'm from Columbia and we have a program to encourage . . ." She felt a little sick to her stomach as she heard herself talk. She was not at Columbia. Not anymore. There was no "we" there.

"It's cool," the taller girl said. "Whatevah." She had a thick Jersey accent. She slid a glance at her friend. "Actually, we was just wonderin' if you lost a bet or something."

Erin blinked, caught off guard. "Lost a bet?"

"Yeah, and that's why you're dressed like that," the short one said, and they both cracked up.

Why is everyone always dissing my clothes? Erin plucked at the sleeve of her blazer. "See, that's the problem," she said. "We women focus so much on appearance when really—"

"Well, *you* sure don't," the tall one cut in, and the short one said, "Woo!" in approval. The tall one head-bobbed in recognition of the compliment.

"Well, at least I'm not dressed like a *hooker*," Erin snapped.

The two young women stopped laughing. They glared at Erin, faces hard, eyes narrowing.

"What did you say?" the taller one bit off.

Erin's synapses began firing. Her brain was giving her mixed messages: flee, fight, mouth off some more, shut the hell up. She started to reply, but before she could get a word out, Abby broke into the conversation.

"Sorry, ladies," she said to the girls, "what we are doing is highly classified and we must ask you to move away."

"This is our street, bitch," the short one informed her.

The tall one slipped her hand into her jacket pocket. *Oh god, she's going to pull out a switchblade or even a gun.* Adrenaline zipped through Erin's body as she looked for someplace to run.

But instead of a knife or a gun, the girl pulled out a top-of-the-line smartphone and checked the screen. "Our Uber is almost here," she announced to her friend.

"Good. 'Cause I am not letting Anderson exercise my

proxy at that meeting," the short one said. She rolled her Cleopatra eyes. "Selling short. What a dirtbag."

Abby took Erin's arm and urged her backward. Erin came along willingly. "Hey, are you guys investors?" Abby said as they retreated. "Because you can get in on the ground floor of something *enormous* here." She bobbed her head, oh yeah. "We are changing all the rules. What you see isn't what you get." She nodded at Erin and Holtzmann. Holtzmann nodded back, her curls of blond hair bouncing like springs.

"Abby, *no*," Erin hissed. "We can't involve strangers. We don't even know *what* we know yet."

"Oh yes, we do. We do know what we know," Abby insisted. "We know that ghosts are re—"

"Uber's here," the short one said to the tall one. They headed for the curb as a Fiat stopped in the street and the traffic zoomed around it. The tall one glanced at Abby over her shoulder. "Try *Shark Tank*. That's what we did."

"Awesome, what is your product?" Abby called after her as they headed for the waiting car.

"Glow-in-the-dark eye makeup," the girl replied. She and her companion both opened their eyes as wide as they could, and then closed them.

"Now you see us; now you *really* see us," they said together.

It had to be a marketing slogan.

"We're breaking sales of six million this year," said the tall one. She looked at Erin and clucked her tongue in disapproval. "We're nakedeyes.com. Use the contact form and ask for Tonya. That's me. We can fix you up."

"You must be a librarian," the short one added as she slid in beside Tonya.

Then the door closed and the Uber sped away.

"I can't believe that," Erin said in exasperation.

"I know. Six million dollars? For glow-in-the-dark eye makeup?" Abby whistled.

"No, they thought I was a librarian," Erin sputtered. With an effort she gathered her dignity. "Not that there's anything wrong with that."

"Come on and I'll show you some real glow-in-the-dark," Patty said, stepping up beside them. "And for the record? I don't believe those two. If you have six million dollars, you dial up your limo, not an Uber."

"Also, I think your dress looks very nice," Abby assured her.

They made their way across town on foot. Not for the exercise—no cabbie would stop for them. When they finally reached the entrance to the Seward subway station, they left the busy streets and headed down the stairs. Patty helped Holtzmann lug the unwieldy proton box and duffel to the mezzanine, where they piled it back onto the cart liberated from Kenneth T. Higgins. She pointed out her ticket booth as they hurried past. "That's me!" she said, waving energetically at the clerk on the other side of the window. "Hey, Milt!" she called out to him. "We got a ghost on track three."

He made a sour face and looked away.

"Nice," Patty said. "Real nice."

The subway platform was thinly populated, and although they drew stares from the sprinkling of commuters, they had no trouble weaving their way to the far end.

Erin looked at the black maw that loomed before them and could not repress a shudder. But Abby, Holtzmann, and Patty had no problem. Abby turned on the PKE meter. Holtzmann pushed her cart. And Patty led the way into the darkness.

"I told my supervisor and he insisted I take a drug test," she said. Her harrumph echoed down the tunnel. "You know the old York prison used to be right up there above us? That's the first place in New York they fried people in the electric chair. But I always knew something was weird down here."

The dim and widely spaced lights flickered and Erin

looked around nervously. She wasn't alone. Even Abby seemed a bit skittish.

"Strong correlation between negative incidents and paranormal presence," Abby said authoritatively. "It's very difficult for anything to pass through the barrier back into our world. So any spirit determined enough to pull that off, well, that's likely an angry ghost."

Staying as close to the others as she could, Erin reviewed the details of Patty's story about the apparition. She claimed to have seen a man floating above the ground wearing an old-timey prison uniform and a sparking skullcap designed for electrocutions. Patty had described his angry, evil smile. Gertrude Aldridge's smile had been angry and evil, too. Erin doubted that Mrs. Barnard had ever smiled a day in her life, but she had angry down. And there was also the strange electronic device Patty said had exploded in the tunnel at the same time she had her encounter.

Erin tried not to breathe deeply. The air smelled bad and it was thick with the fine grit raised by the trains. Plus there had to be rats galore, so decomposed rat poop was in the mix. Between the overhead lights the passage was dark, and under the lights, dirty—more than a century of grime and grease deposits coated everything. She hoped she didn't accidently brush against something, or worse, trip and fall on the floor. Although if she fell, she'd have a good excuse to go shopping and she could buy some different clothes.

But I like my clothes the way they are. Walking along, she had a thought: *No one started commenting on my attire until I was up for tenure. Aha.* That's *the problem. I didn't look conservative* enough. *I was too hip for that ship. That's why Abby likes my style.*

The lights flickered again, plunging the tunnel into darkness for a fraction of a second. Everyone jumped, including Patty. Then she pointed at something just ahead. A guy—who looked human enough—was spraying paint on the tunnel wall.

"Hey! What did I say?" Patty asked him.

Wearing the guiltiest possible expression, the kid tried to pretend he was using a can of spray deodorant. Patty scoffed and advanced on him, arms swinging, jaw set.

"That is not spray deodorant! Have you yet again mistaken me for a stupid person?"

"Is he down here a lot?" Abby asked.

"Oh, this is his art studio." Patty rolled her eyes.

Abby walked up to the kid. "Have you seen a Class Four semianchored entity around here?"

"You might want to try English," Patty suggested drily, but Abby didn't seem to pick up on the joke.

"Have you seen a ghost?" Erin said.

The graffiti artist looked at them coolly. "Yeah, I've seen a ghost."

A ripple of excitement coursed up Erin's spine. "Can you describe it?"

The guy thought about it for a moment. Then he spray painted the outline of a ghost on the subway wall.

"Don't you draw a ghost on that wall," Patty ordered him.

He stopped. Then he added a few more touches, fleshing the image out—so to speak.

"Do not make me tell you again." Patty was insistent.

He stopped. Then sprayed some more.

"I mean it," her voice rising.

He stopped, finally and for real, and stepped aside so they could admire his masterpiece. It was a cartoony outline of a white ghost with a hand outstretched. Its face was winsome and at the same time a bit goofy. It didn't look at all like an evil electrocuted criminal.

"I don't want that damn ghost up there," Patty said.

The kid grabbed another can of paint and quickly drew a red circle with a line through it over the ghost. When Patty grabbed the can of spray paint from his hand, he abandoned his art and ran back toward the station. Patty walked on, clearly pissed. Erin paused while Holtzmann snapped a shot of the kid's work with her phone, saying, "I can make a logo with that," and then they followed.

She and Holtzmann struggled to push the proton box over the rail ties. Too much speed and the vibration as they bounced over the ties could damage the sensitive innards; too little speed and they lost momentum. Ahead of them, Abby had out both her PKE and EMF meters. Patty kept glancing farther down the tunnel; Erin assumed she was hoping to see the ghost again, or hoping that she wouldn't.

"We don't have much time," Patty told them. "No one touch the third rail."

She's more worried about a train coming than the ghost, Erin translated. *If we get hit—or touch the third rail— maybe we'll start floating around down here.* As she pictured them as ghosts, trapped forever in a stinky black tunnel, something tapped her on the shoulder. She shivered and shut her eyes. *Just her imagination playing tricks.*

It happened again.

She tipped her head back and looked up. Something was dripping from the ceiling, and had dripped onto her shoulder. She moved under the light. It was the same green slime that Gertrude Aldridge had barfed all over her. It was running down her blazer.

"Oh, c'mon, I just dry-cleaned this," she protested.

Looking at the splotch of goo, Patty wrinkled her nose. "Yeah, I figured you were gonna get your fancy clothes dirty down here. I should have given you some coveralls. My bad. The MTA won't pay your dry-cleaning bills. Trust me. I've tried. Cheap bastards."

"We've got something over here." Abby gestured to a large discolored splotch on the wall. It looked like something had scraped away the layers of grime. "Are these burn marks?"

Everyone grouped around her.

"That's where I saw that weird sparking thing," Patty said, pointing a finger at the spot.

"What was it?" Holtzmann asked.

"Darlin', if I knew, I wouldn't have said 'that weird sparking thing,' " Patty told her.

There were fragments of metal and plastic scattered in an arc over the floor of the tunnel. As Abby began collecting them, Erin picked up and examined a piece that lay by her foot.

"That looks like fission scorch," she said.

When she held it out, Abby leaned over and sniffed it. "Huh. Smells of both electrical discharge and isotopic decay," she declared. "Holtz, smell this. You agree?" Holtzmann gave the piece a good sniff as well, and then she stuck out her tongue and licked it. "Definite neuron burn," she concurred, smacking her lips.

They all leaned in and smelled the piece again. The sprockets in Erin's mind turned as she tried to reverse-engineer what the components of the device might have been and what it had been constructed to do. It certainly hadn't been a bomb; the explosion was secondary to function. Overall it seemed familiar—power source, materials, construction—yet she couldn't quite put a finger on it.

"All right, if you're all done making out with that piece of dirty garbage, we only have a few minutes," Patty warned them. "For real, I gave us no cushion room."

As soon as she finished the last sentence, the tunnel lights flickered for a third time and went out.

"Huh, boy," Erin moaned. She hoped their high-tech equipment hadn't caused the blackout. No, wait. Maybe she did hope that, because if they weren't to blame, there could be another weird sparking thing hidden somewhere in the tunnel with them. Not knowing what was coming next or from what direction made her knees start to quake. At that moment, she wished she were back at headquarters, prying ancient pot stickers from the linoleum with a butter knife.

"Did you see that? The *eyes*?" Holtzmann said.

Always the joker, Erin thought, bristling. "Holtzmann, please don't mess . . . *oh.*" Suddenly she saw what Holtzmann was talking about—farther down the dark tunnel, it looked like a pair of glowing yellow eyes hanging disembodied in space. Or maybe it was just two lightbulbs that hadn't blown out. But they were spaced about as far apart as human eyes would be.

"That is . . . unsettling," she managed to mutter. An understatement for sure, but it was the only adjective she could summon from the turmoil in her brain.

"Holtzmann, illuminate the subject," Abby said.

"Yeah, get some light on that," Patty said.

Holtzmann aimed the beam of her flashlight down the tunnel. Erin let out a soft little whimper. The yellow eyes belonged to a tall, spindly ghost with a thin, skull-like face. He was wearing a hundred-year-old prisoner's uniform and a sparking electrocution cap, and he was floating in the middle of the tunnel staring at them.

Immediately the antenna on the PKE meter in Abby's hand started spinning wildly. "That is somehow more unsettling," Erin said.

"And fantastic!" Abby cried. "That's another Class Four, but way more ionized than the Aldridge ghost. Look at the meter. I've gotta get this on film."

Erin tried, but couldn't take her eyes off the ghost as it rose into the air and glared down at them. Her mind was replaying the very first time she had laid eyes on the vengeful phantom of Mrs. Barnard, recalling that strange cognitive dissonance that assured her what she was seeing wasn't there, even though she knew it was. She knew . . .

Oops. Erin realized she had missed part of the conversation around her, because Patty was in the middle of a sentence. "You say somebody's trying to bring ghosts back?" she exclaimed. "Why the hell would a person do that?"

"No idea," Abby said. "Let's bring this bad boy back to the lab. Holtz, power up."

Take it back to the lab? A ghost? Erin opened her mouth to suggest a more prudent course of action, such as run and hide, but Holtzmann and Abby were already swinging into action. Holtzmann hit a switch on the proton box and frantically typed into the keyboard on top as Abby pulled out her camera and began to record.

"This is early stages," Holtzmann told Erin and Patty, "so it's a little rough. I'm going to adjust the levels. Erin, hold this."

Holtzmann handed her a large, cumbersome proton wand that looked like the business end of a vacuum cleaner. It was attached to a flexible tube that was in turn attached to the proton box. And even for its size, the wand was surprisingly heavy. It took two hands to lift it.

"This will shoot a proton stream, so just aim it at the ghost when I say. Oh god, I almost forgot—"

Aim it at the ghost? Erin thought incredulously as Holtzmann clapped what looked like a metal neck brace around her neck. A look of horror crossed her face as she realized it was attached with a thick wire to the machine.

"Just a little bit of grounding," Holtzmann explained. "Okay, don't move too much. Or talk. And definitely don't sweat."

Oh god, oh my god. Erin stood stock-still while Holtzmann fiddled with some switches on the box. Holtzmann's flashlight, held tucked under her arm while she tweaked the settings, was pointed down. When she pointed it back up, Erin's jaws clenched and every muscle in her body contracted.

The ghost had cut the distance between them in half! When? How? They hadn't heard a thing. The PKE and EKE meter antennas were whirling in a blur like the rotors of miniature helicopters.

"Hey, look," Holtzmann announced with glee. "He's getting closer."

Without moving her lips, Erin said, *"Holtzmann."*

"Aim the wand at it," Abby told her.

Erin succeeded in unfreezing her muscles just enough to comply. A weak little beam skittered out of the massive tip—a mere fizzle of faint, watery light. *Proton stream, my ass.* Squeezing the wand seemed like her only option, but that had no discernable effect on output. Erin felt the panic rising in the back of her throat.

"Well, that's underwhelming," Abby grunted. "Use more power."

"Trying." Holtzmann played the dials like a deejay. "Okay, Erin, do it again." As Holtzmann straightened up, her flashlight beam once again illuminated the tunnel.

Erin choked back a squeal. The ghost was even *closer.* She could read his prisoner identification number on the strip of scorched fabric sewn to his chest. Abby kept filming. Holtzmann kept dialing. And in desperation, Erin aimed the wand at it again. The beam that exited the nozzle was definitely more intense, more like a set of beams that vacillated from particle to wave and back again, and the wand vibrated against her hands like a runaway chainsaw. The oscillation was accompanied by a sizzling noise, and this time the undulating beam extended just far enough to touch the ghost. He stopped moving, but she couldn't tell if it was from the beam or if he'd just decided to play it coy. The wand was definitely getting heavier, which was impossible, unless the constant force of gravity had changed. No, that was crazy talk. A more likely scenario was that the violent shimmying and the effort to keep it on target were draining the strength from her arms.

I'm dripping sweat, she thought. *She told me not to sweat and I'm pouring sweat. I'm drowning in sweat. I'm going to get electrocuted, too.* The unpleasant irony of that made her squirm.

"Can this thing get stronger, please?" she begged.

Holtzmann shot her a wistful look. "Not at the moment. Live and learn, I guess. I wish I had time to run back to the lab. You couldn't hold that for a while, could you?"

The crackling beam was striking the ghost's chest and

holding it in place no more than a yard away from her. Its yellow eyes bored into hers. Its smile revealed hideous, jagged teeth. It reached out for her, arms waving, stretching. *"No!"* she said emphatically, her whole body shaking from the strain.

When the ghost suddenly pushed forward, the proton beam acted like a solid object between them; like a battering ram, it knocked Erin off balance and onto her tush on the dirty gravel. Somehow she kept the beam focused on the ghost and held him at bay. The ghost no doubt thought he was holding her pinned to the ground. He looked like he wanted to tear her limb from limb. She knew if something untoward happened to the beam she would die in the subway tunnel covered in ghost slime and sweat with an enormous dog collar around her neck. She imagined the headline on her tabloid, front-page obituary: "Defrocked Scientist Commits Suicide in Bizarre Autoerotic Ritual." Talk about laughingstock.

Keep him centered in the beam and you'll be okay.

Suddenly there were more lights, much brighter, focusing in on her, blinding her. *What the—*

"That's the train. We gotta move!" Patty cried.

Even if Erin could have moved under the pressure the ghost was putting on her, she was so sopping wet she didn't think she could summon the traction to push herself back up. She wanted to let the others know, but because she was expending every ounce of strength she couldn't utter a peep.

Abby pulled out a small metal box that she had called a "ghost trap" when they were loading up the duffel bag. "We are not losing this thing. Erin, drag the ghost back to the platform."

The ghost leered at Erin, flailing his arms, fighting to close the distance between them and only succeeding in pushing her harder down onto the gravel. He paused to laugh as Erin stammered, "W-w-what?"

"There's no time!" Patty shouted. "Grab her sides!"

Patty grabbed the back of her metal collar and jerked her toward the platform. The jerk didn't break her neck, but felt like it might have; that's how strong Patty was. Like a mama lion carrying a cub, she hoisted Erin to her feet as Holtzmann and Abby grabbed hold of her arms. For all that, even as she was dragged bodily away, Erin continued to keep the beam on her target and hold the ghost off them. As she was hauled down the tracks, so was the ghost. Until that instant, he hadn't realized that he was being more than just repelled—he was caught in the beam like a bug on a pin. It was something he did not enjoy, and he demonstrated his displeasure by swinging his arms and kicking, and trying to take a bite out of them with his snaggly spectral teeth. Connected to the wand in her hands, the proton box banged along behind them as the subway train bore down.

Clackaclackaclacka.

The ground underfoot began to shake.

"That's express!" Patty yelled. "It's not stopping."

We are all gonna die, Erin thought as she looked into the blazing headlights. She couldn't drop the wand without releasing the specter. And if she didn't drop the wand, the box was an anchor tied around their ankles. There was nothing she could do, nothing to save herself or the others. The ghost seemed to recognize the oncoming danger, too. His face grew monstrous. Then a hard wind slammed into them. The pressure wave pushed ahead of the train in the tight space sandblasted Erin with grit and stink. She sensed the end of the tunnel behind her, but it was too late . . .

Her stomach lurched as she went airborne in reverse. Heaving in unison, Patty, Holtzmann, and Abby yanked her up onto the platform beside them. But the proton box was still on the tracks just inside the tunnel, she was still connected to the box by a stout cable to the collar around her neck, and the train was almost upon them.

She felt Holtzmann's fingers frantically fumbling at the back of her neck.

Train, box, train, box, trainboxtrainbox—

Eyes darting back and forth, Erin could see what was going to happen: train hits box at fifty miles an hour, drags box down track, cable jerks taut, and she is either beheaded or pulled under the screeching wheels.

At the last possible instant, Holtzmann freed her and threw the collar and cable down onto the tracks.

As the train sped into the station it smashed the proton box against the third rail. The incredible surge of electricity shot through the wand Erin still clutched and the resulting beam hit the ghost, dead center. A massive proton discharge enveloped the specter, and for a split second immobilized him. A split second was all it took. When the express train plowed into him, globs of slime exploded in all directions—ectoplasm rained down on the platform, covering Erin from quivering head to curling toes.

The train's impact splattered the ghost against the back wall of the subway—smashed, leaking goo, but being already dead, apparently unharmed. Metal cap still sparking, the bewildered spirit sped back to the safety of the tunnel.

"Guess he's going to Queens," Patty deadpanned.

I want to throw up, Erin thought as the coating of slime oozed under her clothing and into alarming new territory.

"Did you see that? That surge of power really got ahold of it," Abby said. "What a field test! Data-tastic."

The trickle of ectoplasm slowly creeping down Erin's bare back reached the base of her spine and there was nothing she could do to stop it from sliding down further. Not without taking off all her clothes. The very act of breathing sped up what seemed inevitable. *If I wasn't afraid of getting some of this yuck in my mouth, I would so throw up right now.*

"Yep," said an equally jubilant Holtzmann. "We're going

to need a lot more juice. We need to be more mobile, too. I know what to do."

Throw up? Erin filled in, squeezing her eyes shut and clenching her fists as the slime that had gotten under the back of her collar oozed down the inside of her legs. In a faint, flat voice, she said, "We almost got killed."

"Yeah, I know," Holtzmann said. "So awesome. No one looked into that flash, right?"

"I looked directly into it," Erin said.

"Oh, that's fine," Holtzmann said, waving off any reason for her to be concerned, then throwing a look to Abby that clearly said, "Yikes!"

12

The moment they got back to headquarters from the station, Abby had posted her three-minute subway video online. There was shaky camera work like in those "found-footage" horror movies, but many of the images of the ghost were crystal clear. There was no denying the stripes on his prison uniform, his floating above the ground, or his face distorted in demonic fury. It had been hours since the video went up, but they had only thirty views, and the comments so far were all mean:

"So fake."

"My dog liked it."

"You people are crazy."

All indications led to it not going viral.

Erin was stumped. How could a video of them jumping up and down like sugar-overdosed Girl Scouts have gotten so much attention that Dean Filmore felt compelled to fire her, while this truly groundbreaking piece of footage rated nothing more than a handful of mehs?

She heaved a sigh as Abby walked up. "Man. What do people want?" Abby shrugged, and Erin went on. "We really need to get a ghost back to the lab and document it properly. This stuff's all real and we can't prove it to anybody."

"We will," Abby assured her. "You can't read that stuff. You just gotta ignore these people." She scanned the comments. Her face changed to an expression of pure outrage. " *'Bullshit equipment'*?"

Abby grabbed the keyboard and started to pound out an angry response. Erin ripped the keyboard away from her before she could finish and held it out of reach.

"Okay, okay." Abby took a deep breath. "Just ignore them."

Erin watched Abby's shoulders slowly descend from a high point up around her ears. Her face looked more relaxed, but as Kevin walked up to her with a mug in his hand she shot the comment-filled screen a nasty side-glance.

"Here's your coffee," he said.

"Did you remember the sugar?"

Kevin frowned for a moment, clearly struggling with an answer. Then a big smile lit up his face. He took the cup back and sipped from it noisily.

"Yeah," he said, handing it back to Abby. He looked quite pleased with himself as he walked away.

Abby stared down at her cup in dismay, and when she finally looked up, Erin gave her a "what do you expect" shrug.

"Well, at least he remembered," Abby said defensively.

Erin couldn't decide if Abby was loyal to a fault or just stubborn. She had championed Kevin and she was still his champion. Except that Erin was paying his salary from her savings. Not a productive line of thought. She decided to change the subject.

"What do you make of the tech from the subway?"

They moved to a table where the fragments of the device had been spread out. They hadn't made an attempt to organize them yet. It looked like a jigsaw puzzle, without the picture on the front of the box and most of the parts barbecued.

"I've only got bits and pieces here," Abby said. "None of which have any business in a subway tunnel. But look at this." She held up a piece for Erin's inspection.

The part looked like it could be a magnet yoke, only reduced to the size of a Frito. If it was a magnet yoke, then the matching piece she could see on the table was likely a pole shoe, one of two. Erin was impressed, despite herself. Until now, the subcomponent she believed they came from was only theoretically possible. "Was that a miniature cyclotron?"

"Yup. Everything I'm looking at here, it's all things we've associated with attracting ghost particles."

Abby was right, of course; the minicyclotron was an integral part of the speculation they had put forth in their book.

"I'm wondering if someone built some kind of device to bring in an apparition, which is very impressive. And I'll say it . . . a little sexy." She grinned and waggled her brows provocatively.

Erin could see a big downside to what she was suggesting, and it wasn't the least bit sexy: the barrier between the living and the dead was there for a reason. But there was no arguing her conclusion—the device they were visualizing could only have one purpose. "What was that weird thing that guy mentioned to her?"

Looking on from her seat at a computer, Patty said, "The Fourth Cataclysm. Sounded like some spooky ancient shit, but I can't find anything about it online." She indicated her computer monitor with a shake of her head. "*Fourth* Cataclysm. Do I also need to worry about the first through third cataclysms? Who's got that kind of time?" *I think it's cataclysma,* Erin thought as she and Abby traded pained looks.

"Ma'am, why are you still here?" Abby asked Patty politely.

"Oh, I'm joining your club." She spoke as if they had no choice and it was a fait accompli.

Abby's response was interrupted by the ringing of the phone. Kevin, who'd been sitting at a small desk by the door with a vacant look on his face, looked a little mystified. He said, "What is this place called again?"

"Conductors of the Metaphysical Examination," Erin shouted out.

Kevin picked up the phone and said, "Conductors of . . . meta something or other." Then apparently without waiting for a reply, he hung up.

Erin rolled her eyes at Abby.

Abby's expression conceded the point. She cleared her throat before she said, "Hey, Kevin? I'm going to need you to try a little harder. Okay, buddy?"

Kevin was agreeable. "Okay, if they call back, I will."

"There you go," Abby said with forced jovially.

He slid back from his desk. "I've gotta take off, though. I've got a hide-and-seek tournament. We're in the semis."

"Yup," Abby said.

She did not look at Erin. But his comment gave Erin a smidgeon of hope that perhaps he was attending a college part time, or knew someone in college, or knew where a college was. Because a "hide-and-seek tournament" sounded a lot like a game of Assassin to her, which was something that undergrads played at Columbia. They hid from each other and there was running to home base and all kinds of things that she had never squandered precious time doing in college.

She didn't ask him, because she didn't want to be more disappointed in case her hypothesis proved incorrect. Instead, she turned to their new odd duck.

"Patty, right?" she said. "This isn't really a club. We're a research group. Do you have any lab experience?"

Abby and Holtzmann both stopped what they were doing and watched.

"No," Patty said flatly. "And I kinda feel like I was set up to fail with that question. No, I am not a scientist. I understand that. I didn't go to some fancy school like the rest of you. I didn't go to Harvard or Rutgers—"

Rutgers? Erin swapped incredulous looks with Holtz-mann and Abby. Had she really said *Rutgers*? She might as well have said Higgins.

"But I read a lot of nonfiction," Patty continued. "You know, you can be smart about science but straight-up dummy about everything else." She caught herself and winced. "I guess I didn't need to insult you. I apologize for that."

They all nodded to say, "It's cool." But it kind of wasn't.

"Look, I spend most of my time sitting alone in an MTA booth. Thought it'd be nice to pick up an activity that involves other people."

A near-death experience involving the spirit of a murdering psychopath is an "activity"? Erin was flabbergasted. She felt it was her duty to immediately set the woman straight. If they were correct in thinking that some-one was deliberately bringing angry ghosts across the barrier into the world of the living, the "activity" was going to get a lot less "nice" in a hurry.

"Also, I can borrow a car from my uncle so you don't have to keep lugging all that heavy equipment around," Patty said.

"Great. Welcome to the team, Patty," Abby said, essen-tially ending the discussion.

And Erin's chance at setting the newbie straight. What was *up* with Abby? This was the second time she'd brought someone in without checking with her. She cor-rected herself. *This is the third time she's welcomed someone new; I was the first. Who am I kidding? This is Abby's team, not mine, even though I'm the one paying for it.*

Anyway, Patty was in, and obviously happy about it, too. Maybe she was good with all of it, the danger and the freaky scariness? She hadn't been with them a full day yet and she had already led them to their second ghost encounter, and without flinching had risked her own life to protect everyone else.

Erin heaved a sigh of resignation. If Patty didn't have a clue what she was doing, that made five of them—unless Kevin counted double.

13

I t was the dawn of a new day in New York City. And like most new days, this one was greeted by the loud honking of a car horn. Erin ignored it and continued recalibrating the PKE meter she was working on. Some jerks fighting over a parking spot most likely. *It has to end soon*, she thought, giving the adjustment screw a quarter turn, then checking the result against a performance graph.

When the horn continued honking and honking, she kept losing her focus. She looked up from the booth's table in irritation. Abby, who was almost finished sorting the mysterious device fragments, frowned at her from the opposite side; she couldn't concentrate, either. They got up from their seats and went over to Holtzmann, who was over by the window welding something while practicing her dance moves. When they nudged her she tipped up her welding mask and pulled a headset earphone away from her ear. The string of short honks had become an unbroken sustained blast. Holtzmann made a sour face and hooked a thumb toward the door. The car sounded like it was right out front. Without a word, they raced for the stairs to find out what was going on.

A long hearse was parked in the loading zone in front of the Chinese take-out place and Patty was in the driver's seat merrily pounding on the horn. She stopped honking as soon as she saw them. As she climbed out, Holtzmann cried, "Oh sweet!"

Abby clearly did not share Holtzmann's delight. She crossed the sidewalk and said in an uptight voice, "You did not disclose this automobile was a hearse."

Patty took Abby's disapproval in stride. "My uncle owns a funeral home! Would you rather take the subway? What's the difference? We work with the dead anyway."

And it's not like it's the Oscar Mayer Weinermobile, Erin thought, recalling Kevin's bizarre floating hot dog logo. *It's way more normal than that.*

A couple walked by arm in arm. When they saw the hearse they did a double take, then paused to gawk.

"Can I help you?" Patty said. Her tone of voice made "help" sound damn painful.

They scooted away as fast as they could.

Erin watched the pair speed walk into traffic against a red light. *Well, maybe not all that normal.*

Rowan was making his rounds at the Mercado. A door opened at the end of the hall. *Oh, glory be,* he thought. It was Mrs. Potter, in her bathrobe as usual. He'd peeked in her closet once—she had about fifty of them.

"Excuse me," she called. "Maintenance man!"

"Mrs. Potter," he said, acknowledging her with an unctuous grin. "Thank you for using my preferred title. How may I help you?"

His faux officiousness was completely lost on her. She actually thought he was serious. Was convinced that humiliating him was her due. He couldn't wait for the scales to drop from her rheumy eyes, to watch her grovel at his feet . . . and plead for mercy . . . of which there would be none forthcoming.

"Well, for starters," she said a bit crossly, "you could tell me what in god's name this is."

She pointed at something on her apartment door—a shiny, green, gelatinous substance. He could have named it for her, but chose not to, as that would have spoiled the looming surprise. The ectoplasm had materialized out of nothing and traveled along the doorframe. *Excellent*. The eternal barrier was failing just as he predicted, and as a consequence, fundamental elements of the strange new world on the other side were seeping through.

What the stumbling masses thought was forever lost would soon be in their laps, clawing and scratching, and eating off their faces.

"Isn't that something," he said as he leaned down and took a closer look. Mrs. Potter hadn't appeared to notice—perhaps because the rhinestone trifocals she wore on a lanyard were not hanging from her scrawny neck—that the substance was moving of its own accord. "Must be some leakage from the air-conditioning. I'll take care of it immediately." All he had to do was adjust a few dials, and there would be much, much more of it.

"I think it must have touched my skin," Mrs. Potter complained. "It's given me a rash."

She turned her back on him, loosened the sash, and then without another word lowered the neck of her robe. He found her boldness shocking at first, but then it hit him—he mattered so little that it was like exposing herself to her dog or parakeet.

"Does this look red to you?" she asked, glancing at him over her withered shoulder.

With difficulty he hid his overflowing delight. It looked more than red. It looked like one of his recently freed subjects had invaded and taken possession of Mrs. Potter. The full outline of the small ghostly creature was visible just beneath her skin. It was an imp, gnashing its fangs and trying to claw its way out through her back. He could see its features as it stretched the skin like plastic wrap. It was so hideous—and he never used that term lightly—that even he was taken slightly aback. But that was only because, like every other creature on the planet, he had yet to fully explore the wonders of the world that lay beyond.

The place that he liked to call hell.

He pretended to scrutinize her back as she stood patiently awaiting the verdict.

"Well. Uh-huh. I was gonna say no," he began. Then he leaned closer to her, squinting. "But you know what? Yep. It *is* a little red." He took the liberty of tracing a section with his fingertip. Mrs. Potter didn't object to the physical contact, but the little monster's teeth clacked as if trying to bite him. He was sure he could hear it growling. "Right in this area here. Does it look bad? No, no, not at all. But just in case, I'll send up some cream."

He turned and walked away with eyes widened, unnerved by what he had wrought. He assured himself it was just part of the process, the necessary learning curve. He was bringing forth a new world order, but had no way of knowing all the different sorts of creatures that would inhabit it. No matter; they were all his subjects and they would all do their part in the cleansing.

It didn't strike Mrs. Potter as odd that he was giving her something for a skin condition. He was, after all, a generic servant and gofer. Over time, he had proven himself so helpful to the tenants of the Mercado that they came to him with all kinds of problems and ailments. Maintaining their trust allowed him to keep track of anomalous events in what was essentially an Art Deco petri dish. For example, while she was barely complaining, Mrs. Potter had brought the appearance of ectoplasm around her door to his attention. Monitoring ectoplasm transfer rate was critical, as it was a direct indication of his success in supercharging the particles unique to postlife existence. More ectoplasm was leaking through with each passing day, a very positive sign. Until his magnificent accomplishment, only a handful of phantoms had managed to penetrate the barrier—through a fortunate combination of force of will and the unique configuration of their spectral particles. His device would make it possible for any ghost to return to this world.

All ghosts.

He entered his basement kingdom and removed his jacket, hanging it carefully by the door. Deeper inside the room, faint creaking and scraping sounds echoed off the hard surfaces.

Yes, Daddy's home.

He walked over to his workstation, which was cluttered with test equipment and devices in various stages of assembly and development. He gazed into a large mirror on the floor and, his chest swelling with pride, addressed the roiling chaos on the far side of the glass.

"Who put the imp in Mrs. Potter?" he asked. "I know you are all anxious, but we must be patient. The guests are starting to complain. We don't want any spoilers before the big show."

He stared deeply into the mirror, which opened onto the astonishing spirit world. Ghosts, both human and demonic in appearance, phased in and out of what resembled dense clouds of smoke. The other side was easier to see now, another measure of his success in weakening the barrier between existences. The ghosts were scratching and clawing at the glass, so very eager.

It wouldn't be long now.

Not long at all.

14

At the world headquarters of the Conductors of the Metaphysical Examination, Erin and her three colleagues stood around the table admiring the array of Holtzmann's latest accomplishments. She was scaling down the proton cart into a portable pack and working on a few other ideas. Basically, everything she had made was smaller, lighter, more mobile, more powerful—she had definitely upped her game and their arsenal. The phone rang from the other side of the dining room. Erin shot their fifth wheel, AKA Receptionist Kevin, a questioning glance, and on the fourth ring he dutifully picked up the phone.

Yay, she thought. *Progress.*

"Hello?" he said, and then paused, apparently listening to what the caller had to say.

Erin's enthusiasm immediately faded a bit. Kevin had forgotten to mention the five-word name of their organization. All those hours of training apparently had been for nothing.

"Not with me, you don't!" he said, and hung up the phone.

Erin frowned. "Uh, Kevin, who was that?"

"I don't know. I didn't like him."

Good grief, he's like a dog that can't be housebroken. She considered pointing out the incident to Abby, but realized she'd just turn things around and claim he was "using his own initiative."

Meanwhile, Holtzmann was continuing her debriefing. She seemed perkier than usual.

"So based on our findings from the subway field test, I added an amplifier using microfabricated dielectric laser accelerators to speed up the particles before entering the DLA device. Portable and wearable for maximum flexibility. And we're just getting started."

Holtzmann gestured at the inventions-in-progress on her banquet table workstation and was about to continue when Erin jumped in. "Okay, well, one life-threatening device at a time, please. So it fires. Then what?"

Abby picked up the ghost trap they had attempted to use in the tunnel before things got totally out of hand. "Then we add the reversible tractor beam with Holtz's hollow laser inside this guy, and wah-lah. We are gonna catch us a mother-effin' ghost!"

Abby and Holtzmann proceeded to do a high-five ritual as complicated as any cheerleader routine. This was their thing, their we-have-worked-together-forever statement. Erin looked on glumly, aware that if Kevin was the fifth wheel, then she was the third.

Patty didn't seem to care that she was being left out—if anything, she was amused—but Kevin slid Erin a comforting glance and said, "Don't worry. We can have our own high five."

He started high-fiving her. It was crazy and Hulk-like with immense arms, impossible to follow. All she could think about was living through it and avoiding permanent injury. The sequence ended with him lightly slapping her neck.

"Okay, I'm good, thank you, Kevin," she said, her head reeling, fighting to remain upright. He didn't seem to be aware of his own strength.

Holtzmann patted her on the back. "I'll teach it to you later," she promised.

Erin was touched by their efforts to make her feel included, misguided though they were. Kevin was a plug-in night light in terms of brilliance, Holtzmann was a certified genius, but both were kind at heart.

The TV was turned on, but set to mute. They were still hoping their Reddit might go viral, or someone else would report a sighting in the subway tunnel, but so far there had been nothing.

Picking up one of the new proton packs, Holtzmann turned her attention to Patty. "C'mon. Let's get you fitted up with one of these."

"Okay," Patty said. As she took in the hazardous-looking assemblage, her eyes narrowed. "Is it safe?"

Holtzmann's expression grew serious. "To be clear, nothing in this lab is safe."

She led Patty over to her workbench by the buffet table's sneeze shield. The smeared and smudged glass looked like it hadn't been disinfected in years. Erin took their departure as her cue and stepped up to Abby. She steeled herself to do something she should have done a long, long time ago.

First she had to swallow a bit gulp of pride and antipride, which was also known as shame.

Here goes.

"Abby," she began, "that time I didn't show up? I—I didn't try to call." Her face was hot. "I lied. I was just so tired of being the big joke. I'm sorry."

A flicker of a grin crossed Abby's mouth. "I know." There was a beat between them, and then Abby said, "Well, you're here now, right?"

A rush of genuine joy swept over Erin; it had been so long she couldn't remember the last time she'd felt that emotion. It was so good to be back together with Abby again. She'd sacrificed so much to hide who she was and keep a lid on her fears. She had let herself forget how important friends were. Well, no more. She had rejoined the friend zone.

And it was a great place to be.

There were now four portable proton packs hanging from the wall like commando gear. Erin and the other women warriors sat in a booth in front of an open box of New York–style pizza. They were eating it while it was still hot and talking with their mouths full, getting to know each other better.

"So, how did you two meet?" Patty asked Erin and Abby as she deftly folded over a cheese-dripping slice, her second. She took a big bite, tip first, skillfully steering the inevitable drip of olive oil away from her fingers and onto the cardboard box.

"Oh, Abby transferred to my high school junior year," Erin explained.

Abby took up the thread. "We started sharing ghost stories and bonded immediately. All the other kids were getting drunk and going to parties and we were like 'that's stupid.'" She wrinkled her nose.

"Also, we weren't invited to any parties," Erin said.

Abby gave her an incredulous look, as if she had just given away the secret of cold fusion. "Well, we also put out a vibe that indicated we were not accepting any invitations," she said.

Erin shook her head. Abby was rewriting history. If they'd been invited to any parties before the "vibe" went out, she would have remembered it.

"Why were you so into ghosts?" Patty said. "Had either one of you actually seen one?"

Erin pretended to chew what she had just swallowed, stalling. It was *that* sensitive a topic for her. Abby didn't say anything, letting her tell the story if she wanted to, and skip it if she didn't. It had been a long time since Erin had shared Mrs. Barnard with anyone. It seemed weird to hide it from Holtzmann and Patty.

"Yeah," Erin said. "When I was eight, the mean old lady who lived next door to us died. That night, I woke up and there she was standing at the foot of my bed. She was just staring at me, and then blood started coming out of her mouth. She slowly started falling toward me. I pulled my covers over my head and waited until morning."

As she paused in telling the story, she realized her entire body was tense, steeled to defend against the expected and familiar laughter and teasing. Instead, Patty nodded and gave her a sympathetic look. So Erin continued, delivering the astounding punch line.

"She did that every night for a year."

"*What?*" Patty cried.

Holtzmann exclaimed, "Whoa!"

"I told everyone, but no one believed me." Words began to rush out of her in a torrent. "My parents thought I was crazy. They had me in therapy for years. All the kids at school made fun of me. Called me 'ghost girl.'" She looked over at Abby. "But Abby believed me right away."

"Hey, I believe you, too," Patty announced.

"Hmm, I have some questions," Holtzmann said, then winked at her.

Erin smiled back. It was *such* a relief to get this off her chest.

Then it was Patty's turn to let down her hair.

"You know, I never connected with the other kids, either," she admitted. "Mostly because I was into books. I think my experience was perhaps less traumatic than yours."

Kevin stepped up, a thoughtful expression on his face as he casually played with something in his hands. Apparently he had overheard their conversation.

"Erin, if you don't believe in yourself, no one else will," he said.

She was surprised that he had been paying attention. He usually walked around completely oblivious to everything but his own bizarre interior life. Even now, he was goofing around with whatever he was holding.

"Thank you. That's really nice," she said. A bonding moment, unexpected, but welcome.

"Kevin." Abby's voice was measured, strained. "What's in your hand? Now Erin recognized the object—the grenade shape, the folded material in the center that looked like an air filter. It was the piece of equipment she had picked up at the Kenneth T. Higgins Institute to throw across the room when she stormed in to tell them that Abby's upload to Reddit had gotten her fired. The object that Holtzmann and Abby had said would kill them all if she dropped it.

"What? This?" Kevin smiled and began tossing the thing back and forth between his hands like a tennis ball.

"Kevin, no!" Holtzmann shouted.

Abby joined in the panic. "Do not let it fall!"

Their fright was contagious. Realizing that he was in danger, Kevin started juggling it like it was a hot potato, bouncing it on his palms. No longer in control, he overcompensated with one hand, then the other, fighting to keep it in the air. He was on the verge of losing it for real.

"Just stop juggling and put it down!" Holtzmann bellowed.

Erin considered rushing him and attempting to scoop the gizmo out of his hands, but what if that only made things worse and he dropped it?

Kevin managed to slow the back and forth, and keeping his eyes locked on it the whole time, caught it in his cupped hands. He set the thing down on the table and hurried away, his face drawn and pale.

"Jesus Christ," Abby said.

Everyone took a deep breath and hit reset. They slid out of the booth to stretch their legs and walk off the tension.

Patty pointed at something on a round table near the

lobster tank and said, "Hey, what's this?" She picked up the photo and showed it to them.

It was of Abby and Erin as geeky teenagers standing beside the poster describing an experiment. Clad in black turtlenecks, they glowed with happiness and excitement.

"Science fair!" Erin gasped.

Abby grinned. "I found it this morning."

Patty turned the photo to look at it again. A smile spread across her face as she read aloud the title on the poster in the picture. " 'The Durable But Not Impenetrable Barrier!' What does that mean?"

It meant that I had a friend, Erin thought.

15

I t was senior year at C. W. Post High. Erin and Abby
pushed an overloaded, liberated, Felpausch Market shopping cart through the teacher parking lot and onto the
winding asphalt path that led through the little campus. It
had a wonky front wheel that kept sticking and making
them correct course. They circumnavigated the few pud-
dles left over from a late spring rainstorm and headed for
the tallest building on the grounds, the red-roofed gym-
nasium that had always reminded Erin of an outsized
barn. Students with arms loaded with boxes were already
entering through the open double doors. A paper banner
strung over the entrance said: C. W. Post High School
Science Fair.

Their senior guidance counselor, Mrs. Rice, had urged
them to enter a project in the fair because it could help them
nail down scholarships at the University of Michigan. Erin
saw another side of it: simplifying their work for a lay
audience was a way to organize and gain perspective on
the gains and shortcomings of their research. In the year
since she and Abby had met, they had accumulated a
wealth of factual information and had assembled what they
felt was a rational theoretical groundwork to account for
spectral intrusions into this plane of existence.

Entering the cavernous building, they were met by
Mr. Puccini, who stood just inside the doorway behind a
little folding table, bow tie askew. He didn't try to hide his

frown when he saw them. As he handed Abby their location assignment, he glanced at the contents of the shopping cart, and through a forced smile said, "Good luck with that. I think you'll find there's some real tough competition this year."

"Thanks for that information, Mr. Puccini," Abby said brightly, then turned to Erin and gave her "the look," which involved extending her tongue to its absolute limit, crossing then rolling her eyes. Erin had to choke back a giggle.

Their science fair project was largely incomprehensible to the Honors Physics teacher. Even though they tried to explain it to him twice, he got lost trying to follow the Lagrangian mechanics and gauge field theories that attempted to describe what they termed the "spectral ether"—the predicted medium through which spirits interact with our world. The second time they went through it with him even more slowly, but before they finished he threw up a hand and walked away, angry and red faced. Mr. Math-Macho Puccini didn't like being upstaged by a couple of teenage girls.

"Let's do check out the competition before we set up," Abby said.

"Sure, why not."

They pushed their cart down the middle aisle between two rows of long tables lined up on the basketball court. Students were busy assembling components of their projects, plugging in power cords, and sotto voce practicing scripted explanations for the judges.

The high points were: a three-foot-tall papier-mâché volcano complete with plastic palm trees and native huts—presumably prepped to erupt, it was somehow connected to a discussion on global warming; a multilevel, clear plastic maze stocked with glow-in-the-dark mice; chemical extractions of local plants to make fabric dyes; and a science of refrigeration demonstration—which Erin thought bordered on cheating, since the student involved was the daughter of a local heating and air-conditioning contractor.

"*This* is strong competition?" she said.

"Why don't you save time and strain, Gilbert," Carl Lund said from the next table in line. "Push that junk straight to the Dumpster out back."

Abby fake-laughed, but they both stared at his project as they rolled past.

He and his cohorts had constructed a pair of remote-controlled, robotic fighting machines. The combatants faced off on the tabletop. "Blade Face" featured parts scavenged from a five-and-a-half-inch power saw and had an extendable single claw hand, like the Terminator. The legend on the project poster said Blade Face seized hold of its opponent, pulled it close, and then gave it "the kiss of death." Its opponent was "Señor Pain," whose weaponry consisted of a hatchet wielded by a single arm swinging through 180 degrees of arc. According to the poster it could cock back and deliver twenty-five to thirty crushing blows per minute.

"Shit," Erin said under her breath.

"Come on," Abby told her. "Our spot's near the end of the row."

Erin began helping her unload the cart onto the empty table. She didn't want to say it, but she was sure they were going to lose. Their exhibit consisted of a series of posters and drawings with titles like "Spectral Foam," "Positive and Negative Ethereal Polarization," "Proton Countermeasures," and "Gauge Theory for Dummies."

Written across the top of the biggest poster: "A significant coupling may well exist between spectral and Standard Model particles—a total of twelve gauge bosons: the photon, three weak bosons, and eight gluons." The rest of the surface was covered with line after line of equations describing Lagrangian mechanics.

Reading the expression on Erin's face, Abby said, "It'll

be okay. Don't worry, we've got our secret weapon." She took a boom box from the bottom of the shopping cart. "Spooky ghost sounds!"

Abby was so excited she was practically jumping up and down. Erin couldn't help but crack a smile. The cassette tape in the machine was a copy they'd made of sounds supposedly recorded at the sites of documented ghost appearances. Kind of like *The Blair Witch Project,* a film they had memorized, only without the video.

By 10 A.M., the gym had filled with parents and students, who milled up and down the center aisle. Fifteen minutes later the volunteer judges made their entrance. Mr. Puccini handed them clipboards and pens. Shouting over the din to get the everyone's attention, he introduced them to the assembly. Two were adjunct professors from Kellogg City College's Science Department, and the third judge was the science writer for the *Battle Creek Enquirer.*

Erin and Abby had to man their booth, so they couldn't see exactly what was going on at the other end of the aisle. The judges stood in front of contestants' tables listening to their explanations and asking questions.

The three were standing about a yard back from the volcano when it erupted with a roar. Then the back of the cone blew off with a dull pop, sending cold oatmeal "lava" shooting across the court and into the bleachers.

Screams rang out and the audience retreated en masse to the fire exits.

Mr. Puccini rushed forward, waving his arms for calm. "Do not be concerned. There's nothing hazardous," he shouted. "The lava is organic. Our janitorial staff is on hand to clean up the mess . . ."

On his signal, the custodian crew sprang into action with mops and buckets. The excitement was over. People resumed browsing; the judges resumed their task.

When they got to Carl's project, the übernerd gestured for them to step around his table. Waving for people to move back, he and his project partner cleared a wide space between the aisle and the bleachers. Then they unrolled a heavy circular mat, presumably to protect the hardwood from saw and hatchet misfires.

As the audience began to crowd in around the makeshift ring, Carl and his nerd buddy donned crash helmets.

"You know we can't miss this," Abby said. And they abandoned their posters for a spot at ringside.

Carl picked up Blade Face and his partner grabbed Señor Pain. They put the machines facing each other on the mats about four feet apart. Carl and his nerd bud held game controllers in their hands.

"Imagine a not-too-distant future," Carl bellowed at the audience, "where robots fight the wars and we are their slaves!" On his count of three the machines charged each other and music blasted out of a speaker under the table—a rousing hip-hop beat.

"*This is not America . . .*" the chorus repeated over and over.

"That's from the movie *Training Day*," Abby said while the crowd cheered and whooped. " 'American Dream,' sung by David Bowie and P. Diddy."

Erin decided she couldn't root for either machine; she wanted them to mutually self-destruct. Or better yet, go berserk and chase Carl out of the gym.

Much to the amusement of the audience, which was moving to the music, Señor Pain drew first "blood." Apparently it had more mass, because their initial collision turned Blade Face sideways. Before Carl could recover, Señor Pain did a hatchet job on its foredeck, landing a rain of blows.

To Erin, it looked like game over. Señor Pain was going to batter its opponent into smithereens without even getting a scratch. She had to admit that watching Carl Lund so quickly and easily defeated by one of his minions came a close second to seeing Señor Pain chop off the odd toe.

Then in a perfectly timed move, Carl/Blade Face used its hand to snatch hold of the hatchet's handle just below the ax head as it swung down, pinning the sharp edge into the mat. The audience gasped as Blade Face used the power of its arm to drag its torso into attack position. The saw blade whined shrilly and sparks flew as Blade Face planted the vaunted kiss of death, then quite efficiently cut poor Señor Pain in two.

The judges and audience applauded and cheered, dancing and laughing as the music reached its crescendo and faded out.

One of the professors clapped Carl on the back as he removed his crash helmet. "You have a great future in robotics, my boy," he said.

Carl looked over at Erin and Abby and shot them a smug, nasty grin. Then he mimed a hanging, yanking up on an invisible noose around his neck, sticking out his tongue like he was choking to death.

Erin pulled her partner aside. "Abby, we're going to get totally creamed unless we do something quick."

Abby nodded, her expression chagrined. "My bad. I thought we dumbed it down enough."

"The judges are five tables away. Think of something!"

"Clearly we can't change any basic elements at this point," she said. "But we can sure spice up the presentation. Give it some punch. Carl and his crew have music, but so do we."

Abby popped the cassette out of the boom box and slipped in a different one.

"It's our planet dance!" Erin cried.

It was a hip-hop mix tape they had danced to in Abby's bedroom a million times, whirling around like planets and then bustin' their moves. They hadn't done it in forever.

"Remember how jiggy we got?" Abby said. "We were so awesome in the mirror. We know all the cool steps and have our explanation down pat—we can rap it to the judges!"

"But let's dumb it way down," Erin said. "Way, way down. Wait, I thought of something else . . ." She turned over one of the posters and wrote on the back in huge letters with Magic Marker: "There is a barrier keeping ghosts out, and if they are let in they will destroy the world."

"Oh my god," Abby exclaimed, "that's perfect!"

As soon as the judges were in position in front of their table, Abby cued the music and they let it rip. At first Erin couldn't focus on the audience's faces because her dancing was so jerky and violent, and she was concentrating so hard on her footwork. She really got into it. So did Abby. And they hit their marks on the rapping, too.

When Abby dropped down low for her break-dance solo, Erin took in all the people frozen around them, mouths hanging open. *Yeah,* she thought, *you can't top this!*

They finished their routine and the music faded out. There was dead silence in the gym. The looks on the judges' faces ranged from perplexed to horrified.

From the rear of the crowd, a familiar voice sneeze-yelled, "Bull-shit!"

"Do you have any questions for us?" Abby said, panting for breath.

More silence.

Finally one of the professors broke the impasse. "No," he said, "I think we have all we need from you."

The panel of judges retired to the boys' locker room to confer. It didn't take them long to make their decision. The robot fighters won unanimously and would move on to the county finals.

Carl Lund pumped his fists over his head and did a mad toe dance-in-place, shouting, "Yes! Yes!"

"Damn!" Erin said over the din of applause.

"Don't sweat the small stuff," Abby said. "Look at all we've accomplished in just a year. And we're both moving on to the University of Michigan—a bigger stage with better equipment."

"And maybe a more intelligent audience."

Mr. Puccini and another male teacher had hoisted Carl

Lund onto their shoulders and were marching him around the gym, through the cheering crowd.

"Mos' def," Abby said.

At their headquarters, Erin smiled wistfully as she studied the science fair photograph. "Oh, I wish we still had the presentation. It was fantastic."

Abby raised a Spock-like eyebrow as she smirked knowingly. "Patty's wish might just be granted."

Patty shook her head. "No, that wasn't my wish—"

"You still have it?" Erin cried. "What?"

Abby reached behind the buffet table and pulled out the title board of their project. She set the poster on a table and plopped an old cassette tape recorder down beside it. The poster was decorated with pictures of ghosts cut from books and magazines and pasted in place. But Abby wasn't finished. She took a box out from under the table. She opened it and whipped out two more blasts from the past—their black turtleneck sweaters—and they hurriedly put them on. Abby's looked a little tight, but Erin's fit fine.

"Okay, per Patty's request," Abby said, reaching over to push play.

Patty waved her hands. "No, I can't express enough that I don't—"

Abby and Erin stood side by side in their matching pullovers, very serious as they gazed into each other's eyes and silently counted down.

"Good evening," they said, hitting their mark in unison.

"Oh lord," Patty groaned, but she was clearly amused.

Holtzmann smiled, then opened two beers and handed one to Patty. "I've only heard about this," she said. "Never actually seen it. This is history." Holtzmann winked at Patty and then downed her beer.

"Prepare for takeoff into the unknown," Abby and Erin chanted. "Five . . . four . . . three . . . two . . . one."

Abby hit play on the recorder. What they had thought

back then was the coolest science fiction music ever ooh-wee-eww'ed from the little speaker. Erin still remembered their moves, and they began waving their arms dramatically, orbiting like planets, with Abby spinning around her.

"The universe is mysterious," Erin said in a mysterious voice.

"Ninety-six percent mysterious," Abby shot back.

"And what of the topic of ghosts?" Erin demanded.

Abby whispered loudly, "They're real!"

The music boomed across the dining room. Erin and Abby broke into more dancing, happy exuberant you're-my-bestie dancing, and memories of dancing at the fair washed over her. Abby had been a true friend, defending "Ghost Girl" from her tormentors, telling her over and over, "You are not crazy. I believe you."

Erin poured her heart into the re-creation of their spur-of-the moment skit. "Then why don't I see ghosts flying everywhere?"

"For the barrier stops them," Abby declared. "It is the only line of defense in the portal betwixt the worlds of the living and the dead."

Patty shifted a bit uncomfortably. "What century did they write this?"

Holtzmann nodded, ignoring her question, totally into the performance.

Abby said, "Now let's break it down."

The music abruptly shifted to a corny old-school hip-hop beat.

"Yo. How many different types of ghosts we got, A?"

Erin picked up the rap beat. "Humanoids, vapors—"

Abby glanced over and saw Patty's grimace. "You know what, let's skip ahead."

Erin didn't want to admit that she was a little winded. "Yeah, that part is thirty minutes and involves break dancing."

She popped open the tape player and flipped the tape. The booming sci-fi score returned and they both leapt into a rapid crescendo of ecstatic dance and arm move-ment. Erin couldn't believe that she remembered every step, but she did. The routine was elaborate, and holy cow, they were pulling it off. It was as if all the years between the science fair and the present moment had themselves become ghosts. She flew and spun, freer than she had felt in forever.

"So protect the barrier! Protect the barrier! Or mankind will end! Word!"

When it was over, Erin and Abby struck rapper poses. They laughed and hugged, and Erin was overjoyed. They had promised to be each other's lifelong friends. Could they still be?

Holtzmann ran up and threw her arms around both of them.

"I am so goddam happy you two are together again. So goddam happy."

Erin and Abby turned to look at Patty, and her face was radiant. "I was all set to make fun of you. But goddamn, that was actually beautiful." Then she choked up. "Thank god you had each other."

"Hey, look," Holtzmann said, pointing at the muted TV. It was the NY-Local 1 News, and a reporter was onscreen. She hurried over and turned up the volume.

". . . a local team of paranormal investigators released a video of a proclaimed ghost—"

The picture shifted from the reporter to a segment from their video, displayed for the whole world to see. Erin was clearly visible on the screen.

"Hey, they're airing the video!" Patty cried. "We're fa-mous!"

"So," the reported continued, "what do we think of these 'Ghostbusters'?"

Erin grimaced. "Ghostbusters? Why did she just say 'Ghostbusters'? They can't just make up a name for us, can they?"

Abby shook her head. "No, she just misspoke."

But down at the bottom of the screen, crawling text read, "Discussing the Ghostbusters."

"Oh," Abby said, startled.

The reporter continued. "I spoke with Martin Heiss earlier of the Council for Logic and Data, and famed debunker of the paranormal."

"Oh god." Erin had a bad feeling. She braced herself.

"Tell me. Is this for real?" the reporter asked.

Erin had read about Martin Heiss before, but she had never seen him. He was wearing a large hat, very dashing.

"No," he answered flatly.

"Thank you," the reporter said to him, and then turned back to the camera. "Coming up, Mayor Bradley on the rolling blackouts."

Erin glared at the screen. She took a threatening step toward the TV while the others lost their cool behind her.

"Unbelievable," Abby huffed. "Do you know that we only know what four percent of the universe is? How quick they are to say no!"

"Oh man," Patty said, groaning. "Now *we're* the ghost girls. I suddenly feel your pain, Erin."

"No way. Screw that," Erin said defiantly. The phone started ringing in the background. "We are scientists and we rely on controlled tests and provable physical results. And so we are going to catch a ghost and bring it back to this lab and, *Kevin, answer the phone!*"

Kevin, who had stopped watching them and returned to studying what appeared to be two photographs, put down the pictures and answered the phone. They all looked on.

"Conductor something. Uh-huh." He sounded interested in whatever he was hearing. Everyone else leaned in. "Cool," he said. "Thanks. Bye."

He hung up. Then he picked up the photographs. They were headshots of him, and he was shirtless in both.

"Hey, which of these makes me look more like a

doctor?" he asked. He showed them the one with the stethoscope.

"Whichever one tells us who was on the damn phone!" Erin yelled.

"Someone from the Stonebrook Theatre. I don't know . . . something's happening there."

Something? Erin thought. The only person they'd given the landline number to was their rental agent. It had appeared on Abby's flyers as well. Ergo, unless their rental agent was into acting, this was a call from someone who wanted to talk to the Conductors of the Metaphysical Examination!

"Yes!" Erin shrieked.

"I'll get the car," Holtzmann announced.

They whipped into action, Abby pausing just long enough to point to a whiteboard next to Kevin's desk.

"All right, when I get back we're gonna start off with parallel universes and entanglement," she told him.

He blinked. "What?"

"He's curious already!" Abby rejoiced.

Abby, Erin, and Patty dashed outside. Patty was carrying an armload of MTA uniforms along with her proton pack.

"I took these from work and made 'em look all official. Put 'em on if you don't want to get slimed again," she said.

Erin was grateful for the extra barrier of protection. She said, "We'll put them on in the car."

And they were off.

16

Abby, Erin, and Patty raced outside while Holtz blasted their hearse—now fully loaded with proton canisters and other power boosters, a new license plate that read ECTO-I, and a cute little ghost hood ornament—down the streets of Manhattan, the siren wailing like a banshee— a tentative Class 4 soprano full screecher—as pedestrians stopped and stared after them. It was like they were shooting out a paralyzing ray on all sides. Weaving in and out of the traffic, the massive vehicle slewed right and left. Holtzmann drove right up on the back bumpers of the cars ahead, flashing high beams until they yielded, swerving out of the way, more often than not with raised fists and middle fingers stuck out driver windows.

Erin would have felt a wee less vulnerable if Holtzmann had deigned to put both hands on the wheel and stifled the running commentary on the scenery blurring past. Patty nodded her head as if she was listening to the monologue with rapt attention, but rode with one hand firmly gripping the door handle, as if poised to make a quick escape should Holtzmann ever slow down. Or maybe her apprehension was such that she just had to hang on to something.

Abby didn't seem to notice Holtz's erratic driving. She was leaning forward in her seat, eyes wide with excitement, confirming the address and pertinent information with Kevin. Abridged version: it sounded like the Stonebrook Theatre was haunted!

Erin figured they might be facing slime, so she passed
out the uniforms to Patty and Abby, and with difficulty
they pulled them on in the moving vehicle. Holtzmann
braked the big wagon to a stop alongside a trash truck and
illegally double-parked so she could slip into hers. The re-
fuse workers on the truck got a big kick out of that show,
and as the hearse pulled away urged them on with fist
pumps and shouts of, "Go get 'em, MTA!"

When they screeched to the curb in front of the theater,
a few sleepy-looking thrash band fans were straggling
through the doors. Erin could feel the *thud, thuh-thud,
thud, thuh-thud* of a death metal bass line through the side
of the hearse. It faintly rattled the windows. She and the
other Conductors of the Metaphysical Examination piled
out of their sick white ride, proton packs strapped on their
backs and ready to rumble.

As they stepped out into the street, a couple of dudes in
comic book T-shirts walked under the marquee. They
stopped and stared at the fearsome foursome.

"Are you guys the Ghostbusters?" one of them asked,
cutting his eyes to shoot a smirk at his pal.

Oh, that name. That terrible name, Erin thought. "We're
actually the Conductors of the Meta—"

"Yes, we're the Ghostbusters," Abby broke in.

Erin winced but let it pass.

The other nerd grinned. Chuckling at his own sparkling
wit, he said, "Lame. Girls can't catch ghosts. Go use those
vacuums on your back to clean a house."

His Neanderthal prejudice didn't shock or surprise
Erin—that was the reason for STEM. She wondered—just
for a second—how the meeting about the glow-in-the-dark
eye makeup had gone. If there had been a hostile takeover.

The graphic novel bon vivants sauntered away, nudging
each other and cracking up over the stupid comment. Patty
looked intently up and down the street, which was momentarily deserted, and then unclipped her proton wand. Be-

fore Erin could get a word out, the team's newest member gave her wand a quick tap, firing a short blast of pure energy into the joker's backside. He went down as if mule-kicked and the seat of his pants burst into flames. Yelping, flapping his arms, he scooted down the sidewalk on his butt, trying to put it out. He looked and sounded remarkably like a dog with a bad case of worms. Erin tried hard to be shocked at Patty's show of overwhelming force—but she just couldn't quite manage it. And it was just an itsy-bitsy fire.

"Man down! Man down!" Patty shouted in the direction of the theater entrance.

A group of death metal fans ran out of the lobby and came to the wormy dog's aid, kicking him over onto his stomach and then meticulously stomping out the fire on his butt. Erin and the Ghostbusters strutted past them and entered the theater.

The lobby was packed with T-shirt booths and concession stands, and all varieties and subclasses of metal head milled around on the worn carpet. The music fans stopped milling and looked on in awe as Erin, Abby, Holtzmann, and Patty pushed into their midst. Erin got the distinct impression that their snappy uniforms and unconventional weaponry were a big hit. Through the padded theater doors, the music was blaring at an impressive decibel level—roughly that of a 747 revving for takeoff. Erin could feel the vibration inside her chest. From across the room a nervous-looking guy waved wildly to get their attention, and then rushed through the crowd to greet them.

In the process of introducing himself, Jonathan, the theater manager, violated their personal space big time so he could keep his voice down, which was kind of funny, considering all the racket blasting through the closed doors to the auditorium. "Are you the Ghostbusters?" he asked, desperation in his eyes.

"Yes, we are," Abby affirmed.

Erin gave a rueful farewell to the personalized Conductors of the Metaphysical Examination business cards, coffee cups, door sign, and promotional pens she had ordered.

Jonathan's forehead wrinkled. He seemed under a great strain. "But I was told a 'Doctor' Yates was coming."

Not you, too, Erin thought, and she was in solidarity with her sisters as they turned on their heels and began to walk away.

Jonathan raced after them, protesting, "Whoa, wait! It's not because you're women. It's because you're dressed like garbage men."

That would be sanitation engineers, Erin thought huffily, but the overdue lesson in gender-free language would have to wait. All their attention turned to a pair of paramedics wheeling a man on a gurney through the lobby. Firmly strapped down across the chest and knees, he was mumbling to himself in Spanish, and he had a Puerto Rican accent. Erin was fairly fluent and she translated what he was saying to the others: " '*I have looked into the eyes of the Devil . . . I have looked into the eyes of the Devil . . .*' "

Wow. She watched him roll past, and then looked over at Jonathan expectantly. The other Ghostbusters were looking at him, too.

"Follow me," he said. "*Please.*"

He led them through a narrow doorway and down a flight of stairs, which opened onto a maze of dimly lit hallways under the theater. "Fernando was down here when something came out of the wall vent and attacked him. I heard his screams, and when I came to see, some 'thing' was throwing him all over the place."

Abby turned to Erin. "A T-5 interaction?"

So very yes. "Great. This is great," she concurred.

"Not for Fernando," Jonathan said grimly. "I thought it was going to kill him. I shrieked when I saw it, and I guess I scared it because it flew off down the hall." With a smidgen of pride, he added, "I'm told my scream is quite disturbing."

He stopped as they reached the hall of what looked to be the oldest wing of the theater. He stared down the corridor, suddenly hesitant to proceed, perhaps as he relived his recent experience.

"Whatever is down there, I pray to god I never come across it again. It will haunt me every night when I go to sleep. No one should ever have to encounter that kind of evil."

Gulp, Erin thought.

"Anyway," he said, far more casually, "keep walking that way and you'll find it."

"Oh, *good,*" Patty drawled.

"We'll get it. Don't worry," Erin told her. *We are on a mission.*

Abby nodded in agreement, then said, "One thing we might need from you, Jonathan, is some—" She glanced around behind him. "Oh, he's already taken off? Okay."

Individually and collectively, the newly minted Ghostbusters took stock of what lay ahead. The halls under the old part of the theater split in three directions. Make that three gloomy, dark directions. They were much narrower and had lower ceilings than the subway tunnel, which meant less room to maneuver and less room for error. It looked a lot more dangerous. Were they up to it?

This is what we do, Erin assured herself. *I am a spectral warrior. Patty is a metaphysical commando. Holtz is a proton wrangler. And Abby—*

"All right, it could be anywhere," Abby said. "Let's split up. Walkie if you see anything."

Erin headed out. The proton pack hummed softly against her back—she couldn't hear it because of the noise coming from directly above, but she could feel it, and the power at her command boosted her confidence. She walked past a room filled with costumes and heads topped with wigs. Her peripheral vision caught something that wasn't

right. The glaring wrongness of it startled her. As she
whirled to face whatever it was, she pulled out her proton
wand.

It was Holtzmann, standing statue-still and wearing a
purple eighties glam wig she had picked up.

"Holtzmann, this is serious!" Erin complained.

"And I agree," Holtz said convivially.

Patty was on edge, no doubt. As she cautiously advanced
down a dark backstage hall, accent on spine-tingling
with funky aromas, she kept shifting the nozzle of her proton pack, aiming at doorways right and left, sidling up to
corners, then sweeping around them, low and fast, the way
those adorable, stick-thin policewomen on TV did when
they were investigating the bad guys in deserted ware-
houses or abandoned tenements. Only the proton pack
weighed a ton more than a lipstick and compact, and any
gangbangers she ran into down here were going to be
unkillable—because they were already dead. But they
were not unstoppable, if everything worked the way it was
supposed to. A big "if," from what she'd seen so far, but
the pack was humming with power. Nuclear power, she
suddenly recalled. At least there were no subway trains
careening around corners around here, and she supposed
there was something to be said about standing in the middle
of ground zero.

"I thought this was going to be like a book club," she
muttered to herself. "You know, have a glass of wine, talk
about ghosts, that sort of thing."

She stuck her head into a room filled with blank-eyed,
bald, naked mannequins. Her heart stuttered.

"Oh good. A room full of nightmares."

Dolls and mannequins were two of the things that had
always given her the creepy-crawlies, especially after she
and her cousin Marcie had stayed up all night one night,

taking turns staring at Marcie's dolls and convincing themselves that every time they looked away, the darn things moved. On top of that, Marcie owned a ventriloquist dummy, and no one in the world thought that puppets weren't disturbing. Untrustworthy, that was the word she was searching for.

Pulling the door to mannequin city closed, she kept walking, her proton wand primed and ready for action.

Behind the door, in the middle of the jumble of frozen figures, a mannequin head turned slowly on its molded plastic shoulders, following the direction the intruder had taken with painted-on eyes. Rage boiled inside its hollow skull. This was an adversary, *it decided*. This was something that must be destroyed.

And it would be . . .

Abby walked down a cramped hallway, on guard for real, but hey, this was the adventure of a lifetime—of *ten* lifetimes. It promised payback for all those years toiling in the Higgins Institute's basement, enduring the jibes of her colleagues, peers, and students, and way before that, the nonstop bullying of the kids on the playground. Every drop of *I'll show them* coursed through her bloodstream. She was good to go. She gave her wand a little test goose, and a bolt of energy sizzled down the passage ahead of her.

Lock and load, hell yeah.

Beneath the bottom edge of a door in front of her a light flickered erratically. Taking a firm grip on the wand, she opened the door a crack and peered in—*oh double hell yeah*—

A strange, bulbous device sat in the middle of the otherwise empty wardrobe room. It was sparking and humming, and an eerie green waveform emanated from it in all directions. She got a whiff of ionization so strong it made her choke.

Clearing her throat, Abby clicked on her walkie-talkie and spoke into it.

"Guys, I found another device."

On legs that wobbled at the hips and threatened to buckle, the mannequin lurched for the closed door. It couldn't move its fingers because they weren't articulated, so it trapped the knob between immovable hands and leaned, turning the knob just far enough to open the latch. Using the brittle form of the life-size doll as both shell and camouflage, the ghost stepped into the hallway, and turned stiff-legged to follow the tall intruder.

Patty caught Abby's walkie alert and stopped in the middle of the hall. The blast from the subway device was still fresh in her mind. "I had a good job," she recalled wistfully. "Not a great job, but it was a job."

She heard a noise behind her—a squeaky sound like rubbing a thumb across the skin of an inflated balloon. The hair rose on the back of her neck and her arms as she looked over her shoulder.

A mannequin was standing in the hall. It stood rooted, stock-still, while Patty studied it, her heart thumping fast.

"That wasn't there," she said. She knew she had just walked over that same ground—so how does a mannequin get from point A to point B? She took a step toward it. A Holtz joke, maybe? That girl was such a kidder . . .

Keeping her distance, Patty more closely examined the placid doll face. It wasn't a high-end dummy. She stared hard into the blank eyes, searching them for an explanation. The thing about mannequins was, you never knew what they were thinking.

Then, with a loud balloon squeak it broke free of the floor and power-rushed her. It was coming right for her—

"Oh, hell no!" Patty cried as she turned and ran for her life.

Erin and Holtzmann met up with Abby at the wardrobe room where she had found the device. When they looked in it it was still sparking away. Erin was taken aback by the visible wave energy flowing from it. It looked like a sickly green searchlight cutting through a fogbank—it appeared to have *texture*. The ionization was off the charts massive, which meant the little package had a matching power source. Erin had to wonder about the mind that had created it. Who was he or she? What was their training? How had they come up with the design? From the way it was freely arcing, finish work was not the builder's forte. The much more disturbing question was why would anyone smart enough to build it want to use it to lower the barrier and let in demon ghosts?

"It's definitely the same device we found in the subway," Abby said.

"This is some sort of hyperionization device," Erin said. "Somebody's really trying to energize—"

Patty burst into the room and slammed the door behind her. Before anyone could speak, she threw her back against the door, digging the heels of her shoes into the floor. Panting for breath, she looked half crazed with fear.

"I think I lost it," she gasped. "Please don't tell me that thing is unrelated to the ghost that we're looking for. I can't handle two things."

Patty wasn't making sense. "What thing?" Erin asked her.

The answer arrived special delivery. Patty screamed as a bare leg kicked through the middle of the door, splintering the wood beside her. Erin gawked as the limb hung there, half in, half out of the storeroom. There was a bare foot and ankle; it was shaped like a human leg, but there the resemblance ended. The splintered edges of the hole had gouged furrows in the surface from ankle to shin, and the leg shed curls of white plastic instead of sprays of bright blood. Patty looked at it and screamed again, spinning away from the door.

The leg withdrew and a second later its owner smashed through the weakened door, showering the retreating Ghostbusters with woody debris.

There was only so far to retreat in the little room. Erin backed away with the others until she hit the sewing table on the rear wall. The mannequin stood before them, growling. At a signal from Abby, they all fired up their proton packs. The combined noise in the closed room made it hard to think.

"I'm sorry," Holtzmann said to the dummy. "Is this your dressing room?"

Abby was stunned *and* delighted by the thing. "Full paratransferral embodiment. Erin, all our theories on spectral possession are true!" She gave Holtzmann a sidelong look. "Someone owes me a dozen Krispy Kremes."

Holtzmann was equally jubilant. "Ecto glazed or plasm filled?"

Unable to restrain themselves, the two gamblers broke into their elaborate high-five routine.

Patty and Erin didn't take their eyes off the mannequin, and their wands were locked on it in case it made any funny moves.

"That's great," Patty said to no one and everyone. "Can we shoot it?"

"There's a ghost inside that thing and I want it," Erin shouted. "Let's light him up!"

The Ghostbusters powered up their proton wands and did the firing squad thing—blasting in unison. The sizzling energy beams hit the polystyrene mannequin, plowing right through it and the doorframe. It lit up with the same eerie light as Gertrude Aldridge and the ghost in the subway, then exploded with a sharp crack. A winged monster-ghost burst from it. It looked like the demons in medieval literature, almost dragonlike, not humanoid in the least. It flew down toward them, menacing them, then flew out of the room.

"We can't lose it! C'mon!" Erin cried.

"Wow, liking the fire," Abby said. "You heard her. Move it!"

The hideous ghost flew down the cramped hall with Erin and the other Ghostbusters in hot pursuit. Patty huffed and puffed.

"If we live through this," she said, bent over and wheezing for air, "can you make these packs lighter, Holtz? My kidneys are taking one hell of a beating."

Erin jumped the stairs three at a time as Abby and Holtz struggled to keep up. She could hear their groans and the thud of their boot falls behind her. What had Abby said about liking the fire? Oh yeah, she felt the heat, all right. She was burning up the house. She was going to run this bad boy to ground and box it with a ribbon on top.

I am a Ghostbuster. She thought it loud and proud.

B*OOOOOOOOO!*
    Difficult to believe, but the irate shouts of the metalhead audience were actually drowning out the ear-blistering combined output of six Peavey 6505+ amps and a dozen double-stacked speakers. Front man and lead guitarist Adam was blazing through the crescendo in the band's first tune of the set, totally thrashing in the zone. The floor of the stage, the whole building was throbbing to the insistent, thunderous beat, threatening to split apart at the seams, but the crowd in the auditorium was having none of it. They were booing them as loudly as they could. It was his worst nightmare. But the show had to go on. He ended the tune with a leap in the air and a vicious downward slash of his midnight-black Jackson King V.

From hard experience he knew that to let the crowd see how rattled he was would only incite them to worse. Adam ignored the taunts and shouted into the microphone, "Thank you! We are the Beasts of Mayhem! And now let me ask you a question. Are you ready to *rock this—*"

The microphone squealed feedback into all their speakers. Equipment they had yet to pay for. All Adam's credit cards were charged to the max and he had been forced to move back to the basement in his parents' house.

"Oh, sorry about that, my bad," he said.

From the crowd, a dude in a sour orange Mohawk yelled, "You *suck!*"

A fresh chorus of boos erupted as Adam started counting down the beat to the next song. He was covered in flop sweat. This was going so wrong.

A glowing figure rose right up out of the floor behind him and levitated into the air fifteen feet above the stage. It looked like a hologram, only it had a lot more moves and there didn't seem to be a start-over point in the digital loop. The crowd stopped booing and throwing things, and stared up at it slack-jawed. He looked up to the balcony, gave a thumbs-up to the light-board operator, and exaggeratedly mouthed the word "Ex-cell-ent." The board op looked back at him, confused.

"It's not mine," he mouthed back.

Meanwhile, Eugene, the passive-aggressive bass player, leaned in close to the drummer and shouted something in his ear. Adam heard it faintly in his headset:

"Damn, he really did spend some money. That's awesome."

Metal music slammed into Erin as she reached the stage. It made her bones vibrate, and she had to pause for a second to regain her balance and mental focus. Wincing, she waved the Ghostbusters on. She weaved through the maze of pulleys and cables and towering curtains toward the light and found the wings of the stage. Clustered together, the Ghostbusters peered out around the edge of the main curtain as a tremendous roar went up from the audience. The band, framed in blazing spotlights, was blasting out mind-numbing, three-chord black metal, but the loud cheer had nothing to do with them. It was the demonic phantom. As Erin watched spellbound, it flew away from the stage and out over the bobbing heads of the audience. It slowly circled, eyeing the crowd like a box of chocolates as if trying to select just the right one.

"Whoever made that device knows their high energy-density physics. That thing is *super*ionized," Erin said to Abby.

Abby nodded. "And it is not benign."

"It looks like it's looking for dinner," Patty said. She had recovered her wind, but still seemed rattled by the exploding mannequin experience.

The song ended with a raucous crash and wild applause. The lead guitarist strutted up to the front of the stage and pointed at the ghost with his guitar. He seemed completely unafraid of it, which baffled Erin, until she realized that he, like the crowd of metalheads, assumed it was a just an elaborate special effect. She wanted to warn him, but it was already too late for that.

"Behold the power of the undead!" Adam bellowed, his voice raspy hoarse and full of heavy-metal melodrama. "We have summoned Satan himself!"

The ghost turned in midair and looked down at the singer.

The singer threw back his head, puffed out his chest, and spread his arms wide, basking in the glory of the musical history moment. "For we are the kings of darkn—*Oh shit!*"

Like a glowing green fighter plane, the ghost dive-bombed straight for him. The singer froze, mouth agape, arms still spread, and the ghost crashed into him, hurtling the singer and his flying V guitar backward. He cartwheeled over the drummer and the drummer's double bass drum kit, and smashed into a double stack of speakers.

The crowd went berserk, clapping and hooting.

"Ow, ow, ow!" Adam screamed, hitting a new personal best high note, clutching at his backside and writhing in pain. "I think I broke my tailbone!"

The audience thought it was all part of the act and cheered the spectacular pratfall. His band mates, not sure what had just happened, not knowing what else to do— and wanting to keep the precious applause coming—kept pounding out a wall of seething noise.

Some of the audience members were filming the hovering ghost with their selfie sticks. The creature then resumed its predatory circling over the crowd. There was no telling what it would do next, or to whom. They had to stop it. Now.

Erin rallied the troops. "Let's do this. Everybody ready?"

"Hell yeah," Abby and Holtzmann said together.

"Um . . ." Patty began.

They all looked at her.

". . . sure."

They ran out on stage in front of the still-rocking band and aimed their proton wands at the airborne ghost. More or less at the same instant they all fired their beams. They lit up the theater, but the ghost dodged the incoming protons. A near miss, and their beams kept on keeping on, slamming into the elaborately sculpted ceiling and its curlicue embellishments. Plaster exploded from the rococo assembled mermaids, cherubs, and stylized ferns. Paint-gilded bits rained down on the audience, who cheered ecstatically.

The ghost did a barrel roll, reversed course, and dived right at the Ghostbusters. Erin didn't move, Abby and Holtzmann stood their ground; Patty looked really pissed off. They fired again as it flew by, but again it evaded the blasts and their beams hit the side of the theater, taking out a pair of bow-front balconies, blowing out more plasterwork, and drawing black lines of scorch across the walls.

That drove the metal fans even crazier. As they cheered, they pumped their fists in the air and gave the Ghostbusters the sign of the horns salute.

Jonathan appeared from the wings behind Erin. His jaw dropped. He said, "This is Art Deco, people!"

"It's gonna take a lot of firepower to pull that thing down," Holtzmann said.

"Circumvallate!" Erin ordered. "We need to surround it!"

"Patty," Abby said, "let's each take an aisle. Holtz, set the trap and let's reel that thing in."

Erin and Holtzmann got into firing positions next to each other on the front edge of the stage. Abby and Patty ran down the short flights of stairs at opposite corners of the proscenium—but the aisles and the orchestra pit were absolutely packed with pogoing fans celebrating the walkaway winner of the battle of the bands—the Beasts of Mayhem. Try as they might, Patty and Abby couldn't find a place to wade in.

Waving her proton wand like a nightstick, Patty shouted at the gyrating mass of shoulder-to-shoulder people, "Get out of the way! We need to get down to those aisles!"

Erin looked up at the ghost. Its expression was hardening into what she had come to think of as "Gertie-face." Hideous fangs, murder in its eyes. As she watched, its body language turned darker and even more menacing, and Erin knew it was getting ready to attack the crowd and do some real damage. Abby must have seen it, too.

"Guess what, people," she yelled at the grinning metalheads. "You are now part of this operation. Patty, let's hit it!"

Throwing her arms out in front of her and caution to the wind, Abby dove into the audience. The nearest fans caught her and lifted her up over their heads. Immediately she was bodysurfing her way across the top of them.

"Left!" Abby shouted. "Move me to the left! Now back. Keep going! Excellent!"

Patty watched Abby swim over the crowd and into position. She sucked in a deep breath and seemed to steel herself as she looked at the wall-to-wall fans in front of her.

"All right, you freaks," she bellowed. "Time to catch a ghost. Let's do this!"

With that, Patty duplicated Abby's move, and with arms outstretched, dove into the audience. But instead of catching her, everyone moved out of the way and she hit the floor. Hard.

Erin's eyes grew huge. There was a very good reason why—

"I don't know if that was a race thing or a woman thing, but I am *pissed*," Patty shouted. But nobody moved; they just stared at her in disbelief and horror.

Patty got up and glared at them.

Erin opened her mouth to explain why everyone was gaping at her. Patty was in the middle of dusting herself off, hand brushing the chest of her uniform, when she froze. Erin immediately knew she had spotted two otherworldly claws resting on her shoulders.

The ghost was crouching on top of Patty.

"Okay, just stay still," Abby told her.

Erin swallowed. "Patty, I, uh—"

"No need to say anything," Patty told them.

Erin tried to interject. "You—"

"No, I don't want to hear what you're about to say," she said.

Holtzmann tried next. "But—"

"I'm pretty tired. I'm actually just gonna take off. Go back to work at the MTA—"

Erin shook her head. "I really don't think that's a good—"

"Nope. I'm out," Patty said.

As she turned and started to walk up the aisle, the crowd parted for her and stared. A fan raised her cell phone for a quick selfie with her, the demonic-looking ghost, and its ride. Patty forced a smile for the camera.

"Patty, stay still!" Erin pleaded.

Abby moved into position with her proton wand. "All right, ladies. Let's light it up. Fire! Just don't hit Patty."

"*What?*" Patty cried.

As they fired, the ghost leapt off Patty's shoulders and into the air. Patty grabbed her proton wand and joined in. The beams missed the ghost. The specter dodged and wobbled high overhead, but there were four beams coming at it from different angles and it couldn't escape them all. Erin locked on to it first; that slowed it down enough for Abby and Holtzmann to join in. Then Patty had hold of it, too. The ghost went wild as it struggled to escape, and its strength was incredible.

Erin thanked her lucky stars it hadn't attacked Patty when it had the chance. They could barely hold on to it. And they had to fight to keep their footing and their leverage; as it thrashed from one side to another, it was almost lifting their heels off the ground. Erin's ears were still ringing so badly she hadn't noticed the band had stopped playing. It surprised her to see the bass player and drummer standing right next to her. They looked on in amazement, finally having realized that this wasn't a put-on. This was real.

Ghosts were real.

As they continued to grapple, beams rippling, bending, Holtzmann said, "Oh, I forgot to mention. Don't let your beam get entangled with my beam."

"What? Why?" Erin demanded. Her beam had already grazed Holtzmann's any number of times.

"It's too much power," Holtzmann said. "It would cause a counterreaction. The beam will shoot back into your body and each atom will implode."

"What? I'm going to kill you, do you know that?" Erin shouted.

But Holtzmann's attention was diverted elsewhere. She

said, "Okay, I'm gonna open the trap on three. Everyone else hold steady!"

Holtzmann reached out her foot and stomped on the trap's trigger pedal. It popped open into two halves. Then she kicked it toward the edge of the stage. It slid across the floor. As it stopped, the inside of the trap lit up and emitted a tractor beam that resembled the burst of light from the proton wands, only it angled outward at a much wider angle. The ghost was captured, immobilized with an output of maximum effort on all their parts, and Erin had a stomach-churning moment of déjà vu as she relived the relentless fury of both the Aldridge ghost and the electrocution ghost in the subway.

"Okay! Bring it down!" Holtzmann yelled.

Stepping backward, they used their arms and legs to force the ghost to descend toward the stage. It fought harder when it looked down and saw the open trap and the steady tractor beam blasting from it. The four of them could barely hold on to it, and continued to struggle to keep their footing. It was like cattle roping on roller skates. Erin guessed its superionized state was definitely contributing to the battle it put up.

"Turn off your streams as soon as I close the trap," Holtzmann said. "Ready? Okay. Off!"

Holtzmann stomped on the foot trigger. The ghost was sucked right in and the trap slammed shut. The Ghostbusters turned off their proton packs. Steam rose from the ghost trap. It smelled strongly of ionization. Erin stared at the trap, entirely spent, as Holtzmann darted over, then slowly lifted the smoking box by its cord, almost as if it were a dead animal—a possum or a skunk. Erin and the others waited with bated breath for her to say something. Holtzmann just looked at them.

"Are you waiting for me to say something?" she asked.

"Did we catch a ghost or not?" Erin cried.

Holtzmann grinned at her. "Oh, we caught a ghost."

"Yes! Oh hell, yes!" Erin whooped.

Abby jumped onstage and joined them. "We did it!"

Erin and Abby threw their arms around each other and hugged as the metalheads went wild and the band started playing again: *thrashthrashthrashthrash*. Erin and Abby whirled in a crazy-ass victory dance as free and joyous as their science fair neutron dance. Erin was happier than she had ever been in her life. She couldn't even believe what it felt like. They had captured a real ghost! The haunted had become the haunter.

Take that, Mrs. Barnard!

She danced to the front of the stage and, bobbing her head to the thunderous beat, played her proton wand like an air guitar. Abby joined her and they pretended to rip a double guitar solo.

Protect the barrier! Protect the barrier!

Then Holtzmann ran over and grabbed one of the guitars out of its player's hands and smashed it like the legendary Pete Townshend, leader of The Who. Wham! Crash! The guitarist stared open-mouthed at her.

Catching her breath, she said, "Sorry, I got caught up in the moment. Can't buy you another one."

Feeling the love, Erin stopped wailing on her proton wand, ran over and picked up the steaming ghost trap by its cord, and planted a big wet kiss on its side. When she turned back to Abby, her bestie's face was suddenly pale.

"Erin, that's radioactive," Abby shouted at her.

She carefully set the trap back down, feeling suddenly faint. *Oh my god, that was stupid. And it tasted like burned toast.*

Holtzmann stepped forward and said, "It's okay. You'll just take some potassium iodide for the next ten years. It's fine."

In the wings, Ozzy Osbourne, AKA "the Prince of Darkness," stood watching the ruckus, waiting to take the stage next. He was freaking out. "Sharon," he wailed, "I think I'm having a flashback!"

Like victorious gladiators, the Ghostbusters strode out of the theater, holding the smoking ghost trap aloft by its cord. Their new uniforms were ripped and dirty. A crowd had already gathered on the sidewalk; people were cheering and taking more videos of them. The word had spread during the battle as cell phone footage from inside the hall was uploaded to the Internet. Erin basked in the attention and adoration, waving at the spectators.

A NY-Local 1 News van rolled up and double-parked in front of the theater. A reporter and her videographer bailed out the side doors and started shoving their way through the mob. Erin had no doubt the station would air a retraction of what they'd said about the Ghostbusters. This complete validation might open doors that had been slammed in her face. And she had a fleeting thought that maybe Dean Filmore would regret firing her.

"Hey, Ghostbusters," the reporters called out to them, her microphone held high overhead, "Look this way!"

"Ghostbusters!" a photographer shouted. "Who are you wearing?"

We caught a ghost, she thought over and over as they posed, mugging, vamping it up, and she beamed a smile as wide as the Brooklyn Bridge.

17

As soon as they returned to Ghostbusters headquarters and unloaded their gear, they set the ghost-filled trap on a lazy Susan they found in a cupboard, gave it a spin, and got the party started. Abby hit the stereo and music blasted through the dining room.

Erin and Patty immediately got their groove on and started dancing.

They'd not only saved the day, they'd made their fortune. Their meal ticket sat smoking between the soy sauce and the chili paste. Being the first to catch a ghost was as Kuhnian paradigm shifting as being the first to meet space aliens. Erin could see the Ghostbusters on every talk show in the world, the front pages of every newspaper, and the cover of *Time* magazine. Not to mention the supermarket tabloids: "Holtzmann Spends Thirty-Five Mill on Cold Fusion Smart House"; "Abby's Secret Recipe for Ghost Shrimp"; and "Erin and Brad: Say It Isn't So."

Validated and vindicated, Erin dropped into a wide, squatting wushu stance, then she and Patty added a bit of whip to their nae nae.

Erin beckoned their receptionist, who had yet to join in. "C'mon, Kevin!" she cried. "Let's see what you've got."

He shook his head no. Which surprised her. She couldn't imagine that he was *shy*. He was a model and an actor, right? And a semiprofessional hide-and-seek player? He sought the limelight. He loved the limelight. He was all about the limelight.

"Give us *something,*" Patty insisted.

Kevin stared at them stone-faced, as if he had no intention of doing anything of the sort. Then just as Erin had given up on him, he rose out of his chair and busted a move that was all his own. He was incredible, and Erin and Patty cheered. They all danced over to where Abby and Holtzmann sat at their worktable. They had the device they had found at the theater disassembled in front of them, and they looked intense.

"Guys, cheer up," Erin encouraged them. "It's time to celebrate. This is what 'legit' feels like."

Swept up in the joy of the moment, she snatched the trap off the table, puckered up, and gave it another energetic kiss. Kevin stopped busting and peeled off at once.

Abby winced. "Okay, you gotta stop kissing the trap."

"I know," Erin said. "But it's like the more you guys say, 'Don't kiss the trap,' the more I want to kiss the trap. Holtzmann, get in on this!"

Holtzmann held up a wait-a-minute finger as she shifted attention from the heap of parts disassembled from the weird sparking thing on the table, to the different heap of parts on her workbench. "Rain check," she said. "Exciting things happening over here. Newly printed circuit boards, superconducting magnets rebuilt, beam accuracy improved and extended by producing a controlled plasma inside a new RF discharge chamber in the redesigned wand, a cryocooler to reduce helium boil-off. And—wait for it— a mothergrabbin' Faraday cage to attenuate RF noise and provide physical protection to avoid quenches. Can I get a woot woot?"

"Woot woot!" Abby and Erin cried.

Kevin rejoined them. He looked nonplussed. "Ummmm," he said, hesitating as if he was trying to remember what he came over to say. Then he blurted out, "There's a Smartin Christ here to see you."

After a few days of constant exposure, his malapropisms no longer challenged her. Erin adroitly translated the Kevinese: "Smartin Christ—you mean Martin Heiss? The famed scientist? The paranormal debunker? Here? Inside this building?"

There is nothing to be nervous about. We are for real, Erin reminded herself as she and the other Ghostbusters followed Kevin to the reception area.

A very dapper man in a a three-piece suit with a dramatic hat and holding a walking stick was standing with his back to them, scrutinizing papers on the wall filled with scientific notations and crazy-looking squiggles. It was all highly scientific and completely accurate. *Surely he would be able to see that.*

But he had already told all NY-Local 1 News's viewers that they were just frauds. He had a lot invested in making sure the public still saw it that way.

What do we care? We aren't frauds. And the whole world knows it, Erin assured herself.

"Mr. Heiss. Welcome to our laboratory," she said more calmly than she felt. Suddenly she didn't want him looking at their equations.

He turned around, left hand cupping his right elbow, fingers of his right hand touching his chin—a classic speculative pose.

"Is now a bad time?" There was a mischievous glint in his eyes, and his lips formed the faintest hint of a mocking pout.

In person, Martin Heiss was a bit of a jerk. A pompous, smug, self-satisfied jerk.

Could he sense that Erin was weirded out by this uninvited intrusion? Did he think that meant that they had something to hide? She caught herself reverting back to old Erin, the self-doubting, fearful Erin. What the heck did she have to be defensive about? They had caught a frigging ghost, for pete's sake. An empowering image flashed through her mind: her shouldering a proton pack, then beam-smacking his tailored butt down the stairs and out of the building, like what Patty had done to that dude in front of the theater. Liar, liar pants on fi-ahh!

"Actually, it is—" Abby began, but Erin cut in.

"Not at all. Please, have a seat." She turned to Kevin. "Kevin, could you get Mr. Heiss some water?"

The professional paranormal debunker sat down. The Ghostbusters joined him, their expressions ranging from anxious to indifferent to jolly.

"I sure hope you don't mind being recorded." Again he flashed that self-satisfied smirk, as if he thought they were stupid and he was so smart that he was going to make them look even more stupid on TV.

Erin's inner bravado began to weaken—in postproduction editing he could put whatever they said in an unflattering context. "Well, I actually would prefer—"

He whipped out a camera and put it on the table. Then he hit record. He also pulled out a notepad.

Weiss the weasel had played it perfectly, and from the way his smirk broadened into a grin, he knew it. If she challenged him now over the fact that he was recording the interview, he could air her unwillingness to go public. That would make the Ghostbusters seem like charlatans.

"Oh, okay." Erin shifted in her chair. Then Kevin set down a glass of water that was inexplicably only one-eighth full. Just enough for Heiss to choke on?

"Let's start light and easy," Heiss said, actually batting his eyelashes at her. "Ever hear of the One Million Dollar Paranormal Challenge? James Randi offered to pay one million dollars to anyone who can prove paranormal claims under scientific testing criteria. No one has. Why are you pretending to catch ghosts?"

The unprovoked insult and condescension lit Abby's fuse. She said, "We only know what *four percent* of the universe—"

"Breathe," Erin told her gently. Turning to Heiss, she said, "Sir, we believe in the scientific method. I've dedicated my life to it. We have been working on bringing the paranormal into a controlled environment so we can supply that proof. This has been very difficult to do. But we have now done just that." She gestured to the ghost trap. "At 4:23 P.M. today we successfully trapped a Class Three vapor." She said it clearly. Let him record *that*.

"You're saying there's a ghost in the box?" Again, there was glee in his eyes and a smirk on his mouth.

Contempt dripped from his chin like ectoplasm. Mockery, apparently Heiss's forte, was the lowest form of humor, and Erin wanted to make him eat a yard of it. "Yes, I am," she said with confidence. She was proud of what they had achieved, and rightfully so.

There was another flurry of eyelash batting. "Well, I would just love to see it. Wouldn't that be a treat."

Abby stepped in. "You can't. We still have to establish the best method of testing that can contain it in the lab."

"What a shame." Phony sigh. He quickly wrote something in his notebook.

"Otherwise we would show you," Erin assured him.

"Hey. You gotta keep it contained." He shrugged, beaming at her. "What can you do?"

Erin decided to appeal to him, one scientific professional to another. "Listen, I know this sounds like we're making it up." She gestured to their jumpsuits and proton packs. "Obviously, we look a little ridiculous right now."

"You look like the Orkin of Bullshit."

Ooh, she could tell that he loved saying that. His eyes shined in triumph. He had probably worked on it on the way over. What a *jerk*—

"Well, it was real nice of you to stop by," Patty said.

Erin realized it was the first time she had spoken to Heiss. He'd probably riled her up making fun of their uniforms. And who was he, anyway, to sit there and rush to judgment when the scientific method *demanded* that one keep a clear and objective mind when new theories were being advanced? He wasn't just a jerk, he was more than a jerk. He was a scurrilous, slanderous, pompous buffoon who made a living by humiliating people. Well, she was about to put him in his place.

"You wanna see it?" Erin said. Her caustic tone and inflection made it a declarative statement: You don't have the balls to see it.

"I would love to see it," he said, assuming the elbow-resting, chin-cradled speculative posture.

"Too bad. He can't," Abby insisted.

"I think he should see it," Erin shot back.

"This jerk's approval doesn't matter," Abby said. "There are more important things at play."

"I bet," Heiss said. He was just *loving* this.

Erin had already locked in her course. "We're showing him."

As she stood up and started over to the trap, Holtzmann and Patty shot each other looks of alarm. They bolted for the wall hooks, pulled down their proton packs, and shouldered them. The devices made a scary pinging sound that built to a roar as they powered up to max output. Patty and Holtzmann tapped their wands, ready to recapture the freed ghost.

Erin moved the trap from the lazy Susan to the floor in front of the table. "I would stand over there behind us," she suggested to Heiss.

He didn't move a muscle. "I weirdly think I'll be just fine here," he insisted, practically hugging himself with glee.

Abby stepped beside Erin and blocked her hand from the trap's reset. "Erin, no. We finally caught an entity. I'm not letting you do this."

"Okay, fine, fine, I get it," Erin said.

Abby said, "Good," and backed off.

Just as Erin knew she would.

She immediately hit the release button and the two halves of the trap snapped open with a loud clunk. A cloud of steam puffed out and rose to the water-stained ceiling. Then . . . nothing.

No ghost.

Heiss's bemused expression was terrible to behold—it looked painted on.

"Oh come on," Erin said after a few very long seconds passed. She tapped the side of the box with her toe. Still nothing. Gave it a harder kick. Nada. She was baffled. How could the specter have gotten out? Had the force field broken down? Had the power supply failed for a micro-second? Had that caused the polarities to reverse? Had its not-of-this universe molecules simply evaporated? Had it found an unknown way to return to the other side?

Shaking their heads in disbelief, Patty and Holtzmann lowered their wands.

Heiss stood, and with a flourish turned off his camera. "Well, it was lovely meeting you—"

In the span of a single heartbeat, a crushing and humili-ating defeat became something infinitely worse. Without warning the theater ghost burst out of the trap, and fangs bared, in full demonic mode flew straight at Heiss, who seemed rooted to the floor. The intervening distance was less than ten feet. Before anyone could say or do anything, it swung the debunker into the air and threw him through the window. Right through it, with tremendous force— window frame blown out, glass shattering. Glittering frag-ments hung in the air as Heiss's shoe soles toppled out of sight; his warbling scream presumably cut short by un-yielding pavement. The ghost darted through the emptied window frame and disappeared.

"Oh my god!" Patty cried. They ran to the window, and as they stuck out their heads the ghost vanished over the rooftops across the street. Erin stared down in shock. How far the mighty had fallen.

Shortly after they put in a 911 call, sirens began to wail in the distance, and a few minutes later an FDNY EMT ambulance and NYPD squad cars arrived, lights flashing. Then the second part of the ordeal began.

A patrol officer named Stevenson took charge of the scene. He pulled aside and interviewed the Ghostbusters. He quickly made it clear that he was no more accepting of the existence of the paranormal than Martin Heiss was. It was still too soon to know how to refer to TV's favorite debunker. "The late" seemed somewhat premature. Heiss had been rushed away in the ambulance with screaming sirens and spinning lights. Erin recalled that when the firemen left with dead Mrs. Barnard, there was no such fanfare, but rather a quiet, leisurely departure.

"I'm going to ask you one more time," the officer said. "And if you tell me a ghost threw him out the window again, I swear to Christ, you're all answering this behind bars." He stared hard at Holtzmann. "Okay, here we go. What happened?"

Holtzmann muttered, almost inaudibly, "Ghost did it."

Stevenson cocked his head and glared at her. He looked like a Tasmanian devil about to take down a wombat. "Say that louder, please? I just want to be sure I'm hearing you right."

But this is supposed to be our day, Erin thought. It wasn't fair and it wasn't right. In a few unforgettable seconds, hard-earned glory had slipped through their fingers. Their ghost was gone, and Martin Heiss was just another stain on the sidewalk of life.

The police officer was about to put on the cuffs when several black SUVs pulled up. Two men in suits got out and flashed wallet badges at the cops.

"Official business. We've got this," said the red-haired man, stepping through the line of uniformed police.

"You need to come with us," his dark-skinned companion told them. He had a very intense and soulful expression, not angry or hostile. It took a second for Erin to put her finger on it: the expression in his eyes was disappointment. Like he could see through every layer of a person's façade and into their private thoughts, and what he saw saddened him.

Erin balked. "Why? Who are you guys?"

"The mayor would like a word," said the first man.

The Ghostbusters were packed into one of the black SUVs and driven at high speed through the streets of Manhattan. When pressed, the black agent finally identified himself as Frank Hawkins, and his red-headed partner as Rorke but that was all he would reveal. If Martin Heiss hadn't just been thrown out of their window, Erin might have been more assertive about her rights as an American citizen and demanded to know what was going on. Even Abby seemed cowed by the way they had been scooped up, and she kept glancing warily at the other black SUVs, one leading and one following their vehicle. Holtzmann said something self-deprecating about her streak of putting men in comas, and Patty asked the back of Hawkins's head if he'd seen her on TV.

"We're famous, you know," she added.

"Yes, ma'am," he said, and that was all he said. He didn't look up in the rearview mirror. Patty rolled her eyes and crossed her arms and went on at length about how *some men* felt threatened by strong women. After that, everyone fell silent as it sank in how weird it was to be driven to an elected official's office after almost being arrested for attempted murder on the same day that you captured and lost a ghost. Erin wondered if these guys were two of the mythical "men in black" who went around threatening people who had seen UFOs not to say anything about it. Which would make them factual. "Mythical" thereby being inaccurate . . .

The dreamlike sense of reality accompanied her as they were let out of the SUV and shepherded to a reception area outside the mayor's office. Before they stepped through the double doors, Hawkins told them the mayor's assistant, Jennifer Lynch, would be also present.

Lynch was a very striking young woman. She stood

beside the mayor, who was seated, as Erin and the others entered and lined up like good soldiers to discover what they were here for. The mayor seemed almost merry as he regarded them, which eased Erin's mind greatly. Maybe he wasn't going to throw them all in jail.

"There they are," he said in a friendly tone. He had a very thick New Yawk accent. "Sorry for all this drama. Please, have a seat."

They sat uncomfortably in the comfortable chairs.

Erin felt compelled to speak, to justify the Ghostbusters before the meeting started. She leaned forward in her chair and said, "Listen, something big is happening. We're not frauds. We are scientists—"

"We know you're not frauds," the mayor said. "Because we've been monitoring the situation as well."

It was difficult to imagine something topping what had already happened that day, but there it was, right in their laps. It turned out they were not alone. Bombshell! At first blush, it was wonderful, exciting news, and then a barrage of questions started popping into Erin's head. From their expressions, the others were clearly puzzled, too.

"Agents Hawkins and Rorke are with Homeland Security," Ms. Lynch said. "We've been investigating this extremely quietly."

Erin was pleased to learn she had guessed correctly.

"So what do you know?" the mayor asked her.

Erin looked at Abby, then Holtzmann, and then Patty. Evidently they were cool with her acting as spokesperson. "Um, just that we believe someone is creating devices to attract and amplify paranormal activity."

"And this activity could be escalating toward a large-scale event," Abby added.

Well put, well put, Erin thought. It was just supposition at this point, but it was a scary supposition. The mayor concurred.

"Well, that sounds terrible," he said earnestly. "I certainly don't like the sound of that."

Ms. Lynch nodded in agreement. Erin sagged with relief. If he believed them, if he really bought into the whole nightmare scenario, then that meant he would—

"Okay. Well, listen. Thank you. Great work. Really." The mayor beamed at them warmly. "But it's time to knock it off."

Abby said, "Excuse me?"

After the build-up, Erin was flummoxed and flabbergasted.

The mayor gestured to the two unsmiling agents. "These gentlemen are on it. Let the government do its work."

"The mayor's concern is that you're drawing way too much attention to yourselves," Ms. Lynch elaborated.

Erin couldn't believe what she was hearing. "I think we keep a pretty low profile," she argued.

Agent Hawkins spoke up. "You drive a hearse with a ghost on it. You use an unauthorized siren. Do you know how many federal regulations you are breaking on a daily basis?"

"We're going to have to make the public believe you're frauds," the mayor added.

"*What?*" Erin cried, her voice cracking shrilly.

Ms. Lynch took over again.

"The human mind can handle only so much. If people knew what was happening right now, there would be a panic. We'll have to put out information that the concert was a hoax. Otherwise, there would be mass hysteria."

To Erin's shock, her three friends nodded in agreement.

"Listen," Abby said. "All we care about is being able to continue doing our work."

"Now, that's true," Erin said, trying to recover a reasoned, convincing tone. "But it just seems like all those people already saw what happened anyway and what we did. It must be all over the Internet by now."

The others seemed to accept her premise, but Agent Rorke shrugged.

"You mean a bunch of whacked-out metalheads who

saw a high-tech prop that went out of control? And then their cell phone photos were all erased by a magnetic wave blast? We've got it covered."

"Jesus," Abby blurted.

Men in black. Not mythical. Erin filed that away.

She was not finished. "It's just . . . if we could back up one second . . . can't there be both things? And I'm just spitballing here, but like, what if we told people what we did but then said it's all under control now?"

"I think Miss Lynch here made it very clear we don't want mass hysteria," Abby reminded her.

"Okay, okay. Fair enough." Erin thought a moment. "But what is 'mass hysteria'? I mean, is it really that bad?"

"Let me show you a clip of it," Ms. Lynch offered. She hit play on a video on her laptop labeled MASS HYSTERIA and showed it to the group.

It was a montage of selected incidents from around the world. Not pretty. People running around in circles, waving their arms in the air, tipping over vegetable carts, and yelling at the top of their lungs.

Erk. Erin felt queasy.

Patty said in horrified fascination, "Why would you even have that on your laptop?"

"Right, right," Erin said, trying to find her way back to solid ground. But why *would* someone have that on their laptop? "It's just, I feel like the cat's already sort of out of the bag."

"Are you finished?" Abby sniped.

"The cat's been out of the bag before," Agent Rorke said, "and yet people always get bored and put it back in. A police officer in New Mexico reports a UFO encounter. The crew of the SS *Ourang Medan* mysteriously dies. The entire town of Langville, Montana, goes missing."

"What?" Erin raised her brows. "I never heard of that."

Agents Hawkins and Rorke stared at her, waiting for her to draw the obvious conclusion.

"Time to get back to work," Hawkins said.

"Well, on that horrifying note," the mayor said, "thank you all so much for what you've done. We will always be grateful for your service. Please think of me as a friend." He smiled reassuringly, then added, "A friend who will ignore you on the street, but a friend nonetheless."

"A long-distance friend," Ms. Lynch emphasized.

"Exactly," the mayor said. "A pen pal. But without letters. Or any kind of contact. Never send me anything in writing."

She remembered the cheers from the audience when they had sprung into action to catch the hideous, demonic theater ghost. The way the media had converged on them outside, asking about their fashion choices. But most of all, she remembered how good it felt to prove to the entire world that ghosts were real. And now that had all been taken away as if it had never happened.

It wasn't that she was advocating mass hysteria. Far from it. If they could educate the world about the reality of ghosts and do something about the dangerous ones— She caught herself. Were there any that weren't dangerous? Granted, their experience was limited, but so far they hadn't run across any nice, happy ones. Which made her wonder if the good ghosts went to heaven and had no urge to return here. She and Abby had made a point of avoiding the philosophical and religious in their research. They were too emotional subjects for most people, and emotion tainted data. Plus they were both faith-based, which was all well and good, but that didn't meld well with the scientific process and controlled experimentation. If she and Abby had included that sort of material in their book, it would have raised even more red flags among their peers.

The idea that ghosts could be divided into good and bad categories was comforting in a way because it reduced the number of likely homicidal intruders waiting on the other side for their chance to cross and cause havoc. But it didn't change the fact that there were a lot of them—half of the historical total of roughly a hundred billion dead people was still seven times more people than were alive today—and the fifty billion evil spirits were, well, lined up and waiting. Erin felt it would be better to let the world know what it was up against than to leave it to the mercy of spectral rage. Especially when the whole thing was being facilitated by some mad scientist. Hawkins and Rorke *said* they had the situation under control. But everything she had seen was out of control. They *claimed* to have made people forget all kinds of things, but had they? Where was the evidence? Then she had a chilling thought. Could "make them forget" be a department euphemism for "terminate?" It would be a low-tech, low-cost solution to a complex problem.

Talk about scary.

The unsmiling agents drove them back to their headquarters and silently rejected Patty's offer of an autograph. When Abby asked them if they wanted a copy of their book, Agent Rorke said, "That's been effected."

Erin had no idea what he meant by that, but honestly? She was relieved when they left.

When they turned on the TV, Ms. Lynch was being interviewed on NY-Local 1 News. Below her, the crawl read "Jennifer Lynch—Mayor's Office" to leave no doubt on whose behalf she was speaking.

"It's fraudulent and unsafe," she told the reporter. "These 'Ghostbusters' are just creating an unnecessary panic in a sad grab for fame. We went to their lab. There's absolutely nothing there. People can rest assured that these women are just bored and sad."

Erin, Abby, Holtzmann, and Patty stood transfixed by the character assassination and invective. Then Erin lost it; with a sweep of her arm she shoved a bunch of equipment off the worktable. It crashed to the ground. Glass shattered. Tendrils of white smoke rose from the linoleum.

It didn't make her feel any better that she had been warned the cover-up was in process. She *knew* she was right, and had been all along. She had had unquestionable proof that she had never lied, that these brave women in their cockamamy uniforms had saved lives and could save many more.

She should have had tenure at MIT, never mind lowly Columbia! Speaking engagements, books, their own show on the History Channel—those should have been the rewards coming their way, not claims by their own government that they were pathetic, delusional liars. Every discovery they had made had been confiscated and then publicly savaged by people in authority who had no idea what they were talking about. It was like one of those recurring nightmares, except that Erin was not naked. Or flying. Or both.

She watched Kevin take in the mess on the floor, then the mess she was becoming. A kind of light came on behind his eyes. Like he was waking up from a daydream and fully aware of his surroundings for the first time.

He said, "Guys, what the hell was that thing before?"

"It was a ghost," Abby said impatiently. "What do you think goes on here?"

Kevin seemed a more little lost than usual. "I didn't know. I answer phones in a Chinese restaurant where four women sit around in painters' outfits. When people ask me what I do, my response is, 'I have no idea.' I guess I knew it had something to do with Chinese food and science. I couldn't put it together."

Erin did not feel smug. Just kind of dazed at the revelation.

"I asked you in the interview if you believed in ghosts," Abby reminded him.

"Yeah," Kevin said. "I thought that was weird."

Abby persisted. "Just yesterday I was telling you all about a Class Three with distinct human form!"

"I don't know what that means," Kevin responded.

Holtzmann spoke up on his behalf. "That's fair."

"Listen," Kevin insisted, "we have to get ahead of this thing."

The sudden change in his demeanor and tone of voice was remarkable, almost as if in this moment of crisis he had reached deep into some previously untapped reservoir of strength and intelligence.

"Form a group to study it," he continued assertively. "Clear out all that kitchen equipment and build something to fight the ghosts."

"Oh my god, this is what we're doing," Abby said.

"Well, we need to do more," Kevin said emphatically. "Okay, look, we sell the restaurant. We don't really get any customers anyway. It's time to face it. This restaurant isn't working."

Erin gaped at him. So did Abby.

"Are you serious right now?" Abby asked.

"I just—I'm really confused," he confessed.

Kevin had run out of steam. Erin completely understood why. That was a whole lot of words he had strung together. And many of them would have made sense in some other context. He seemed to be taking everything in and processing it, but very, very slowly, and of course, incorrectly.

"For now, could you please get some baking soda out of the fridge?" Holtzmann asked him. "Erin just spilled hydrofluoric acid all over the floor."

Whoops. That was what was making the caustic white smoke. It didn't help the smell ambience that the hydrofluoric was burning up decades of ground-in cooking sauces, shrimp shells, and fortune cookie crumbs.

Kevin donned rubber gloves and started cleaning up the mess Erin had made. She imagined the top of her head smoldering, too; that was how massively she was still pissed off.

"They think we're a laughingstock," she said.

"I don't think anybody's actually laughing," Patty said. "That's a very serious news report."

"Painting us as delusional frauds," Erin replied.

"So what?" Abby said. "We're not."

"But nobody knows that!" Erin said. "In fact, look, it says 'Frauds!' Right there on the screen."

It did say that—directly under a group shot of them mugging under the theater marquee.

"But that doesn't make it true," Abby reiterated. "Kevin, sweetheart, don't rub the baking soda in your eyes," she added.

"But they burn," Kevin whimpered.

Abby gestured for Holtzmann to help him and she rushed to his aid, guiding him over to the sink, which was full of dirty dishes from days gone by. Bending him over it, she sprayed water on his face.

"Last week we saw a Class Four malevolent apparition," Abby reminded them. "And then we came back here and we figured out how to catch one. And it worked. Who cares what anyone else says? We know what we're doing. And there's bigger issues at play here. Look."

She crossed to one of their computers and gestured to the screen. "A wailing spirit sighted on Sixth and Twenty-sixth. A spectral polar bear on Park and Forty-fifth. Weeping walls at a thrift store in Chelsea. Someone's clearly trying to open the barrier and unleash the dead and we need to—"

Then Erin had a thought. "Wait," she said. "Sixth and Twenty-sixth . . ." The synapses started to fire. She ripped down the map of New York and with a pen started marking off the addresses that Abby had read aloud.

"Where did we find the first device?" she asked.

"At the subway," Patty replied.

Seward Street, Erin thought. *Right.* She scanned the map. "Here's the theater. Give me the other sightings . . ."

Abby obliged, sliding the computer toward her. Erin

notated all the locations and drew two lines straight through Manhattan. They intersected.

She indicated her handiwork. "What do those look like to you?" she asked.

"I can't see," Kevin replied.

"Ley lines," Abby and Holtzmann said together.

"What are ley lines?" Patty asked.

"A hidden network of energy lines across the Earth. Currents of supernatural energy. Let me see if there's a map of New York City."

While she hunted, Erin took up the thread of her explanation for Patty. "Supposedly if you look at sacred sites and weird events around the world, you can draw a line between them. And where lines intersect create an unusually powerful spot. Abby and I always dismissed it because it seemed too likely to happen at random to have any merit."

Holtzmann pulled a book out from under a pile of stuff. Erin recognized the cover; it was a copy of a ley line map book she and Abby had used for research in the olden days. As she flipped it open to the page showing the city's ley lines, Abby put their marked-up New York map next to it. The ley lines matched up.

"I guess there is some merit," Abby muttered, shaking her head.

Erin felt tension building in her stomach as the implications dawned on her. This was not good. Not good at all. "He's been using those devices to charge up the ley lines." Erin jabbed a finger on the intersection. "He's creating a vortex."

"If he has something powerful enough in here"—Abby pointed to a block under the crossed lines on the map—"he could rip a hole right through the barrier."

Holtzmann picked up the thread. "Letting everything out there come in here."

Patty swallowed, then said, "I feel like I should say something, too." But she didn't. That was it.

"What's there now?" Erin asked Holtzmann, again tapping the intersecting lines.

Holtzmann squinted at the city map. " 'The Mercado.' "

Erin typed the name into the computer search engine.

"The Mercado," Patty drawled. "Well, that makes sense."

Holtzmann looked at her. "Why's that?"

Patty turned to them. "The Mercado has one of the weirdest histories of any building in New York City. Check out these online reviews." She clicked a tab and began to scroll down through them.

"Half a star. 'I felt strange noises there,' " she read aloud.

" 'Loud noises in my closet throughout the night.' "

" 'I took a man back to my room and the next morning he was missing.' "

Patty clucked her tongue. "Oh girl," she said, "that was a one-night stand."

"So it's a haunted building?" Holtzmann asked Patty, trying to maintain the course of their conversation.

Patty shook her head. "Nah, this is even before it was a building. All sorts of massacres happened there. Like a peaceful trade with Captain Warren and the Lenape Indians and suddenly everyone dies. You know, no other section of New York has more power outages? My cousin got hit by a car in front of there." She shrugged. "But he's an idiot."

Erin processed that as she scrolled down the current Web site of the Mercado. There was a picture of the entire staff standing in the lobby. Everyone was smiling except for one person: a guy with a high forehead and big blue eyes. He stood straight-faced and humorless wearing what appeared to be a short-sleeved doorman's uniform.

Patty looked over her shoulder. "Hold on!" she cried, pointing at the screen. "That's the dude from the subway! Talking about cataclysms."

At the intersection, trying to create a vortex; they had their mad scientist. Erin said, "Bingo."

"Fire up the car and let's get over to this high-rise of horrors," Abby said.

They piled into ECTO-1 and, siren blasting, barreled down the street. Patty called out the directions to Holtzmann from her phone's GPS.

They found a place to double-park and headed through the massive front doors into the Art Deco building's lobby, dominated by a dramatic swirling floor, a double staircase that joined at a landing, towering gilded ceiling columns, and sculpted light fixtures. A clerk in a snappy uniform jacket stood with her back to them behind a wide, highly polished service desk. She was speaking on the phone. A walkie-talkie sat on the desk in front of her.

She said into the phone, "And did you try adjusting the thermostat before making this call? Oh, what a wonderful tone you've decided to use with me. I see the cold draft has not cooled your temperament."

This person is not from the Midwest, Erin thought as she took in the clerk. *We are far more polite than this.* She said, "Excuse me?"

The clerk half turned and gave the group a hold-on-a-sec hand gesture.

"Uh-huh," she said into the phone. "Well, that sounds more like a your problem. Hold on." She looked up at the Ghostbusters. "What do you want?"

Abby said, "Where's your janitor?"

The clerk sighed and made a face. "Ugh, that guy. What has he done?" Then she waved a hand as if throwing in the towel. "I don't care, take the stairs down, get him."

The four rushed over to the door that she'd indicated and headed down a flight of stairs. Walking along the hallway below, they found a sign on the wall that read GENERATOR ROOM. A blinding light flashed from underneath the metal door. It was *that* kind of light, weird and sparkling. They exchanged knowing looks and, fanning out, powered up their proton packs.

They pushed open the door and rushed through it, sin-

gle file. The generator room had been redecorated, turned
into a chamber of mirrors of various sizes, all crackling
with intense supernatural energy. In the dizzying reverse
reflections, Erin glimpsed an incredible Byzantine hell-
scape stained with clouds of burnt-orange smoke, brimming
with ghosts that looked like demons, ghouls, and regular
ghosty people, all scratching and clawing against the glass,
frantic to break through the assembled mirrors and enter
this dimension.

At the center of it all, a man stood bent over a strange
round machine that looked kind of like a large brass
boiler adorned with glowing windows and large conduits
and wires protruding from it, some of which dipped into
jars of burbling ectoplasm at his feet. Two long poles,
one on either side, were ringed with dark metal coils. He
was working a set of levers like a concert maestro. It was
the same man whose unhappy face had caught their attention on the Web site. Rowan somebody. Erin wondered
what had prompted a scientist so clearly gifted to take
such a drastic step over to the dark side. She highly
doubted it was a failed bid for tenure. Not that it mattered,
except as a reminder to self—whatever happens, don't go
bonkers.

"Stop!" Abby said in a commanding voice. "Okay, I
know you're having a ball bringing all these ghosts into
New York, but the thing is, we happen to like this world
the way it is."

Rowan looked up and smirked at them, surprisingly
unruffled by their intrusion. "I don't. I think it's garbage,"
he said. "And when the barrier is destroyed, the armies of
the undead will pester the living."

That gave Erin pause. She cocked her head and said,
"Okay. I mean 'pester' doesn't sound too bad—"

"They will pester the living with unspeakable pain and
torment. Everyone will be eliminated."

"Different meaning of pester," Erin said. As in make up
your own definition and run with it.

"Yeah, that's something else," Holtzmann concurred, deadpan.

Abby was not done berating him. "You don't like people? I get it. People can do terrible things. Don't get me started on this one." She nodded at Erin, which, hey, like wasn't that over?

"But then there's good things!" Abby continued. "All sorts of good things like . . . like soup and . . ." She paused. Struggled. "Jesus, why is the only thing I can think about right now soup? I'm very stressed out. Just stop the machine, damn it!"

Rowan hurriedly stepped toward a power coupling. There were two, one on either side of the massive chassis. Abby aimed her proton wand at him and he froze. Not that she had immobilized him literally, but because he didn't want her to use it.

So he knows what it is, Erin thought. *Has he seen us in action? Was he there in the tunnel or the theater, watching?*

The wail of approaching police sirens pierced the air. Erin wondered who had called them. The desk clerk? Or had certain scary quasi-terminators been watching from afar?

"Don't take another step!" Abby shouted. "The police are on their way down."

The strangest look passed over Rowan's face. How could he be *excited* about the police coming to take him to jail?

"Well," he said, merrily, "in that case, bye." With that, he turned around and placed a hand on each of the metal poles. Thus the circuit was closed, and electricity zinged through his body. It sucked so much juice from the system that the room lights actually dimmed. His legs straightened abruptly and he shot up on tiptoe like a ballet dancer, convulsing in a wild straining dance. When his body collapsed to the floor, smoke rose from his hair. His eyes were wide open and staring at nothing. He wasn't breathing. He looked dead.

"What?" Erin cried, unable to fathom this turn of events.

Abby said, "Turn the machine off!"

Holtzmann ran over and shut down the power grid. The tiered mirrors all went instantly blank.

The Ghostbusters bent over Rowan. His chest still wasn't moving. He was totally, irredeemably dead.

"Weird move," Holtzmann opined.

"Holtz, are we okay?" Erin asked, gazing anxiously at the normal-looking mirrors.

Holtzmann read the machine's meters. Erin had never been more grateful to have an engineer on the team than when she reported, "Yeah, I think so."

"Well, at least it's over," Erin said, although she was still massively shaken.

The sirens outside reached a crescendo, then stopped. They were replaced by the sounds of police officers storming onto the lobby floor directly above them.

"Let's get out of this room," Abby said.

Erin was only too glad to leave.

When they reached the stairwell, Abby cupped her hands to her mouth and shouted, "Hey! Down here!"

A short while later, after the scene had been secured, they all joined police and Homeland Security in the mad scientist's cramped basement laboratory. Erin walked over to Abby, who was studying the setup on Rowan's worktable.

"What's up?" Erin asked her.

"It's so strange," Abby said. "A lot of his technology isn't that different from ours. It's the same science behind our apparition catching."

Erin took that in. "That *is* strange."

"I think I know why that is," Holtzmann declared. She held up Abby and Erin's book.

"Oh my god." Erin was floored.

"Well, it's a very powerful book," Abby said with pride in her voice.

Yeah, but, Erin thought.

Then, like a toothache that just wouldn't go away, Jennifer Lynch stepped through the doorway and approached them. Erin looked around the windowless room; there was no escape.

"Thank you. For everything you've done," Ms. Lynch said with what seemed genuine feeling.

That was unexpected and Erin dropped her guard a little.

"The mayor privately thanks you as well. Let me walk you out."

As they left the room, Erin saw techs from Homeland Security begin disassembling Rowan's machines. Proof positive that the crisis was truly over.

They went upstairs to the lobby, where agents Hawkins and Rorke waited for them, unsmiling. Ms. Lynch told them, "Now get some rest. Let these guys get you out of here." She seemed warm and concerned, and Erin was grateful.

"That sounds nice. Thank you," Abby said, speaking for them all.

"I just have to say a few words. You know how it is," Ms. Lynch said with a conspiratorial wink.

When she opened the door and looked out into the street, Erin saw the mob of press waiting for them. Even more than at the theater! They had saved the world and were finally about to get their due.

As Erin was about to step out, her hands were pulled behind her back. She wasn't alone. Agents Rorke and Hawkins yanked all their hands behind their backs like they were being taken into custody and then perp-walked them in front of the bank of cameras. Jennifer Lynch immediately headed over to the press, who surged around her with microphones held high and camera flashes popping off.

"Everything's fine," Ms. Lynch assured them with a beatific smile on her face. "Just another publicity stunt by these incredibly sad, lonely women. I mean, give it a rest, am I right?"

The Homeland Security techs finished their assignment and stretched yellow crime scene tape around the disassembled machine. Then they packed up their gear and left.

But what they did not see . . . what no one could anticipate . . . was that the short, loud one had accidently left behind her PKE meter . . . and as it lay on the floor of the generator room it slowly lit up and then started spinning like a top.

The Fourth Cataclysm had begun.

18

Dissed again, Erin thought glumly as she and the other
Ghostbusters walked down the street away from Times
Square. Her friends appeared to be shrugging off
the latest effort of the powers that be to discredit and
disgrace them. As the kids said these days, achievement
unlocked.

"Well, mission accomplished." Abby sounded philosophical and proud. "Let's get a drink and celebrate."

Holtzmann and Patty high-fived. Abby turned to her.
"Erin, you in? My treat."

Just as she was about to answer, a guy Erin recognized
from the press conference ran up alongside her and started
recording her with his iPhone. He wasn't a real reporter
or he would've had a real camera, and probably a news
outlet windbreaker with a logo, front and back. She decided he had to be a blogger.

Not that there was anything wrong with that.

"How do you feel about wasting taxpayer money and
government resources with your pranks?" he said.

Abby jumped in. "Back off, buddy. We've got nothing
to say to the press."

Erin began a slow burn. Really? She couldn't even defend herself? The guy dogged her, but she ignored him and
kept walking.

"Miss Gilbert, I asked around your hometown. Talked
to someone you went to school with. They told me when

you were a kid you made up a ghost. Tell me, were you born a fraud, 'Ghost Girl'?"

Erin turned.

Don't, she warned herself.

Faced him.

Do.

Then she lunged at him.

IT!

Abby tried to catch her by the sleeve. "Whoa, whoa! Let it go!"

Erin went berserk, shaking off Abby's hand and grabbing the jerk by the front of his shirt. Patty and Holtzmann jumped in to hold her back, but she had come completely unhinged.

Enough was enough. Enough was *too* much. She had had it.

Adrenaline surged through her; she broke free of her friends and chased him down the street. Nothing on earth could have kept her from tackling him, not even a monster ghost from outer space. She dove at his knees, wrapped her arms around his legs, and they both went down hard on the pavement—she landed on top, squashing him. The others came up from behind, trying to pull her off, but she wouldn't be restrained.

"They should put you back in therapy, you freak!" the blogger wheezed.

And that sent her sailing right over the edge.

Eyes full of rage, she cocked back her fist and punched him square on the nose. It didn't break the bone, but the impact made his eyes cross, and then he started to cry, really cry. He was still bawling as he scrambled to his feet and ran away, clutching his face.

The next morning, Erin stared dully at the cover of the *New York Post.* Front and center was a photo of her—who had taken it?—punching the blogger. The headline read "Nosebusters!" She put it back on the table and buried her face in her hands. *Why* had she let him get to her? She'd made them all look bad.

Holtzmann walked in, taking off her proton glove as she said breezily, "I'm working on some new treats. No spoilers. But let's just say a lady needs a sidearm, and I've always wanted to throw a proton grenade."

Holtzmann grabbed a seat at the table and sipped her coffee. She casually reached over for the *Post* and began to read it. Erin braced for a bad joke at her expense, but Holtzmann didn't say a word. She just sipped her coffee and cleared her throat every now and then.

"These guys really have their finger on the pulse," she remarked.

Erin sighed. "Just read it to me."

"Okay. 'Midtown movie theater owner claims basset hound regularly attends matinees by himself—'"

"The story about me," Erin said dully.

Holtzmann flipped through the pages, then flipped back to the front. "Oh wow. I really didn't notice. Huh." She skimmed. "It's not that interesting."

She kept reading as Erin turned on the TV. A news reporter was staring earnestly at the screen.

"We spoke to Harold Filmore, Physics Department chair at Columbia University, where Ms. Gilbert used to teach."

"Oh no." Erin gasped.

There was Dean Filmore's office, and the dean was watching a replay of the video of her attacking the blogger—evidently the pest had taken it with his cell phone. She looked like a maniac.

"It's unfortunate that we have these former ties with Miss Gilbert," Filmore said. "At Columbia University, we're about real science, discovering truths, not lying for a sad moment of fame."

The cell phone footage froze on an especially unflattering shot of Erin. She looked like one of those demon-things trying to break through to the other side. She wanted to barf.

"Doesn't matter what these people think," Abby insisted as she watched, too.

"We also spoke with the dean of the Kenneth T. Higgins Institute—"

The report cut to Abby's surfer-dean's office as he finished his sack lunch.

"A terrible shame on the Kenneth T. Higgins name," he said. "But I want to rise from this opportunity to tell you about an album I'm about to drop—"

Patty clicked off the TV.

"Forget those dudes. You gotta just walk that off. Think about how many people you saved."

Holtzmann nodded. "Yeah. Let's just grab something to eat and find that basset hound."

Erin appreciated the effort, but she was done in.

"I think I'm going to take a walk," she murmured.

Abby sighed as Erin got up and left. The trouble was, Erin just couldn't stop caring about what people thought. She'd figured once they'd proved the existence of ghosts, Erin could lay Mrs. Barnard to rest. Literally. That she would be free of the intense need to be thought well of. Erin had nothing left to prove, no one to answer to, and yet she couldn't stop herself from craving validation. It was as frustrating as the mayor's insistence that the only way to prevent mass hysteria was to continually drag the Ghostbusters' names through the mud.

"Hey, Abby," Kevin said. "Can we talk about the paranormal? I got a bunch of ideas and theories about—"

"Not now, Kevin," Abby said glumly.

Erin walked through Times Square on the way home to her apartment. She still had on her proton pack, having forgotten to put it back on the wall. Maybe that was symbolic.

She was all alone in the bustling crowd. People were staring up at the signs advertising Broadway musicals. Locals dressed in superhero costumes posed for photos with tourists for tips.

"Who are you supposed to be?" asked a woman with two small boys in tow. The kids were maybe five and seven years old. They were eyeing her suspiciously. "Are you from a movie? I know we've seen you in something."

Erin was startled. She didn't know what to say.

"How much do you charge for a picture?" the woman persisted, opening her purse. She pulled out a cell phone and a five-dollar bill.

"Mom, no," said the older of the two boys. "We want a good one."

"Yeah," said the little boy.

"She's not in anything," the older boy insisted. "She's nobody."

The woman made a face. She said to Erin, "I'm sorry." She gestured to the busy square. "It must be very difficult to compete."

"I'm not in competition with anybody," Erin replied. But that felt untrue. If that were the case, would it matter so much what other people thought? Her jaw set, she turned and began to walk away.

Then the woman called after her, "Oh, I know who you are. You're a Ghostbuster!"

"Big liar! Big faker!" the older boy shouted.

Erin sighed and kept walking home.

Once there, she tossed her Ghostbusters uniform into the laundry basket, walked over to her computer, and stared at the monitor. Then she typed a URL she had memorized. A YouTube video came up and she shrank inside. It was the University of Michigan show, *Best Reads "On the Quad,"* that she hadn't shown up for. The show she had tried to watch live, but couldn't. Abby was sitting alone facing a snarky man in a tweedy jacket. She was wearing a nubby black-and-white turtleneck sweater. The two of them had spent hours discussing what to wear. What looked authorial. She looked lost and uncomfortable.

I didn't even call her, Erin thought. *I didn't warn her that I was bailing. I was such a coward.*

The host smirked at Abby as he said, "So you're saying that ghosts are actually real? And you can back this up with science? What could be less scientific than that? Have you actually ever even seen a ghost?"

Abby was squirming like a bug under a microscope. "We have . . . um . . . I mean, I have experienced . . . um . . . theoretical contact with the, um, spirit world—"

The host was practically laughing in her face. "I'm sorry, but I find that hard to—"

Erin turned off the clip. She felt terrible again, queasy.

I was the one who experienced actual contact. And I couldn't bring myself to say that in public anymore. But that was why we did all the research. I was tormented, terrified that I was crazy. From day one, Abby believed in me. But I didn't believe in us.

What other people thought of her had been far more important to her than keeping her word or backing up a friend. And that was still true. She had walked out on the Ghostbusters, hadn't talked about what they should do next.

She picked up the copy of their book. That crazy picture of the two of them on the back jacket—so young and nerdy, but full of hope. Then she opened it and began to flip through it. She stopped. There were physics notes scribbled inside. Her lips parted in shock.

This is Rowan's copy of our book. The one Holtzmann found.

She shuddered. How had she ended up with it? She didn't even like touching it. But as she stared at the scrawled equations, she realized this was the key to how he had created his superionization device and that machine for breaking the barrier and letting phantoms into this world. She began to page through the book, looking for more notations. She studied them as she went, trying to follow the inherent logic and direction.

And then, in the chapter they had titled "Attracting the Paranormal," she found a sketch of a rough design for his barrier-breaking machine. He had scribbled a caption next to it: The First Cataclysm.

She went past that and saw a drawing he had made of an electrocution. She thought of the first ghost they had seen in the tunnel, and then, of course, of Rowan himself.

He was insane, she thought. *But the machinery he devised was successful.* What would have happened to the world if he hadn't died?

She reached the chapter with the header "Vengeful Spirits and the Dangers of Their Return to Our World."

We guided him every step of the way, she realized. *The only person to believe us almost destroyed the world because of our book.*

She continued to page through the book, and when she got to the back, on the blank end pages she found another drawing of ghosts terrorizing New York City. Some wore historical clothes—colonial, Civil War, the Roaring Twenties, and the gangland thirties. Still others were strange, frightening wisps, or looked like demons and monsters—like the ghost at the rock concert. There was a massive being in the background, vaguely drawn and distant. On the next page it drew closer. Then closer.

She turned the page.

And froze.

"Oh no," she gasped.

On that final page, the being that was terrorizing the city bore Rowan's face. The note beside it said, *"The Fourth Cataclysm. I will lead them."*

19

At Ghostbusters headquarters, Holtz was tinkering and Patty was paging through a map book. Kevin had gone off to do something Kevinish. Abby studied a picture of Erin and her holding the smoking ghost trap in front of the rock concert theater. Both of them were beaming and proud. Erin had allowed other people to take that pride away from her. Abby was still proud. But she was also very bummed.

Holtzmann and Patty put on their coats. Patty said, "Holtz and I are gonna pick up a snack, something light. Probably a cheesesteak. Want one?"

Abby briefly wondered in what universe a cheesesteak was "something light," but she didn't have the strength to make the comment. "I'm good, thanks," she said quietly.

The two left. Abby saw the empty space on the wall where Erin's proton pack should be and sighed. Erin had finally apologized for bailing on her all those years ago. *Maybe I should apologize, too.*

She got up and headed toward the bathroom. Then two distinct slow, loud knocks sounded on the restaurant's front door, a large Chinese character divided into two arched halves that led out onto the stair landing. She stopped, called, "Did you forget your keys again? Wear them on a lanyard. Christ." She sounded cranky, but it was all bluster. She just didn't want those two to see her so down.

She walked back and opened the door. There was

nothing there. She leaned out over the threshold, looking around at the landing. She could see all the way down the stairs to the street entrance. Nuttin'. Completely empty.

It had to be Holtz, trying to tease her out of her funk. It wasn't working.

"Very funny. So spooky," she said.

She shook her head and shut the door, then headed back toward the bathroom. But before she arrived there was *another* knock at the door.

"Oh my god, what are we?" she groused. "In kindergarten? I'm not in the mood."

She walked back to the door and opened it. Now it was dark, all the lights off.

She listened. There was no one there. It was as quiet as a tomb.

Ghosts, she thought, but no, there were no ghosts hovering in the darkness. No Gertie, no Phantom of the Rock Opera. She shut the door, and this time she locked the dead bolt.

Unbidden, the scene where Rowan had electrocuted himself replayed in her mind. What had Erin said? That troubled, delusional people would read their book? She'd been right about that. Tomorrow Abby was going to find out what she could about that man—what had driven him to do what he did—not only the suicide but breaking down the barrier. Did he have followers? Was he part of a cult?

She couldn't deny that she was scared. She hurried into the bathroom, locked the door, and flattened her back against it. Her hands were trembling a little. She whooshed out a breath, seeking calm.

There was another loud knock.

This time on the *bathroom door*.

"Who is that?" she shouted.

No answer.

There was a noise coming from the sink—something rattling the drain. On alert, adrenaline pumping, she approached the sink. *I am a Ghostbuster,* she reminded herself. *Right. Unarmed, without backup.*

The rattling continued. Then something green glowed inside the sink end of the drain. She reached the edge of the sink and, summoning all her courage, moved in for a closer look. Her chest was so tight she couldn't breathe.

Then a shape flew out of the drain and into her face. It moved so fast she couldn't see what it was; it hit her hard and she fell backward onto the floor. For a second she was too dazed and hurt to move. Then she stood up painfully, joints suddenly throbbing, and felt something on her face.

No. In my nose. Something is in my nose.

She touched her fingertips to her nostrils. Green ectoplasm was dripping out of her nose. Ropes of it. *Out of my nose. There is ectoplasm in my body. Oh my god! I've been invaded.* Then her ear bubbled with thick goo. It streamed down her earlobe. There was so much of it. And more from her nose. Lots more. She paced anxiously around the bathroom.

Got to tell them. Got to warn them. Need help!

Her abdomen contracted hard. Pain seized her. She grabbed her stomach and winced. A plume of ectoplasm spewed from her mouth across the bathroom floor. She doubled over in agony, vomiting again.

And again.

From the crack beneath the bathroom door, ectoplasm oozed across the room. Then it seeped around the doorframe, climbing up to the ceiling, and ran down the walls. Gallons of it, burbling and puddling. Infecting, eddying . . . On Kevin's desk, the old answering machine clicked on:

"Hello. You have reached the Ghostbusters hot line. Please leave your name, number, a description of your apparition, a description of what you were doing at the time of encountering the apparition, and a description of the actual encounter with said apparition . . ."

20

Erin paced impatiently as the Ghostbusters office line greeting went on and on and *on*. She remembered when Abby had recorded it, how proud the two of them had been of devising such a painless way to capture anecdotal data. How wonderfully clever of them.

And long-winded.

Finally she heard the *beep*.

"Abby!" she yelled. "Jesus, shorten that greeting. It's Erin. Call me back! I think killing himself was just the next step in his plan!"

She hung up, massively frustrated. She'd tried Abby's cell phone and she didn't have Holtz's or Patty's. She had to get hold of someone who could help avert the Fourth Cataclysm!

Then, out of the corner of her eye she caught sight of a familiar face on her TV. It was the mayor. Below his image was a crawl reading "*Dinner with the mayor.*" It was an NY-Local 1 News broadcast, and the desk anchor was saying, ". . . Mayor Bradley is meeting with the diplomats at Lotus Leaf on . . ."

She *knew* where that restaurant was. She disconnected the call and ran for the door.

"It's interesting that we all call you Holtzmann," Patty said as they collected their cheesesteaks and headed back to headquarters. "Jillian is a nice first name."

Holtzmann smiled and shrugged. "It started in engineering school. Most of the other students were guys. Shy guys. I think they called me Holtzmann so I'd seem less like a girl." She mock-shivered. "Because you know a girl is pretty scary."

"And that's also why you became a practical joker?"

As Holtzmann pondered her answer, the sweet, heavenly smell of the bag full of food overwhelmed the familiar stench of their run-down neighborhood. "I was an oddball growing up. I think my teachers were actually a little afraid of me. I think outside the box. I'm kind of outside the range of social norms." She smiled when Patty nodded her head in acknowledgment of the truth to that.

"I've always like putting things together. Inventing things. I had the best mentor in college. I really impressed Dr. Gorin when I nearly disintegrated everyone in the classroom."

"Yikes," Patty said, laughing. "Like I said, I was pretty normal except for how much I like to read. Studious kids still get teased, you know?"

"I've always wanted everyone to have a good time," Holtzmann said. "I try not to judge people. Abby and I sure had fun in our lab at Higgins," she said dreamily. "I was so happy when we snagged most of our equipment, and then those Homeland Security guys carried off most of it."

"Agent Rorke is a hottie," Patty said with a lilt in her voice.

"Even if he is a jerk," Holtzmann replied. They grinned at each other.

"You know my uncle runs a funeral home," Patty said. "That place always gave me the willies. Still does. You'd think that'd scare me off reading ghost stories and such, but I liked 'em." She cocked her head. "You know, I worked down in the subway for a lot of years. Saw a lot of crazies. But nothing prepared me for what we've seen." She shuddered. "What was *in* those mirrors, Holtz—I mean, Jillian?"

"You can call me Holtz," she said. "I'm so used to it now that if you called me Jillian I probably wouldn't realize you were speaking to me." Her smile faded. "I know. What we saw today . . . it had to be hell, I think. Someplace where angry ghosts are contained, or imprisoned. They wanted to come back here to wreak revenge, I suppose." She blew the air out of her cheeks. "Now *they* were scary."

"Amen," Patty said earnestly. "Thank God it's over."

"It occurred to me that he might have planted devices in other places," Holtzmann said. "But that machine appears to have been the instrumentality required to break down the barrier. It's shut down now. But someone else could try again, you know?" She looked at Patty. "That's why I'm sticking around. That plus the working-for-free part." She wrinkled her nose. "I can't get enough of that."

Patty chuckled. "That's what I like about you, Jill—Holtz. You've got a sense of humor." Her amusement faded. "Unlike *some* folks."

"I *do* enjoy pushing the buttons of uptight people," Holtzmann admitted. "Especially Erin."

"Do you think she'll come back?" Patty asked.

"I don't know," Holtzmann replied. "I mean, where else does she have to go?"

When they reached the door of the restaurant it opened easily and Holtzmann made a note to remind Abby to lock it when she was in there by herself.

They set down the food and Holtzmann looked around. Everything was as they'd left it. The bathroom door was shut.

"Abby," Patty called. "We got you a sandwich because we don't want you picking off of ours. Come and get it."

There was no answer.

Holtzmann called to the bathroom door, "Hey, Abby,

you in there?" She walked to the door and tapped on it.
"Abby? Everything all right?"

Just as she made a fist to knock, the door opened. Abby
stood there with a slightly blank look on her face.

"Hey," Abby greeted her.

"You okay?"

"I'm quite well," Abby said pleasantly.

"Well, good," Holtzmann countered.

Abby walked off.

Holtzmann shrugged. She said to Patty, "Not our best
back-and-forth."

She and Patty unwrapped their cheesesteaks and sat
down to eat. Holtzmann looked over as Abby crossed to
the far wall where their proton packs were hanging. The
absence of Erin's pack poked a big hole in the symmetri-
cal arrangement.

Abby walked over and picked up a long metal pipe. She
looked down at it, weighing it in her hands.

"I found that in a Dumpster yesterday," Holtzmann told
her. "Figured I could use it for a new idea I'm playing with.
Proton shotgun. Awesome, huh?"

She hoped the idea would cheer Abby up. Make her see
that their ghost-busting days were not over, far from it.

Abby sauntered back over to the proton packs and removed their protective housings. Holtzmann watched, intrigued, wondering what the heck she was doing. Maybe
she had come up with some cool new modification. Holtzmann was about to ask her, when suddenly Abby reared
back and started beating the proton packs with the pipe,
seriously wailing, throwing all her weight into it. It sounded
like a blacksmith pounding on an anvil. Parts were breaking off and flying everywhere.

"What are you doing?" Holtzmann cried.

She ran over and grabbed Abby's arms, squeezing hard
until Abby let go of the pipe. It clattered against the floor
and rolled away. Abby grabbed Holtzmann by the throat;

her feet crunched on broken bits of the proton packs. Then, seemingly with no effort at all, Abby just lifted her up into the air by the neck.

How is she doing this? Why is she doing this? Holtzmann thought as she struggled, both hands prying against Abby's superhuman grip. Then Abby thrust Holtzmann's entire body through the window. The glass shattered outward and Holtzmann found herself dangling two stories up. Her windpipe was cut off and the world was turning shades of gray and yellow, fading to black. Abby was going to kill her!

This is not Abby, she realized. *This cannot be Abby.*

"Oh my god, you guys aren't playing a game, are you?" Patty cried, rushing at Abby from behind.

When Abby let go of Holtzmann, she started to fall and her life passed before her eyes: the joy of detonating her first explosive device. The excitement of her first kiss, which coincided with detonating her first explosive device. The prototype nuclear-powered skateboard . . . Then her full weight fell on her arm, practically dislocating it from the socket, and she realized she wasn't falling anymore, she was swinging against the side of the building—Patty had reached out the window and grabbed hold of her hand. With her left arm, Patty slap-punched Abby in the chest, bouncing her off the wall. Holtzmann scrambled, scraping her toes against the building's masonry, trying to gain a foothold, as Patty strained to pull her back in through the window. Holtzmann was level with the ledge when Abby jumped up and rushed them again.

Holtzmann looked on helplessly as Abby and Patty had the world's most awkward catfight. Open-hand slapping, pushing and missing, shoving and missing. Even though Patty was much bigger, she was at a serious disadvantage because she was still holding on to Holtzmann's wrist, fighting with her left hand, and she wasn't possessed by a ghost demon.

Holtzmann couldn't see it ending any way but badly.

Then, as Abby lunged again, Patty caught her behind the heels with a kung-fu leg sweep and cleanly flipped her onto her back. Abby hung in the air for a frozen instant, as if floating. Using her own momentum, Patty yanked Holtzmann headfirst through the window, let go, then spun and jumped on Abby before she could get up from the floor. She leaned over Abby as Holtzmann choked and gasped for air. Cocking back her arm, Patty bellowed, "Get out of my friend, evil spirit!"

Patty smacked Abby across the face hard with her open hand, making her head snap to the side. Even Holtzmann saw stars—

No, not stars, she realized.

It was the ghost of Rowan, exploding out of Abby. The sudden emergence created a sonic boom so loud that the rest of the windows shattered and the entire building shivered like they were caught in an earthquake.

Ghost Rowan was horrifying to behold, even more so since Holtzmann had seen him when he was alive. The transition to spirit had amplified his least attractive features and made her wonder, *Am I going to look that hammered after I'm dead?*

With a deafening snarl, the freed ghost shot out the window as Patty and Holtzmann looked on in shock. He became a black dot against the sky that shrank and shrank, until it finally vanished in the distance. Holtzmann was still rubbing her bruised throat as Abby came to, a bewildered expression in her eyes as she saw Patty on top of her. She touched her own cheek and cried, "Yeeeooowwch!"

Reacting instinctively, Patty smacked her across the face again. Abby flailed her arms at her. "Stop! It's me! What part of 'yeowch' didn't you understand?"

"Hey, guys! Check it out!" a voice filtered through the broken-out window.

Holtzmann and Patty leaned out the window as Abby struggled to get to her feet.

It was Kevin, calling up to them from the street. Dressed in a subway uniform like a Ghostbuster, he stood beside a junky old motorcycle that had been painted white and decorated with decals, a biohazard warning with a little pink heart in the center, red triangle showing radiation turning one person into a skull and another running away, with exhaust flames added in marker, and a Ghostbusters logo was affixed to the gas tank. A proton wand and a laser had been taped to the handlebars, and a license plate identified the poignantly close-but-no-Ghostbuster-cigar contraption as ECTO-2. Kevin was more excited than Holtzmann had ever seen him.

"I figure you're going to need my help," Kevin shouted to them. "I just need my proton pack, if you could—"

Abby scrambled to the window, looked up, and pointed into the sky. High above them, the ghost of Rowan was circling, just as that ghost had circled above the crowd at the theater. The evil spirit appeared to spot Kevin below, because it banked a tighter turn, craning its neck downward. It folded up, stooping like a hawk, and dive-bombed Kevin just as Abby yelled down to him, "Kevin, get inside!"

Kevin still didn't see Rowan's onrushing ghost; he was looking in the wrong direction. Crestfallen at yet another rejection, he pouted and said, "I really don't appreciate being yelled at like that. It's emasculat—"

His words were cut off as Ghost Rowan slammed into him and disappeared inside. Kevin's face instantly went blank. Or blanker. A second later, the lights turned back on behind his eyes. When he examined his arms and body, he seemed awestruck at his state of buff. Then he looked up at the three Ghostbusters in the gutted window frame.

"Thanks for the upgrade," he said. It was Kevin's voice, but it sounded weird, otherworldly. "This will be very helpful."

Then he jumped onto the motorcycle, revved the engine, and peeled off, disappearing down the street.

"Oh, that's not good," Patty groaned.

No kidding, Holtzmann thought. *He isn't wearing his helmet.*

Beautifully coiffed and formally dressed, Jennifer Lynch sat with the mayor and the diplomats who were his dinner guests, and reflected on all that had happened to her since becoming his assistant. His Honor had insisted that she attend tonight's gathering to, as he phrased it, "make sure I don't say anything undiplomatic." She was the soul of tact—when tact served the mayor's interests. Sometimes you had to be blunt and tell it like it was—like with the Ghostbusters, for example. What sad and lonely women.

Well, not really. We made that up, she remembered. But not out of whole cloth. The four of them were manless, careerless, styleless, and thanks to her efforts, very likely to stay that way. But she was confident they understood what was at stake. The mayor's office *had* to portray them as crackpots. Otherwise, mass hysteria—

Her train of thought was derailed by something moving on the other side of the restaurant's plate glass windows. It was someone in a tan uniform with orange bands across the chest. *Dear lord,* she thought, strangling the linen napkin in her lap. One of the Ghostbusters was running around wildly outside. She kept darting forward, pressing against the glass, then darting forward a few steps further down. Jennifer realized with a start that she was looking for a door.

"Oh boy," she said quietly to Mayor Bradley, nodding her head toward the windows. "Code red."

When the mayor followed her line of vision, he blanched. "Oh, what the shit is this?"

The woman was still bounding around like a gazelle, banging into the glass, looking for a door. The good news was, she couldn't seem to figure it out. Amazing. *They* had saved New York City?

"What is this woman doing?" the mayor murmured.

As Jennifer and His Honor looked on, a couple exited the restaurant, revealing at last where the door was. The Ghostbuster brightened and sprinted toward it before it could swing closed.

"Maybe she just really likes the restaurant," Jennifer said hopefully.

The Ghostbuster burst into the restaurant and put on the brakes when she spotted Jennifer and Mayor Bradley. Both of them tried to hide their faces behind their menus—great minds certainly thought alike—but it was no go; she ran over to them, face red, eyes wide, waving her arms like a standard-issue Manhattan maniac.

"You have to evacuate the city!" she yelled at the top of her lungs.

The diplomats stared at her. His face darkening, the mayor said through clenched teeth, "Don't say that word. *Never* say that word."

Restaurant patrons were looking over now. Jennifer knew it was very likely that at least one of them was recording this with a cell phone.

In a louder, public voice, Mayor Bradley announced, "Ma'am, I don't believe we've met."

The Ghostbuster leaned closer to the group. Her eyes were practically spinning in their sockets. Was she Karen or Gabby? Jennifer had trouble keeping their names straight.

"It's not over!" the woman wailed. "It's just beginning. I don't know how he's going to do it, but you gotta send every officer over to the Mercado and you have to shut down the power to the city."

Jennifer put on her public face. "I'm sorry. As you can see, the mayor is eating right now."

A loud rumbling erupted outside. The Ghostbuster gasped and put her hands to her head. "It's starting!" she shrieked with full-on drama.

Everyone turned and looked, including the diplomats.

What they saw was a pair of white-liveried and aproned workers straining to wheel an overloaded Dumpster past the window.

"Oh, okay," the distraught woman said as she realized her mistake. Then she tried to recover the intensity of the moment. "It's still starting, though."

Of course the mayor was accompanied with heavy security wherever he went. Jennifer gave the signal for them to cautiously approach, and two plainclothes guards moved up and grabbed the woman from behind.

Mayor Bradley blew out a breath and said, "That took way too long."

"No!" the Ghostbuster cried. She wasn't going to go quietly. She grabbed on to the edge of the table. The guards tried to pry her off, but she wouldn't budge. "*No!*"

"This is crazy. You're embarrassing yourself," Jennifer said in a tight, measured voice. The statement didn't faze the woman, who clung so tightly to the table that even when the guards pulled her body parallel to the floor she would not be moved.

"I . . . don't . . . care!" she growled.

At a signal from the mayor, his guards stopped messing around and really put their backs into it. She still wouldn't let go. Something had to give. And it did: with a screech the table began moving across the floor—along with Jennifer, Mayor Bradley, and all the mayor's guests, who were slowly dragged through the crowded restaurant. Everyone was watching. *Everyone.* Jennifer realized if she kept her job until tomorrow it would be a miracle.

Finally the woman could hold on no longer; her arms gave out and she let go. She hit the ground running. The security detail chased after her. She bobbed around as she had before entering the restaurant—apparently she couldn't find the door *again*. Jennifer began to seriously wonder if the Ghostbusters had lied about their involvement in the resolution of the Mercado crisis.

Then the woman located the door and, scrambling,

stumbled outside. The restaurant patrons looked on in fascination as the door swung shut. It was so quiet that you could hear a soufflé fall.

Mayor Bradley smiled and said in a voice loud enough for all to hear, "Never a dull moment."

That seemed a signal that the strange event was over. Silverware began to clink, soft chatter resumed, and everyone relaxed.

This is not on me, Jennifer thought, twisting the napkin in her lap. She prayed the mayor would see it that way, too.

21

Rowan pinned the motorcycle's throttle wide open. Buildings and trees blurred past and the wind ripped over the face of his new toy, making the eyes stream hot tears down its cheeks. He had no concern for his own safety at high speed, nor the toy's for that matter—why would he?

I have survived my own death. And I have possessed a second living human body. I have become an immortal god. The Fourth Cataclysm has begun, and no one can stop it.

An image of the Ghostbusters coming to the rescue flared in the usurped brain and Rowan twisted the slack mouth into a smirk. *They're just smart girls in sanitary worker outfits.* He thought of all the females who had humiliated him, calling him a dork and a nerd, or worse, pretending he didn't exist. He remembered Angelina Beltrano, the vivacious, curvaceous Latin pixie who had burst into giggles when, after four years of loving her from afar in high school, he had finally asked her, stammering, sweaty-palmed, to go to an after-the-football game dance in the gym with him.

"You're not kidding. You really aren't," she'd said, looking at him as if she couldn't quite believe it. Then she had run off to tell all her girlfriends. Her boyfriend heard about it within minutes and had dragged Rowan under the bleachers and beaten him to a pulp.

I'm going track that jerk down to the ends of the earth, and when I do, he'll beg for my forgiveness. But he won't get it. None of them will.

"What did you expect?" his father had said when Rowan had dragged himself home, broken and bloody, wearing nothing but his grass-stained underpants. "You're a weirdo, kid. You gotta face it." Then his father had chuckled at the sight of him, and his mother, unable to maintain a straight face, turned back for the kitchen. He hadn't shed a single tear when he learned his father had died of a heart attack. And he'd left his mother to fend for herself when he'd gotten accepted to MIT.

Let her see how it felt.

At MIT, he had focused solely, obsessively on his studies, and his dedication paid off when Professor Gupta took an interest in him and encouraged him to pursue a career in advanced physics. Dr. Gupta said he was a genius. A new world was opened to him! He had finally found his calling.

But he still had no friends, his own age or otherwise.

One evening as he was hiding in his dorm room bunk bed, browsing the Internet, he came across a post on a physics site that mentioned a "hilarious" TV interview on the University of Michigan station about the science of the paranormal. There was a link. It didn't take long for him to find other clips of it online. That was how he first became acquainted with the radical theories of Erin Gilbert and Abigail Yates, the woman he had recently possessed.

He found nothing about the interview hilarious; the razzing Yates endured on camera was uninspired and doltish, the kind of abuse he'd encountered from nose pickers in fourth grade. The content of her talk, however, was revelatory and revolutionary. The underlying principles of an entirely new branch of physical science, though they were hastily described in a venue designed for mockery, made perfect sense to him. His face flushing and his ears turning red, he jotted down the title of their book, and with considerable effort and no small expense acquired a rare copy under the table from its print-on-demand publisher— actually it was from a janitor, and it was passed to him through a crack in the warehouse door.

After much reading and study, and his own experimentation, he came to the conclusion that the authors had far underestimated the power requirements of the systems they described. He set out at once to find ways to boost power input exponentially, and reach the theoretical "bridge point," where the eternal barrier between the living and the dead became as substantial as smoke.

The authors had used an analogy in their book to explain the principle. A rock could be ground to powder, and that powder would still be recognizable under a microscopic or in a spectrometer as the same rock; but if the rock's temperature was raised sufficiently, and under specific conditions, its molecular characteristics would change: it would re-form into something else, something with new and different properties. Rowan had reasoned and independently proven that adding energy of the correct type and at the correct level was the key to cracking open the gates of hell.

Despite Dr. Yates's contributions to his own breakthroughs, or perhaps because of them, it had been a great pleasure to torment her, and it seemed appropriate that she be the first living human his spirit invaded. In a very real way she had instigated her own demonic possession. He was looking forward to overseeing her final and utter destruction.

Up the street, he could see the towering façade of the Mercado. His exhaustive study of ley lines had shown that the structure sat on the nexus of paranormal power and supernatural intrusion into this world. If he was to take his rightful place as sole lord of the dead, the coronation had to take place at the Mercado.

He parked the motorcycle at the curb and strode into the Mercado and through the ornate lobby, unrecognized, unrecognizable. He had put up with untold abuse from the tenants, even more from his boss. Repairing air conditioners. Cleaning *toilets*. Rage coursed through him. No matter. That life was over. Rowan North was dead.

And he had been reborn a god.

In his fine new body, he stepped up to the door of the generator room. Two uniformed cops left behind to protect the equipment sat drinking coffee, guarding the door. One of them looked at Rowan, who of course looked like the moronic Ghostbusters receptionist, Kevin.

"Hey, you can't come back here," the cop said.

"Interesting," Rowan-as-Kevin said. "Is that so?"

In a swift move, a move he'd never practiced or even seen attempted, he raised both well-muscled arms and punched them both in the jaw, one with each fist. The heads of the two cops snapped back, and they slumped unconscious.

Rowan was glee-struck. He stared at the meat puppet's biceps and said, "Oh, I should have worked out more when I was alive."

He kicked open the door to the generator room and walked inside, prepared to face irreparable damage. But there was nothing of the kind. The fools had only partially disassembled his device, and they had left the pieces lying about! Even better, they had made no move to destroy any of it. They had assumed that "dead" meant "dead," and that the original owner would not be returning to claim anything. Idiots! He bent down and picked up the heaviest pieces easily, like they were made of Styrofoam.

"Oh, I *definitely* should have worked out more."

He began to reassemble the device piece by piece, something he could have done blindfolded, as well as dead. He needed to hurry, though. The Ghostbusters knew he hadn't left this world, and it wouldn't take long for them to figure out what he was doing and where he had to be doing it.

The meat puppet had deft fingers, and putting everything back in place didn't take long. It was oddly amusing to watch its reflection in the banks of mirrors, doing his bidding like a robot. He wanted to make it pull down its pants and dance a jig, and certainly would have, had he not been so pressed for time. Holding the usurped body's breath, he made its finger flip the power switch.

There was a horrible pause. It lasted so long that Rowan began to have doubts . . .

Then it fired up. The room blazed with light as the machine pulsed and glowed, and bolts of lightning crackled out of it. As the intensity grew, raw electrical energy snapped and swirled around the room, building, building . . .

Ka-boom! Every one of the mirrors exploded outward, sending a mist of sparkling fragments cascading from all directions, and in the same instant, supernatural lights and spirits blasted, howling through the empty frames and into this world! Wisps of phantoms and skeletons; imps, ghouls, banshees, zombies. The ghosts of evil people who had died centuries ago—mass murderers, serial killers, hit men, assassins.

The deafening cacophony summoned a security guard, who raced past the still-unconscious police officers and into the generator room. His eyes grew huge and his jaw dropped at the spectacle before him. His arms and legs began to shake. Rowan-as-Kevin shot him his most menacing glare—in a shard of mirror still stuck to a frame, his eyes were glowing red. And then he growled like the fiend he had become.

The guard staggered backward with his hands up in a gesture of surrender.

"Hey, man," he said, "you do you."

Then the insect ran out of the room.

22

Erin ran down the busy New York sidewalk. Passersby, oblivious to her frantic urgency, snarled at her as she jostled in front and cut them off. She paid them no mind; her one and only goal was to reach the Mercado before it was too late. The stitch in her side was killing her, but she pressed on, ignoring the red lights, ducking through the auto traffic. She had no choice. Abby wasn't answering the phone and she was almost positive that Rowan was back. The world was in terrible danger and she seemed to be the only person on the planet who knew it. And of course, if she shouted it at the people who yelled at her and made obscene hand gestures, they wouldn't believe her.

A terrible thought crossed her mind. What if *Abby* didn't believe her? What if that was why she hadn't called back? Erin had no proof. It was just another theory. All she had was a picture Rowan had drawn in their book. But no, Abby had always believed her. And believed *in* her.

Then suddenly the sidewalk started to tremble and ripple underfoot like the surface of a rushing torrent. The complacent and inward-looking expressions on the faces of her fellow pedestrians switched to alarm—and then to sheer panic as a loud *boom!* tore through the air. Erin looked up ahead. In the distance she saw the distinctive outline of the Mercado building. Brilliant lights were shooting upward from it, impossibly bright lights that illuminated the afternoon sky.

Erin had no doubt what was going on. And what was going on was the worst thing she could conceive of. It was the end of the world.

Sucking it up, she ran faster, pumping her arms and high-kicking.

At the Ghostbusters headquarters, Abby looked on uncomfortably as Holtzmann worked to repair the proton packs that she had wrecked while the spirit of Rowan possessed her. She had no memory of how that had felt or what she had done. Part of her was massively grateful for that, but the objective scientist part was curious, wishing they had more data about what Rowan had become so they could find a way to defeat him. All signs pointed to a resumption of his plan to destroy the barrier and unleash hell's whirlwind.

Fighting for calm, she punched in Erin's number again. No answer again. She could picture Erin holed up in her apartment with bedcovers pulled up to her chin, soggy tissues strewn everywhere, pouting and/or grieving for her lost days of approval from people who had never met her and never would.

Patty was fretting, too. Abby could see it etched in her eyes. Abby finally glimpsed the full horror of the word "impotent" and why men feared it so.

A *snap* came from Holtz's worktable and Abby glanced over. "Are they ready?" she asked hopefully. "We've got to get to the Mercado and save Kevin." She shook her head in sympathy. "As if he hasn't been through enough already."

"If you weren't so strong, you would have done much less damage to these," Holtzmann informed her.

"I'm sorry I got possessed!" she lashed back, frustrated beyond words. "I guess I should have thought that through more." Her sarcasm underscored just how worried she was. She suddenly realized that the phone had finally stopped ringing at Erin's end and that she was about to get her voice mail. "Erin! Where are you? Rowan took Kevin. We need your help!"

She hung up. "What a surprise," she said to no one in particular. "Never there when you need her."

The Fourth Cataclysm had arrived.

And it was exactly as advertised.

Panicking pedestrians filled the sidewalk, all of them running away from the Mercado as fast as they could. Their eyes were huge, their mouths gaping. Erin fought to keeping moving against the flow. A man tripped and fell and people just stepped on him in their haste to get away. He managed to crawl into a doorway, out of the torrent. He sat there, clearly in shock, clutching the torn knees of his business suit. What she saw around her was mass hysteria, and it was every inch as ugly as the video on Jennifer Lynch's computer. Then she spotted someone she sort of knew in the throng sweeping toward her. It was Tonya, the glow-in-the-dark eye-makeup mogul of nakedeyes .com. She was wearing leopard-print leggings, a nubby lime-green car coat, and teal flats. How did that even go together? Erin felt a microsecond of reassurance about her own history of fashion decisions. Despite all the subtle digs she had endured of late, conservative clothes never went out of style.

Unless of course the world ended; then all bets were off.

Tonya swept past, her signature eye makeup melting, running in fluorescent stripes down her cheeks. Car horns blared as drivers wedged their vehicles into the already packed streets, bumping bumpers, jockeying for a few inches of space to get the heck out of there. And no wonder: huge red clouds had formed above the structure, billowing and pluming until they spread across the entire sky and turned day into night. The Mercado was shimmering with evil light, as if it was straddling the dividing line between the world of the living and the world of the dead, containing the vast energies beneath it like the towering cone of a volcano.

And then the volcano blew.

Ghosts poured out of the building and flew up into the roiling sky—phantoms of all ages from all eras: a child from Victorian times, a flapper from the Roaring Twenties, a mobster, and a pot-smoking hippie. And in varying stages of decay—limbs missing, eyes hanging from sockets—and in all manner of diabolic manifestation: fangs, claws, glowing eyes, eager to tear and rip and destroy. As Erin looked on, they dispersed to all parts of Manhattan.

He had done it. Rowan had succeeded. The barrier was down. And with it down, it wasn't just Manhattan that would bleed and die. It was the entire world.

"I need my gear," she said aloud. She had to get to Ghostbusters headquarters as fast as she could.

She waved down a taxi that miraculously pulled up beside her. Erin couldn't believe her luck. The cabbie pulled over, surprisingly relaxed given the complete uproar around them. But he was going in the opposite direction of the fleeing traffic.

"Where're you going?" he asked her.

"Chinatown," she told him.

"Nah." He drove off, leaving her to throw her hands up in impotent frustration. Then she watched as he came to a red light and braked. A ghost flew over to the cab, swung open the backseat door, and got in. The cabbie screamed.

The grim satisfaction she felt was wrong, so wrong . . . but so, well, satisfying.

The mayhem continued all over New York:

A couple ran around a corner, screaming as a ghost opened his trench coat and flashed them. But as he was only a skeleton, what he had to expose was nothing.

A woman fled to the entrance of a subway station, then stopped dead in her tracks as a ghost rat floated up from the stairs, squeaking and confused. Then a stream of ghost rats joined the first one and she fled in terror.

In a nearby Clark's Coffee, a group of patrons ran to the window to check out the commotion. Nursing a coffee, Dean Harold Filmore was thinking deep thoughts about his application to work at CERN and make some real bucks, since university administrators were still, in his opinion, woefully underpaid, and sexy babes were unlikely to seek him out for his intellectual prowess. Therefore he was blissfully unaware of what the ruckus was about, aware only that some kind of flash mob or something was gathering outside.

"Huh. City College must've let out."

He smirked, turning to the patron next to him to gauge his reaction. But the man sitting next to him was not a man at all. It was a hideous thing.

Filmore screamed. It growled back, face expanding into an elongated nightmare of glowing eyes and fangs. Then it went on the attack, coming right at him. He leapt from his stool and the ghost harried him out the door and into a maelstrom of multidimensional entities phasing in and out of existence.

She was right, Gilbert was right. He fled down the street, grabbing on to people who were as frightened as he was and crying, "Help me! You've got to help me! Hide me!"

But at this point it was every New Yorker for themselves and his pleas for help went unanswered. The ghost was still tracking him, bearing down; he stumbled along and slammed into a newsstand. He fell into a row of fanned-out copies of the *New York Post* with Erin's face plastered on them. "Nosebusters!" the headline proclaimed, and as he crashed into the shelf, his own nose smashed hard into the unyielding wood and pain shot into his skull.

The irony was not lost on him as the awning on the stand collapsed and the rest of the shelves fell over on top of him. Newspapers, cartons of cigarettes, and candy bars cascaded over him. He prayed that the ghost would move on, deciding it would be too much trouble to search through the debris for him.

A ghost chased me down the street.

Then suddenly the layers of debris above him began to shuffle skyward, like dirt clods being dug up by a busy dog, and he began to whimper. *A ghost is looking for me.*

If only he had believed her. *But her sources were suspect. Nonexistent. In this day and age, evidence can be manufactured so easily . . .*

Copies of *Newsweek* and *Sports Illustrated* shot into the crimson air. A cascade of loose cigarettes and a rain of Jolly Rancher hard candies pelted him.

I was wrong, he thought.

And he was wrong again.

The ghost was not looking for him.

The ghost had found him.

Eyes bulging, huge, toothy maw opening, it attacked.

The showdown at the Mercado was under way: police, SWAT, and National Guard troops had massed in front of Rowan's stronghold. All weapons were trained on the building, but so far, the order to open fire had not come. Open fire at what? There was nothing to aim at except the building itself. Large glowing fissures had erupted from underneath the structure, as if something so large that it could not be contained was cracking it open like an egg. The soldiers and police officers were braced for battle, but the standoff was working on their nerves. The mayhem in the streets surrounding the building was monumental; it seemed like a waste of time to stand on alert when demons or ghosts or whatever they were wreaked havoc all over Manhattan. Scores of targets presented themselves most tantalizingly, but eyes and gun barrels remained focused on the Mercado, where the ultimate threat was housed.

Homeland Security Agents Hawkins and Rorke strode toward the building, confidently waving to the troops.

"Don't worry," Agent Hawkins assured those within hearing range of his mic. "Everything is going to be okay." He spoke into his headset. "Bring it out."

A big military truck rumbled down the rows of personnel. A giant weapon was affixed to it. It was a proton cannon that had been produced after reverse-engineering the objects confiscated from the so-called sad, lonely Ghostbusters. The cannon was aimed up at the building and Hawkins, for one, couldn't wait to see it in action.

A police officer ran up to the two agents and gestured to the cannon.

"What is that thing?" he demanded. "Do you guys know what you're doing?"

Another cop said, "You've tested this thing, right?"

Rorke was impatient to get under way. "Stand back, friend," he said to the second cop. "We've got a city to save."

When Agent Hawkins gave the order to fire, a beam shot out of the cannon and hit the building. The cracks from underneath the building got larger. The Mercado shone brighter. The proton charge was definitely making things worse.

"Huh," Hawkins said, surprised.

Rowan's borrowed body glowed a beautiful green as he directed it to step out onto the top ledge of the Mercado. Wind from the brewing storm buffeted its face as he scanned the broad street in both directions. The turnout of adversaries pitted against him was impressive, too many to count, and why bother. Puny mortals couldn't hope to defeat him now; it was too late and too little. The masses of the once dead storming into this world awaited his command, awaited their chance for payback—some of which was a long time coming, centuries, in fact. Every single living person gazing up at him now in awe was dead as well, but didn't know it. And if he had anything to say about it, they would all die horribly.

And . . . guess what? He had *everything* to say about it!

He spread wide his body's arms and gazed down pleasantly at the soldiers and cops.

"Dear brave men of the protection services industry," he began, "thank you for coming to my party. But instead of fighting . . . I would like to see you dance."

From out of the supercharged ether, through the boiling columns of light, the Bee Gees's "You Should be Dancing" began to play because Rowan willed it so. The music was so loud that as it traveled away from the paranormal nexus, the circular shock wave broke every window on every street, one after another. Even at a great distance he could see the cops and soldiers below him shifting anxiously, clearly confused and disheartened by this unforeseen development. Glee thrummed through the borrowed body's bones, even as it responded to the plucky disco beat. The broad shoulders twitched, the torso twisted almost imperceptibly this way and that, and the feet began to rhythmically backpedal.

It was show time.

He pointed the puppet's hands down at the assembled humans and a barrage of psychic energy shot out of the centers of the palms. The blurs of supernatural power were like guided missiles, seeking out and blasting into the chests of the agents, cops, and soldiers. At the instant of invasion, their bodies jolted, their weapons fell from their hands, and they stood frozen. But their minds remained free to puzzle out what had happened and what might happen next. Fear radiated upward in delicious waves from the street below.

With a flourish, Rowan struck a familiar disco pose: one arm extended in the air, finger pointed, hip thrust out, chin pulled in. Billboards filled with his image. From below there was a rustling of movement, like wind stirring piles of autumn leaves, as every person for as far as he could see in all directions assumed the same pose. The instruments of social control were in his command, to do with as he pleased. And it pleased him to make a mockery of their power, of their deluded sense of personal freedom and ambition. He could have made them kneel before him and bang their foreheads against the ground, but where was the fun in that?

Taking his cue from the music, he fell into the dance routine John Travolta had performed in *Saturday Night Fever*. For a physicist and nerd, Rowan had always been quite light on his feet. And he could tear up some of that Bee Gees. Unable to stop themselves, the massed troops followed his dynamic lead, dancing the same steps, spinning the same arm movements, and making the same facial expressions in unison. Fifty thousand or more mirrored his every gesture. Their eyes were the only things he allowed them to retain power over. And that was so they could gaze up at him and cower as their limbs and bodies jerked uncontrollably, knowing that the humiliation would stop only when he made it stop, imagining with dread what might come next.

A terrible laugh bubbled up from his throat. A laugh perfectly mimicked by the helpless thousands below. A laugh that echoed like a roar.

Oh yes, it was good to be a god.

23

Out of the garage and into the street, siren blaring, ECTO-1 blasted at top speed: a red and white hearse, apparently late to a funeral—perhaps even theirs. The early afternoon sky had turned dark as midnight and jagged crackles of lightning arced through it. Holtzmann lead-footed the gas and the heavy car roared away from Chinatown. As the g-force of acceleration squashed Abby into the backseat, she couldn't help but notice the extra room beside her. For what had to be the two dozenth time, she wondered where the heck Erin was. Surely she was seeing all this on TV if not in person. How could she not get in contact with them?

Unless she can't. Abby pictured the vengeful ghost of Mrs. Barnard as Erin had described her. Erin had told her that Mrs. B had "gone away," but what if Rowan had let her back in? What if she was hunting down Erin at this very moment? Or had already done something horrible to her? And it didn't have to be Mrs. Barnard; there seemed to be a bottomless supply of evil ghosts available.

Fear for her friend's safety overcame her disappointment and hurt at once again being abandoned. This was a rescue mission, that was for damn sure, and the list of those to be rescued had doubled from one to two.

Ay, chihuahua, she thought but did not say, as Holtzmann rounded a corner on two wheels and the long, straight street ahead came into view, a canyon of gray buildings pressed side to side, and way down near the end, an incredible brilliance, like ten thousand klieg lights were blazing up into the sky. It was so bright it hurt her eyes to look. They drew closer and she could see it had to be the Mercado, a throbbing, glowing tower of supernatural light. Abby knew the shimmering was an artifact of supercharged particles, and the sheer scope of what they were dealing with rattled her a little. Unnatural clouds roiled above the building, blood red tinged with black, a sky soiled by the upwelling of pure evil. Hell had come to Manhattan.

From the looks of the Mercado, the number of people in need of rescue had jumped from two to a minimum of eight and a half million. And that was just for starters.

As long as the gates stayed open, there would be no end to the invasion. The meltdown they were facing would quickly go global.

As they drew closer to the nexus, the street became more and more crowded with fleeing pedestrians, and even though the siren was howling, they had to slow down. Holtzmann tried to swerve around the swarms of panicked people flowing in a river against them, but made better progress driving straight ahead. Patty grabbed the bullhorn microphone and hit the on switch. Her voice bellowed out of the speaker atop the roof, "Respect the siren, please."

No one did. The pedestrians continued to pile up in front of the hearse, waves of them, bodies bumping off the hood and fenders, impeding their way. Patty got back on the loudspeaker.

"Hey! We're trying to save your asses, so *get out of the way*!"

The crowd thinned a little, but as it did, and as ECTO-1 crept forward, they came upon a cluster of overturned pretzel and hot dog carts blocking the street from curb to curb. Holtzmann stopped, and the three of them hopped out of the car to move the nearest ones out of the way. As they took hold of a hot dog cart and started to lift it up-

right, a fat green ghost with an enormous mouth and a ro-
tund stomach flew out from under the lid of the warming
compartment.

"Whoa!" Abby cried, as they all jerked backward.

The ghost—Abby immediately nicknamed him
"Slimer"—flew past them and dove into the driver's seat
of their idling hearse. Before they could do anything, it
peeled off and drove off wildly away. Abby, Holtzmann,
and Patty just stared as it sideswiped cars all along the
street.

"Well, I guess we're walking," Abby deadpanned.

On foot, proton packs shouldered, the Ghostbusters
set off up the street. Fleeing Manhattanites swept past
without giving them a second look. They hadn't gone far
when they heard strains of odd music riding the hellish
breeze. It sounded like an old-timey marching band, only
twisted and scary. The tune lurched and the drums stumbled, and some of the instruments played crazy solos
full of sour notes.

Up ahead, Abby saw a huge crowd of ghosts watching
what had to be the Macy's Parade. But it was the parade
from the 1920s. There were huge parade balloons floating
above the street, figures of weird, psycho-looking cats,
frightening insects with stingers and teeth, and a Pinocchio with a nose like a gigantic russet potato. Abby noted
that just like the current parade, there was that disturbing
fat Santa and demented elf.

"People had a much higher tolerance for creepy back
then," Patty said.

"Still," Abby said, "at least a parade is something happy.
Keep them busy and in a good mood."

As she spoke she had an uh-oh moment. The weird balloons all turned as one and appeared to stare right at
them. Abby felt a twinge in her stomach as they all started
floating down the street toward them.

"Uh . . . guys . . ." Holtzmann said.

The faces of the balloons had gone from creepy weird

to chillingly murderous—and they were accelerating. It was clear from their inflated body language they meant the Ghostbusters no good.

"Pop some balloons! Now!" Abby said.

She fired her proton wand and an immense homicidal kitten exploded with a loud whap! Patty grazed the ear of the creepy elf, and the resulting pinhole leak caused it to fly wildly up, up, and away, a black dot lost in the red clouds above them. Haunted parade balloon versus proton pack was really no contest. The Ghostbusters worked methodically, and in a few minutes the street was strewn with strips of brightly colored rubber skin. Working together, the three of them popped a honking big one that was bearing down on them. When it went boom, the Stay Puft Marshmallow Man balloon in its sailor suit floated forward from behind it. Before they could get out of the way, the immense white balloon toppled onto them, knocking them down. It pinned them flat to the street, then pressed its torso down like a gigantic pillow, trying to smother them. They were trapped within inches of each other, but unable to move. The squeaking of the balloon skin made it hard to hear.

"I can't reach the trigger!" Abby cried.

Struggling to breathe, Holtzmann said, "This is always how I pictured my death . . ."

"Smothered by a Class Six possession with temporal displacement?" Abby said.

"Oh, it's a Class Six? No, never mind."

Then the sidewalk rocked with a tremendous bang and the crushing weight lifted. The haunted Stay Puft inflatable exploded in all directions.

Erin stepped through the shower of shredded ersatz marshmallow waving her proton wand around like a gunslinger.

"Proton guns are all well and good. But sometimes you just need a little help from the Swiss Army," she said, holding up a Swiss Army knife with the blade extended.

"Oh, there you are," Holtzmann said.

Erin grinned at Abby. "Couldn't let you have all the fun."

Abby smiled a good-to-have-you-back smile, then said, "Okay, let's go save this city and get our receptionist back."

F rom his perch atop the Mercado, Rowan had a clear view of the street in both directions. He could see four ants moving against the tide of refugee ants. They were wearing familiar sand-colored uniforms with orange chest stripes and had angular packs on their backs.

His voice boomed down from the Art Deco heights. "Girls are always late. Finally, here they come. Let's give them a proper New York welcome, shall we?"

"G irls are always late . . . late . . . late . . ." echoed between the rows of tall buildings.

Erin, Abby, Holtzmann, and Patty shared a look of disgust as they crossed a suddenly lifeless Times Square. On the other side of it, the Mercado loomed, glowing with an unearthly light as bloodred storm clouds roiled above it. Row upon row of police and soldiers stood frozen next to it. From a distance they looked like statues to Erin, with one hand all pointing up—to or at what? Or was it a salute? No way to tell, she decided. But that they apparently couldn't move deeply concerned her.

She wasn't alone in that. They advanced more cautiously, on full alert. With a bright flash, Kevin's face appeared on the video screens around Times Square. His dazzling teeth were ten feet tall.

"Ah, there they are," his voice said. "The Ghostbusters. All dressed up and nowhere to bust. I'll tell you what. I can help you out. Oh, and nice not knowing you."

Suddenly, all the buildings and modern electronic billboards started to melt and dissolve away, revealing the

Ghost of Times Square Past—shabby, squalid, all glowing and otherworldly.

Erin took in the shimmering panorama of its entire history—stables, carriage houses, music halls, hotels, theaters, brothels, pawnshops, flophouses, and seedy bars. The ghostly denizens of the place across time were there, too, armed for close combat and itching for some bloodshed. There was a dude in a Revolutionary War hat with a cavalry sword, a mobster in a fedora and overcoat wielding a bloody ax, street criminals with knives and broken bottles, mumbling psychopaths with claw hammers; in other words, the full spectrum of homicidal bilgewater.

The scariest of the ghosts stopped harassing the somewhat less scary ghosts, and glared as if the Ghostbusters had invaded their sacred turf. Growling and shouting, they seemed to be working themselves up for a battle.

"I've never been good in a fight," Erin said.

"Well, you'd better get good at it," Abby said. "Power up!"

Erin and the others switched on their proton packs just as the ghost army rushed them, a mob of incorporeal monsters out for blood. Terrified but with nowhere to retreat, the Ghostbusters battled them with their proton streams and all the wonderful toys Holtzmann had recently invented. Erin used her beam to grab hold of a pimp ghost in a ridiculous wide-brimmed fuzzy hat and bell-bottoms, and threw him into the gang of deceased street punks. They kicked up like bowling pins, flying backward and into the ghosts behind them. Abby and the others picked up on what she was doing immediately, and started using ghosts caught in their beams like clubs, bashing the trailing evil spirits left and right. It was a messy but effective technique; using it, they managed to keep the waves of ghosts from overrunning them.

Patty used her "ghost chipper," a device that sucked in

a ghost, chopped it up into ectoplasmic bits, and shot the debris out the back like a burst of exhaust. She also had a proton sidearm that Holtzmann had made for her. Abby put on her proton glove, which she used to punch holes in the "bodies" of her oncoming phantom attackers. Holtzmann had also created two kinds of grenades—"air filters" and "test tubes"—plus a proton grenade launcher for Erin and a "drop-down" gun for herself.

As Erin sent a drug pusher ghost cartwheeling off toward Rockefeller Center, Abby used her proton wand to smash the face of a flasher pervert ghost that had broken through their guard and was almost on top of her. The beam made ectoplasm burst in a plume from its head and it rained down on them in big, gooey spatters. Explosions rocked the square. Erin cut her gaze and saw Patty throw a second grenade behind the line of approaching ghosts. When it went off with a resounding crack, it sent the spirits flying, arms and legs flailing, ectoplasm exploding.

Holtzmann hit a trigger on her proton pack and two smaller weapons popped out. She caught both and, a skilled deadeye, started taking down ghosts with dual-hand ambidextrous precision.

Patty gave her a look as if to say "Where'd you get those?"

"Just a little bonus I gave myself," Holtzmann told her. "I'll whip you up a set if we manage to not die right now."

Patty sent another ghost crashing into the crowd of surrounding ghosts, knocking them off their feet. The mob of spirits hesitated as they picked themselves up from the street. Instead of regaining their courage, they seemed to have lost it. The remaining winos, hookers, and purse snatchers shrank back, scared of the Ghostbusters.

Abby looked at the cowering ghosts, completely charged up. "All right! Anybody want a piece of this? Bring it on!"

"Okay, amp it down, tiger," Erin said. "Miles to go."

Abby nodded, but then walked totally badass through

the crowd of ghosts toward the Mercado building as Erin and the Ghostbusters followed her. The ghosts made way for them, and as the evil spirits melted back, they looked very intimidated.

Approaching the Mercado, the Ghostbusters filed through the frozen ranks of police and National Guard. They had not moved a muscle; all were locked in what looked like the famous John Travolta disco pose, finger pointing up into the air. Right out in front were the two Homeland Security agents, even more tight-lipped than usual.

"Seems odd," Abby said.

Odder still, Erin could see the eyeballs of Hawkins and Rorke moving in their rigid faces, tracking them as they passed.

A familiar roar from behind made her whirl around. Slimer tore past them in ECTO-1, and a group of partying ghosts had piled into the coffin compartment and clung to the roof of the car. They sang and yelled drunkenly as Slimer sped off.

"Well, at least somebody's having a good time," Abby said.

When they reached the closed doors to the Mercado's lobby, Erin noticed a crack in the ground directly underneath them; the crack pulsed with unnatural light.

"All right, stay back," Abby said, lifting up her proton wand to fire at the door.

Before she could do that, the doors slowly, eerily opened for them. Clouds of smoke rolled out of the lobby onto the sidewalk. It smelled like a mixture of burning hair and sulfur. The Ghostbusters wrinkled their noses— and went in.

The lobby had been transformed since Erin had last seen it. Everything was covered with ectoplasm: walls, stairs, furniture, and floor. Erin took a step and immediately slipped and fell, butt-planting in a puddle of slime. She got to her feet without comment; there were more pressing matters. A whirlpool of evil energy was slowly churning in the middle of the floor.

"All right, let's get down to the basement," Abby said. "We'll start by turning off his little experiment."

As they started over to the basement stairwell door, a grand piano shot past them, its lid propped up. Skiing on the goo on the floor, it crashed into doorway, completely blocking it, and the lid came down with a bang.

Erin shuddered as the keys began to move of their own accord, tinkling out an inappropriately merry tune.

All heads cranked around at movement from the lobby's grand staircase, behind and above them.

Erin looked up and saw a glowing, shirtless figure. It was Kevin, and it wasn't. He was much paler, his face was drawn, and there were circles under his ferociously beaming eyes.

"Kevin?" Abby said.

"Is this what this thing's name is?" It was Kevin's voice, only roid raging. "He seemed more like a Chet to me. I see there's five of you now."

Abby, Holtzmann, and Patty looked as confused as Erin felt, then they all saw the Mercado tenant standing next to them, his eyes bugging, jaw dropped.

"Who are you?" Erin said.

"I was napping, I just came down to get my mail—"

"Get out of here!" Abby said.

The tenant ran out the front doors. A second later they heard him scream outside.

"Probably should've given him a heads up as to what's out there," Patty said.

"Well, you've had a long journey," Rowan-as-Kevin said. "You look winded. Have a seat."

From all corners of the trashed lobby, chairs slid over the slime and came to a stop behind the Ghostbusters. As Holtzmann slowly sat down, her chair pulled out from under her. She dropped to the ground on her backside with a muffled "Ooooof."

Kevin/Rowan chuckled and his blue eyes flashed.

"I appreciate the joke," Holtzmann said as she struggled up. "It's a classic."

"I have to compliment you," Kevin/Rowan said. "I'm surprised you made it this far. You're intelligent, courageous, and I'm impressed. I'm willing to let you remain as my sex companions."

"I'm willing to shove my foot up your ass," Abby said.

"I saw your grandmother on the other side," Kevin/Rowan told her. "I kicked her in the face."

"Yeah, listen," Abby said. "I know you're real cozy in the form of Kevin, but time to hop out. We like him."

"Yeah, he just started figuring out our phones!" Holtzmann added.

"As you wish," Kevin/Rowan said.

Rowan exited Kevin's body in a flash of vapor. Kevin was left unconscious; his body began to go limp and crumple, toppling forward. Erin and the others raced up the stairs and caught him as he fell, but were off balance and couldn't hold him. All five of them tumbled down the stairs, landing in a tangled heap on the lobby floor.

"What form would you prefer I take?" Rowan's voice said as they regained their wits.

"Nothing fancy," Holtzmann said. "Just keep it simple."

"I'll tell you what I prefer," Patty said. "A nice little friendly ghost. Like in a sheet."

"Oh?" Rowan said.

Before their eyes he transformed into a smiling white cartoon ghost. It looked very happy and nonthreatening.

"Is this what you want?" Ghost Rowan said. "Adorable clip art?"

"Yes," Patty said, clearly relieved. "I have no problem with that. Thank you."

Ghost Rowan's smile remained, but the expression in his eyes—which shifted from happy to way, way too happy—made it seem suddenly sinister.

"I don't know," Erin said. "That looks a little murdery to me."

The smile was so happy and so frozen that it indeed looked murdery.

"Hmmm," Abby said. "It *is* starting to feel different."

"This works for me," Ghost Rowan said.

And with that, the ghostly form began to grow larger, the sinister look so pronounced there was no denying it.

"All right," Patty said, "I didn't know this was going to be a development."

Ghost Rowan grew bigger and bigger, towering over them. Erin and the others started backing up—memories of being squashed by the Stay Puft Marshmallow Man were still quite raw.

"This isn't good," Abby said.

When Ghost Rowan shoved his cartoon hands toward them, it was like being hit by a Category 6 hurricane; the blast of 175-mile-per-hour wind blew them off their feet and through the open doors.

Sailing backward out the lobby entrance, they landed on their proton packs and, shooting showers of sparks, skidded at high speed across the pavement. Helplessly, they slid into the front line of agents, soldiers, and cops. Like dominoes, the frozen figures toppled into one another and fell to the ground.

"Strike!" Rowan said, mixing metaphors.

When he laughed again the hurricane returned and there was a shrill crash. Erin looked up to see every window blown out of the Mercado, shattering sheets of glass followed closely by furniture and personal belongings. The accumulated junk of all the building's tenants smashed down onto the sidewalk and everything was dusted in glittering fragments—it was a massive, simultaneous eviction.

Then the whole building began to shake, and with it the sidewalk they were lying on. As they tried vainly to scramble to their feet, the Mercado itself exploded, disintegrating into an immense swirling cloud of dust and debris. Terrifying cartoon ghost Rowan emerged as if from a cocoon, out of the middle of the churning chaos—he was bigger than a skyscraper! Terrifying Ghost Rowan roared down at them.

"Run!" Erin cried.

They jumped up and ran with the gigantic ghost in hot pursuit. Erin ripped a page from the few action films she'd seen, turning around and backpedaling while firing her proton pack at it. The beam hit Ghost Rowan in the side, lighting up ten stories of his happy spirit body. He let out a scream of pain and stopped, bent over clutching the ectoplasm-leaking wound.

Seizing the moment, the Ghostbusters raced for the next corner, then cut down a narrow alley and hid behind a Dumpster.

"My man was taking some real creative liberties with what we agreed upon," Patty said, puffing for breath.

The ground shook as Ghost Rowan approached. They crouched lower and flattened against the wall as he appeared at the mouth of the alley. Erin only got a glimpse of him, because thankfully he didn't stop and look their way, but that was long enough to see his cartoon sheet was badly scorched and he was limping along and snarling like a zombie—a fifteen-hundred-foot-tall zombie! As he passed, his foot came down on top of a parked car and crushed it like an aluminum can.

"See, that's just off-brand," Patty said as the ground-shaking thuds grew more and more faint.

"What do we do now?" Erin said.

"We need to get back there and fire into the portal with more power," Abby said. "If we can do that, then it could cause a reverse reaction."

Ghost Rowan wailed in the distance, still looking for them. It sounded like he was flipping cars and tearing buildings apart—Godzilla style.

"More power?" Erin said. "Do we not have our packs set to max now? Because it does feel like this would be the time for that!"

"We're at max," Holtzmann said. "Rowan's got everything too energized. Which is why I suggest the following . . . Now, it's a little risky. It's called 'crossing the stream.'"

"The thing that was so powerful our atoms could implode?" Erin said. "That's 'a little risky'?"

Patty looked around the corner and reported back that Ghost Rowan was turning his head in a full circle like an owl scouring the intersecting streets for any sign of them.

"I mean, he's really just doing his own thing now," Patty said.

"Holtz is right," Abby said. "If successful, it could cause a reverse reaction that would pull any ionized ectomatter back into its dimension of origin."

"And if it's not successful," Erin said, "then this is most likely not only a suicide mission but one that involves the most painful death conceivable of all time."

"That's definitely a downside," Abby said.

"Well, we don't have much of a choice, do we?" Erin said.

They dashed out of the alley and retraced their steps to what had once been the front of a Manhattan landmark. There was virtually nothing left aboveground. The lobby floor had disappeared, revealing the cyclonic supernatural portal below. Awestruck and disoriented by the rotation, Erin stopped short, lost her balance on some rubble, and for a terrible second leaned out over the edge of the maelstrom. The power emanating from it withered her and made her knees go soft. Holtzmann grabbed the collar of her uniform and quickly pulled her back to safety.

"Okay," Abby said, "fire them up!"

With their customary whine, the packs powered up, and all four Ghostbusters discharged their wands into the spinning portal. As Erin aimed her beam she saw Ghost

Rowan down the street—a hundred stories high, he was hard to miss—and at the same moment he spotted her. Ghost Rowan started lumbering toward them like a maniac skyscraper.

"He's coming!" Erin said. "Cross them up!"

He was already on the far edge of Times Square.

Erin entangled her beam with Abby's, Holtzmann's, and Patty's. With a tremendous jolt four beams became one, and everything began to shake. Their arms. Their legs. Their heads. And the focal point of the beam shook as well, but straining, they managed to keep it near the center of the whirlpool. A fraction of a second later the portal lit up like Christmas in hell, but it didn't reverse.

"The portal's too strong," Abby said as they quickly stood down. "We still don't have enough power to reverse it."

"How do we get more?" Erin said.

"We need to one-eighty the polarity with a high-concentration electron blast," Holtzmann said. "We just need my negative-charge containment canisters."

"Where are they?" Patty said.

At that instant ECTO-1, still driven by the hearse-jacking Slimer, sped around the corner and raced toward them. A gaudy female Slimer was hanging all over him. There were even more drunken ghosts hanging off the car, which swerved wildly.

"On top of our car," Holtzmann said.

"Erin, remember how we used to flush cherry bombs down the toilet in high school?" Abby said.

"Just light 'em up and toss 'em in?"

As they watched the oncoming car, Slimer veered with one hand on the wheel and the other squeezing Slimer babe, this to avoid the looming portal. The unsmooth move sent the hearse into a four-wheel skid, which the drunken passengers cheered.

"Yep," Abby said. "Let's narrow the target." She pointed with the business end of her proton wand, indicating a pair of streetlamps across the street from the portal. No other instruction was needed. They took aim and fired at the bases of the streetlights. When the beams hit the bottoms of the lamp poles, they exploded, and the streetlights crashed down across the road next to the portal.

Slimer was in the middle of a lip-lock with Slimette when the poles went down, blocking his intended route. He cut the wheel over to miss the collision without touching the brakes. Big mistake. His ghost eyes grew wide as he realized there was no way to avoid the portal.

The ECTO-1 zoomed up a ramplike piece of tilted cement on the edge of the abyss and went airborne. As the car nosed down toward the spinning eye of the portal, Slimer and his lady friend screamed a duet in the front seat.

"Aim for the silver canister!" Holtzmann said. "Now!"

They blasted their beams into the canister on the car's roof an instant before it plummeted into the portal. Half in, half out—*ba-boom!* A blinding flash of light and a shockwave sent the Ghostbusters flying backward. Erin left her stomach on the ground while her body once again arced helplessly through empty space at high speed. *This is really getting old,* she thought, then hit pavement with a bone-jarring crash and slid out of control on her back.

Shakily, she regained her feet. When she looked up she saw the portal had stopped spinning and changed color. Then it started to turn slowly in the opposite direction, rapidly picking up speed. The ground beneath her rumbled, a howling wind rose up, and the portal started sucking everything incorporeal back toward it. The creepy balloon floats—Potato Nose Pinocchio, the Strong Man, Uncle Sam, Crazy Rabid Chihuahua—went in and vanished down the spinning drain. All the ghosts they had encountered—including Gertrude Aldridge—were sucked past them, windmilling, clawing, and screaming, back into the bottomless pit whence they came. The biggest, baddest ghost of all, Ghost Rowan was clinging desperately to the side of a skyscraper while the lesser spirits he had summoned were vacuumed up like ants.

"It's working!" Erin said.

Buffeted by the supernatural wind, they watched the incredible number of released spirits tumble by. A creepy clown ghost they hadn't seen before flew past their heads.

"Glad we didn't have to deal with that one . . ." Patty said.

The clown suddenly reappeared above them, fighting wildly hand over hand to hang on and not be swept away. It got right up in Patty's face, straining to keep its grip.

"*Ahhhhh!*" she cried.

The suction was too powerful; creepy clown let go, and like a leaf in a hurricane it zipped away so fast it was like it had suddenly disappeared. Ghost Rowan was hanging on to the building with both arms, fighting the force.

"He's too strong," Erin said. "We can't close the portal with him still there!"

"I'll get him in!" Abby said.

"What are you talking about?"

"I'll get him to chase me into it. Keep firing and hold it open."

"That's crazy. How would you make it back?"

Abby ran over and picked up the end of a cable from a winch on the bumper of an overturned fire truck.

"This thing runs pretty long," she said as she pulled out the cable and tied the free end around her waist.

"That's insane," Erin said. "You can't expect that to work!"

"I gotta try."

"Abby, no—"

Abby's expression softened. "Erin, I don't know if you've noticed, but I haven't done much else besides this. I've been wondering what's on the other side my whole life. And I get a peek!" Looking away, she added, "I'm gonna come back! You just gotta pull the cable. Okay?"

Erin studied Abby's face. She knew what this moment meant and was suddenly filled with regret.

"Listen, I—" What she wanted to say was, *I'm sorry for all my shortcomings as a friend. And I'm grateful, so grateful, that you believed me way back then.*

Abby shook her head. "Hey. No need to even say it. All right, let's do this! Once I'm in there, you just pull me out!"

Abby gave Erin a reassuring smile. As she walked out to the center of the street, trailing her lifeline, Erin, Holtzmann, and Patty cut loose, firing their beams into the portal to hold it open.

"Well, this is a real choice I made," Abby said. "Isn't it."

Erin wasn't sure who she was talking to, but watched over her shoulder as Abby stepped out into the middle of the intersection, in plain view of Ghost Rowan, and started waving her arms. "Hey!" she hollered.

Ghost Rowan's head swiveled and his eyes lit up. He saw her, all right.

"Yeah, you, you dumb idiot."

He swung around the skyscraper like Jack's giant on the beanstalk or supersized King Kong on the Empire State Building and faced her, glowering. What humanity he had once possessed was gone. Abby was staring into the face of evil incarnate . . . and evil incarnate was a big honkin' cartoon ghost.

"Look at yourself!" Abby shouted. "You look ridiculous! Running around here. Can't even catch a bunch of girls. You don't seem very powerful."

Abby powered up and zapped him a little with her proton pack. He growled back and then snapped at her with a mouth big enough to swallow a small airplane.

"Yeah, you don't like that, do you?"

She zapped him a little more, a little longer. Same spot. He growled louder, and clearly pissed off, moved out from behind cover to try to grab her and smash her like a bug.

Erin knew what was coming; it was exactly what she

would have done. Abby fired her proton beam right into his interstate cloverleaf of a crotch. Howling in pain, Ghost Rowan let go of the beanstalk.

"Okay, I have his attention—"

Abby turned and ran, flipping him the middle finger behind her. Ghost Rowan boomed after her, the suction of the portal helping him gather speed. Abby was almost to the sidewalk when the fire truck cable came up taut, stopping her cold and jerking her backward.

"Oh no—" Erin said. Abby was stuck in place with Ghost Rowan bearing down fast. There was enough cable before. Erin looked closer. A loop of it had gotten caught under the fire truck. As she started to run to it, she shouted, "Hold on! I'll get it loose!"

Abby looked over her shoulder. Ghost Rowan was only two giant ghost-steps away.

"There's no time," she said. And with that, Abby untied the cable from her body.

"No, wait!" Erin cried.

Freed, Abby ran and without hesitation jumped into the portal's spinning eye just as Erin unsnagged the cable. Propelled by the vortex's suction and his own insane fury, Ghost Rowan dove into the portal right behind her.

Patty, Holtzmann, and Erin stood there in shock and disbelief as Ghost Rowan vanished. They were both gone. Forever. Erin took a step forward, suddenly choked up and at a loss for words.

"Abby—" she said. Then . . .

No way. Not like this.

Picking up the end of the cable, she charged toward the portal. As she ran she tied it around her waist, cinching the knot tight as she leapt off the sidewalk, legs driving for distance like an Olympic long jumper. She fell through the portal opening headfirst.

"Erin!" Patty cried in horror as the portal's spinning slowed and it finally began to close.

Its final blast of unearthly light and sound knocked

the two surviving Ghostbusters off their feet. Over-head, the dark clouds faded and daylight returned. It was over.

They sat up and watched smoke rise from the sealed portal; it grew thicker and thicker, obscuring their view. Neither of them could speak. Then, *shooomp!* As if they had been shot out of a cannon, Erin and Abby burst from the portal and crashed to the ground.

Holtzmann and Patty ran over to help them. Both were covered in ectoplasm and looked bewildered. Also, their hair had turned stark white.

"Oh!" Patty said, looking at their hair.

The Mercado building re-formed, all the chunks of plaster, shattered glass, and tenants' possessions—clothes, body creams, Bee Gee records, and porn magazines—streamed back into the structure, ostensibly returning to cabinets, nightstands, and between mattresses and box springs.

"What did I just see?" Abby said in wonder.

"What year is it?" Erin said, dazed.

"Twenty forty," Holtzmann said, keeping a straight face. "Welcome back."

Abby and Erin looked around, then said in unison, "We did it?"

"You did it," Holtzmann said.

"We all did it," Erin said.

It was a truly joyful moment.

"That's right," Kevin said, leaning casually against a building. "We all did it." He smiled proudly.

"All right," Erin said, "we didn't *all* do it. What did you do?"

"A lot, actually. I'll have you know I went over to that power box"—he gestured—"pushed a few buttons, then everything got sucked into the portal and it closed up."

"That had nothing to do with anything!" Erin protested.

"No," Abby said, "that may have helped. Good for you, Kevin!"

"It did not help!" Erin said, noticing that he was holding a half-eaten sub. "Where did you get that sandwich?"

"I was looking for you and I looked in that deli over there." He smiled kindly and wisely at her, like a cut-rate version of Obi-Wan Kenobi. "Listen—let's not turn on each other now. That's not what the Ghostbusters are about."

"He has a good point," Abby said.

On a TV, the channels kept changing.

Click:

The reporter was saying, "—in the aftermath, still trying to understand what happened—"

Click:

The reporter on another channel: "—the government trying to claim the event wasn't supernatural—"

Click:

A man on the street: "I'm telling you, I did not evacuate. I saw this shit. I got in a cab being driven by a skeleton. Don't tell me that was no science experiment gone wrong."

Click:

A reporter was asking Mayor Bradley: "You're honestly going to sit here and tell me that we didn't see ghosts and our water was tainted with hallucinogens by terrorists?"

"Yes," His Honor said firmly. Then he blinked. "Wait. What?"

Click:

Another reporter: "—the Ghostbusters have been quiet about taking credit—"

A smiling woman shook her head. "Oh, it was the Ghostbusters. I saw them. It was *bad. Ass.*"

Click:

The channel changed to a Yankees baseball game.

The TV was hanging on the wall of a crowded

family-style restaurant. Erin watched tables of people talking and laughing while others got into the game. Then
she turned her attention back to her tablemates: Patty,
Abby, and Holtzmann. She and Abby had dyed their hair
back, but it looked a bit off—the same, but different somehow. Holtz said they looked edgy. Erin wondered if she
could embrace the edge with as much enthusiasm as she
had embraced the cusp.

Abby was craning her neck around looking for a wait-
ress. Erin figured that if hottie Kevin had shown up by
now, they'd certainly have drinks and probably free
snacks, too.

"Saved New York and we still can't get someone to
serve us," Abby grumbled. Holtzmann stood, raised a
drink, and said, "I'd like to make a toast."

Erin made a show of rolling her eyes. "Oh, here we go."
She prepared herself for a sly joke or maybe even a Class
6 prank.

"When I first met Abby," she began, "I was so happy to
finally have my first real friend. And now with all of you,
I have my first real family." Her eyes gleamed. "I truly love
you guys."

She sat down. Erin could see that the others were as
startled by Holtz's lack of teasing as she was.

"Damn, that was like a real thing," Patty said.

It was a bonding moment, sweet and real. Their relation-
ships had been tested in the crucible of an interdimensional apocalypse, and they had come out best friends
forever—"forever" being a metaphorical term . . . or maybe
not . . .

Then who should come crawling out of the varnished
oak woodwork but Jennifer Lynch. She snaked over in her
snaky way and said, "What did I tell you? People always
move on. We want to thank you for your discretion. It's not
working at all. But thank you."

Erin smiled good-naturedly at her. "It's better to keep a

low profile. Who cares about credit? Let's just focus on the important stuff." She loved how Abby smiled at her in return. *I've learned my lesson. And boy, was it the hard way.*

"I'm sorry we can't give you any kind of formal recognition," Ms. Lynch continued, "but please know that what you did was phenomenal."

Patty spoke for the group. "We appreciate that."

"Mayor Bradley also sends his thanks. He couldn't voice that out loud, but he said it with his eyes," his assistant added.

Holtz went next. "Tell him I said . . ." And she stared back at Ms. Lynch with her eyes.

I love that sassy woman, Erin thought.

"Well, we'd like you to continue studying this . . . subject," Ms. Lynch said. "We need to be better prepared. Just in case. Whatever you need to keep you going. Anything at all."

Holtz got a calculating look. "Anything?"

The hive mind buzzed as the Ghostbusters pondered the vast possibilities of "anything." They exchanged looks. And smiled.

A few days later, they stood across the street from the beautiful firehouse with its loft sleeping accommodations and its monthly rent of twenty-one thousand dollars. They had taken the mayor at his word and now this beauty was theirs.

"Oh, hell yes," Patty crowed.

She and Holtzmann ran off toward it, with Holtzmann shouting, "I claim the upstairs!"

"You can't claim an entire floor!" Patty protested.

"Just did!" Holtzmann riposted.

Erin and Abby shared a moment. This was their doing. Victory was so very sweet.

"Not bad, Ghost Girl," Abby drawled.

"Thank you." Erin inclined her head graciously. "I will proudly take that title."

After exchanging warm smiles, they attempted the elaborate Abby/Holtz handshake. Fingers, thumbs, and elbows went every which way—a total disaster.

"We'll get our own," Abby promised her.

Their reverie was broken when a black hearse with a red roof slowly rolled up to them. Both of them blanched, and Erin said under her breath, "Oh no. Is that . . . ?"

"Patty's uncle," Abby confirmed.

Patty's uncle Bill hopped out of the hearse. He was not smiling and telling them they were awesome. He was frowning.

"Where is it?" he demanded.

Patty marched out. "I already told you."

He scowled. "I don't want to hear that my hearse is in another dimension!"

Patty was indignant. "Look, if I could cross over and get it for you, I would!"

They began to argue. Abby nudged Erin and said, "Let's let them work it out."

And they did just that.

Over the next two weeks, they had mostly moved everything in. Although there were still a few boxes to unpack, they had settled into their new home.

The more things changed, the more they remained the same: that evening, Abby was standing outside the main door dealing with Benny, the Chinese food delivery guy. He favored her with a knowing nod as he handed her their take-out order. Abby pulled out her soup. It was packed tight with wontons. It was all wontons and no broth.

"I know what you did," Benny declared. His eyes sparkled with hero worship.

Abby flushed. "All right, don't get weird on me."

"You're very brave."

"All I want is a healthy ration of wontons to broth, not this madness. This is just a science laboratory. Keep it cool."

He nodded, his eyes still sparkling. Abby walked over to Erin, who was opening up a box.

"The new book?" Abby said excitedly.

"It's here." Erin was just as excited. She pulled out a copy of their brand-new book and examined the back cover. They had updated their author photo. They'd decided on black turtlenecks again. You don't mess with the classics.

Abby took it and read the cover.

"Ah," she began. "*A Glimpse into the Unknown*—"

"Oh, did we go with the shorter title?" Erin asked, confused. "I thought—"

Abby gave her a look and continued. " '*A Journey into a Portal: Catching Sight of the Other Dimension: Discovering the Undiscoverable: A Curiosity Piqued* and *Peaked*.' "

Erin smiled. She had gotten her way.

"I still think we should've gone with *There and Back Again: A Scientist's Tale*."

"Well, next time." *No way.*

The phone rang. Kevin was at his desk and he picked up the phone on the first try. He was finally getting it right.

"Ghostbusters," he said into the speaker. "Please give a detailed description of your apparition."

Abby gave Kevin the thumbs-up as she and Erin passed his desk. As they continued walking, Abby handed Erin an envelope. It was from Columbia University. Erin deliberately did not react.

"Something fancy for you there," Abby said, and there was uncertainty in her voice.

"Not really interested." Erin tore the envelope in half.

Abby's brows shot up. "Really? Wow."

"What would I want with those people? We've got a

good thing here." Then, because she didn't want to fly under false colors, she revealed the truth. "Also, I recognized that envelope. It's just the alumni office asking for contributions."

Abby ducked her head. "But still. I can't help but notice how you've been keeping it real low key. Working hard getting this place together."

"Well, we've got a lot to do."

They reached Holtzmann, who was tinkering with some new gadgets. Everything looked very impressive and rather fanciful.

"Speaking of which," Erin said, "how are you doing over here?"

Holtzmann's natural enthusiasm could not be suppressed. "I am working on some next-level stuff. Real outside the box, like 'put me back in the box because I'm scared of what I'm doing' sort of stuff." She made an "eee" face.

Abby checked out the large containment unit. "This thing running?"

"Quite smoothly," Holtzmann said with pride. "I would say don't be in a room with it for longer than an hour at any one time."

"Well, I think we can probably aim higher," Erin ventured. She was about to go on when she noticed a woman in gloves studying some wires behind the unit. She had steampunk stylings—a brown waistcoat over a white blouse and flared trousers. Also, the same "Screw U" pendant as Holtz.

"Oh, I'm sorry," Erin said, alarmed. "I didn't see anyone there."

"You haven't met?" Holtzmann asked. "This is my mentor."

Elizabeth Gorin, Erin filled in.

Abby said, "Oh, it's so nice to finally meet—"

"This is reckless, Jillian," Dr. Gorin admonished her protégée. "You're breeding fissile plutonium with insufficient criticality moderation. All someone has to do is sneeze too hard and everyone in this building is disintegrated. Do you know how powerful that is?"

Holtzmann shuffled her feet. "I was bad."

Dr. Gorin thwacked off her gloves, put them on the counter, and stared at Holtzmann.

"And I've never been more proud of you," she said warmly, gathering Holtzmann up in a hug. "Now let's make this more powerful, shall we?"

"Yeah." Holtzmann was totally in.

Erin smiled, but she was a little freaked. "Yay . . . power within reason."

"But don't limit yourselves," Abby said.

"Definitely not," Erin amended. "But at the same time, imagine a 'responsible cap.'" She made air quotes.

Just then, Patty ran downstairs. She wore an ear-to-ear grin.

"Hey, you gotta check this out! Come up to the roof!" she told the group.

Erin, Abby, and Holtzmann headed up, while Dr. Gorin stayed behind, smiling after them.

Once they were all assembled on the starlit rooftop, Patty opened her arms to the skyline of midtown Manhattan. She said, "I guess it's a thank-you from New York."

It was a panorama of gratitude written in lights on the tops of buildings, in lights on the sides of buildings:

We ♥ GB
We ♥ New York
Thank you GB
You rock GB
GB Forever

Even the Empire State Building was lit up with the Ghostbusters logo on the side.

Wow, Erin thought, *and we're not even in* Star Wars. It was a truly special moment.

"That's very thoughtful of them," Holtzmann said.

"Well, that's not terrible," Abby deadpanned.

"No, it's not." Erin was happy, so happy. "Not terrible at all."

As they admired the show, more lights came on up and down the city, revealing dozens of logos—and more messages of thank-you from the people of New York. People who knew that four intrepid women had literally saved them from a fate worse than death.

And that's why we did it, Erin thought, *and if need be, why we'll do it again.*

The expressions on the faces of her sister Ghostbusters assured her that they were all thinking the same thing:

We will protect this city from ghoulies and ghosties and things that go bump in the night.

EPILOGUE

And so they kept researching the paranormal and fine-tuning their PKE readers and taking lots of notes and eating lots of wonton soup. Benny the delivery guy had developed a massive crush on Abby, and Erin was trying to get her to agree to go out on a date. Dr. Gorin was helping Holtzmann refine the containment unit.

About a month after New York had thanked them, Patty was listening to EVP recordings they had made during their initial consultation with a new client, a woman who claimed to hear whispering at night in her living room.

She sat wearing headphones listening to white noise. Nothing. Then . . . something. Her brows rose. She rewound the tape and turned up the volume. Then she wrote a note, her forehead furrowed, and took off her headphones. She looked at the other Ghostbusters with consternation.

"What's up?" Erin asked. "Did you get something?"

"Yeah," Patty replied. "What's 'Zuul'?"